BRIE'S SUBMISSION

Bound by Love

Our Love is
Epic

Red Phoenix

Red Phoenix

Bound by Love: Brie's Submission
17th of the Brie Series

Cover by Shanoff Designs
Formatted by BB eBooks
Phoenix symbol by Nicole Delfs

Dedication

This has been quite a journey! I went from writing a simple short story "Brie's First Day of Submissive Training" to an entire series of seventeen novels to date within Brie's world.

Like Brie, I have been changed since joining her on those adventures at the Submissive Training Center in March of 2012.

I have made life-long friends, experimented with tools and scenes in BDSM I never thought I would have the courage to try, and I have fallen even more in love with my husband–the inspiration behind Brie's Submission.

To all of you who have been with me since the beginning, and to all those who are just joining now, I hope you continue to find inspiration and life truths within the pages of Brie's story.

Like you, I have fallen for all the characters in Brie's world. I am eternally grateful that I met a humble genius, Anthony, who advised me to continue in this world, exploring the different characters in more depth.

I want to thank my two kids, Jon and Jessica. They joined me last year and have since spent hours behind the scene getting Brie out to as many people as they can. Both of them are smarter than their mom, and I couldn't be prouder to have them on my team.

I also have fans who work tirelessly for me and have been doing so for years.

While I can't name them all, here are some that have made a huge difference:
Brenda H, Brandi RS, Marilyn C, Becki W, Missy V, Felicia A, Emily E, Mary W, Jennifer RH, Marianna S, Jacque B, Christina G, & Autumn D.

I also want to acknowledge my editors through the years:
Amy Parker, RJ Lockesly, Jennifer Blackwell, K.H. Koehler
My book designers:
CopperLynn, Viola Estrella, and Shanoff Designs, as well as Paul Salvette, of BB Books, my awesome formatter

A quick shout-out to two of my teachers!
Miss Fushimi and Mr. Glenn:
Your enthusiasm for my writing sparked something beautiful in that shy little redhead you had in class. Thank you from the bottom of my heart!

Naturally, I must thank my husband, whom I affectionately call MrRed.
He has been my inspiration from the beginning.
All these many years, he has supported and encouraged my writing. I would not have begun this journey if it hadn't been for his support.
He continues to inspire by creating scenes for me to experience and write about, but more than that, his love has made me a better woman.

I can't wait to find out what the future holds as we all continue on this journey together!
Much love,
Red Phoenix

YOU CAN ALSO BUY THE AUDIO BOOK!

Bound by Love #17

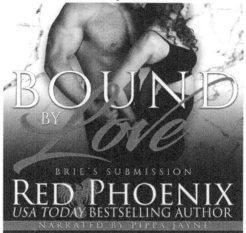

Narrated by Pippa Jayne

SIGN UP FOR MY NEWSLETTER
HERE FOR THE LATEST RED
PHOENIX UPDATES

FOLLOW ME ON INSTAGRAM
INSTAGRAM.COM/REDPHOENIXAUTHOR

SALES, GIVEAWAYS, NEW
RELEASES, PREORDER LINKS, AND
MORE!
SIGN UP HERE
REDPHOENIXAUTHOR.COM/NEWSLETTER-
SIGNUP

CONTENTS

Best Laid Plans 1

Time for Whoopee 7

Secrets to Keep 27

Too Hot to Handle 46

Candles & Kinbaku 64

I'm Not a Masochist! 86

Hello 98

Gift of Memories 108

The Sheik 122

Lea for the Win 136

Me Too 154

Oh, Rhett. 177

Meeting Liam 201

Written in the Sky 215

The Switch 231

Force 239

Aftershock 250

Her Christening 265

The Isle 2.0 287

Blood Moon 309

Coming Next 321

About the Author 323

Other Red Phoenix Books 326

Connect with Red on Substance B 331

Best Laid Plans

B rie looked over at Sir as they sat in the backseat of
Rytsar's vehicle, unable to hide her concern for
the baby as they rode in silence to the hospital.

He took her hand and squeezed it gently. "There is
no reason to be worried, babygirl."

Rytsar bellowed from the front, "But I'm not
ready!"

Sir chuckled under his breath. "This isn't about
you, old friend."

Rytsar turned his head, looking back at Brie in desperation. "I wanted to be healed for her."

Brie rubbed her belly lovingly and shrugged. "I
think this little girl has a mind of her own, Rytsar. She
must take after her *dyadya*."

He gave Brie a self-satisfied smirk and sat back in
his seat. "You're right. She takes after me."

Brie let out a nervous sigh, and Sir immediately
wrapped his strong arms around her. "While we may
not be mentally prepared for an early entrance, everything is ready for her."

Brie squeezed Sir's hand. She smiled, thinking back on the moment the two of them found out they were having a girl. He'd held her hand then, too.

Cold gel covered her stomach as the technician glided the transducer probe over her belly. She'd had an ultrasound while Rytsar was watching over her but, at the time, it had been too early in her pregnancy to determine the sex.

Although Brie was certain she was carrying a girl, she'd come today hoping to find out for sure. She trusted that Rytsar, who'd insisted from the very beginning that she was having a girl, would be able to make the mental adjustment if it turned out she was actually carrying a baby boy.

"Now that you are far enough along, Mrs. Davis, we should be able to tell if it's a boy or girl," the technician informed her.

"Wonderful! I can't wait to find out."

Sir was sitting in a wheelchair beside her, holding her hand tightly as they watched the screen.

While she trembled with excitement, Brie noticed that Sir appeared exceedingly calm, considering the importance of this ultrasound. When he caught her staring at him, he gave her a wink.

Her heart just about melted. How was it he still held that kind of power over her?

The technician first made the required measurements, pointing out unidentifiable body parts while they both watched the monitor intently. Once finished, he smiled at Brie. "Now we get to see if your baby will cooperate with me today."

It took a few moments for him to isolate the area before he was able to point out an unrecognizable blob on the screen. "Although we won't know for certain until the birth, it looks as if you're having a girl."

Brie stared hard at the image, unable to make out what he was showing her, but trusted the technician's expertise. She glanced at Sir with awe in her voice. "A little girl…"

He nodded, wiping a tear from his eye.

"Is it what you were expecting?" the technician asked them.

"Yes," Sir stated confidently.

Afterward, Brie questioned Sir about it as they headed back to his hospital room. "I have to admit that you surprised me back there, Sir."

He chuckled. "How so?"

"You didn't seem a bit surprised that we are having a girl, even though there was a fifty-fifty chance it might be a boy."

Sir nodded thoughtfully, but did not explain himself until he was settled back in the room and they were alone. Brie became worried when he took her hand, his expression serious. "Babygirl, I never told you about something that happened on the plane as it was going down."

They had promised each other not to keep secrets, and she opened her mouth to protest but he spoke first, explaining, "I kept silent because I wanted to preserve this special moment for you."

Brie looked into his eyes, asking with trepidation, "What happened on the plane?"

His smile faltered, and Sir's eyes suddenly had a haunted look—as if he were reliving those last seconds before impact. He cleared his throat. "Just before the plane crashed I *knew,* beyond a shadow of a doubt, that you were carrying a girl."

"How?" she asked, looking at him in wonder.

Sir placed his hand on her stomach, shaking his head. "I have no idea."

Tears pricked Brie's eyes. She imagined the terror he must have felt with everyone screaming around him just before the plane smashed into the ground.

"And now, I have been given the miracle of a second chance." Sir smiled, gazing down at her round belly. "I'm going to get to meet our little girl."

Brie looked at him with a mixture of gratitude and heartache. She'd been so close to losing him...

"I love you, Sir."

He cradled her cheek. "I love you, too."

Tears filled her eyes when she confessed, "Today would be even more perfect if we could tell Rytsar the news. It's killing me inside."

She saw the same level of pain reflected in Sir's eyes. "It is the only thing that tarnishes this moment for me. The overwhelming helplessness of not knowing if he's alive...it eats at me like a cancer."

Brie nodded, her bottom lip trembling.

"But our duty as parents is to separate those feelings from the miracle that is our child." Sir laid his hand on her stomach again. "I am a lucky man..."

Brie gazed into his eyes as he grasped the back of her neck and pulled her in for a kiss. She couldn't help grinning the moment their lips touched, and the perfect name suddenly flashed in her mind.

"Do my kisses amuse you?" he asked teasingly.

"I know what her name is, Sir," Brie announced, and she whispered it in his ear.

Sir leaned back against the pillow, nodding his approval. "I agree. That *is* her name."

Brie felt chills of providence coursing through her when he kissed her again. The name not only reflected the two of them, but it also honored Rytsar's devotion to their baby.

When Sir pulled away, she tried unsuccessfully to keep the tears from falling. Sir reached up and wiped them away. "He *is* coming back, babygirl. And when he does, Durov will appreciate the name we have chosen for her."

Brie forced a smile, taking strength from his assurance. She imagined the moment when Rytsar finally met their child face-to-face. It would be so beautiful...

She *chose* to believe it would happen, and to honor that belief, she asked Sir, "I think you should be the one to make the formal introduction between them when she is born."

"Certainly, if that is what you wish."

Brie felt the baby kick, and glanced down at her

stomach, mesmerized by the wonder of the tiny human growing inside her. Truly, motherhood was a miracle—this ability to create a life born of love.

Time for Whoopee

B rie forced a nervous smile as Maxim sped them to the hospital. Trying to distract herself from her mounting worries, she said to everyone in the vehicle, "I sure hope they were right about our baby being a girl, or our little boy is going be dressed in a lot of pink lace."

"*Moye solntse* is not a boy," Rytsar insisted.

Sir chuckled, patting her hand. "No need to worry about that now."

"You're right." Brie sighed, looking out the window. She was feeling unsettled and mumbled aloud, "But I feel like I forgot something…"

"Do not fret," Rytsar advised from the front seat. "Whatever it is, my men can get it for you."

She nodded, but the nagging feeling wouldn't go away, so she went back to staring out the car window to hide her unease. When she saw an orange tabby running across the street, it suddenly came to her.

"Master Anderson!"

"What about him?" Sir asked.

"I need to call him! He was planning to join us at Rytsar's place after he finished his paperwork at the Submissive Training Center."

Rytsar snorted. "It would be funny if he arrives and all of us are gone."

"No, it wouldn't, Rytsar," she said, laughing. "He *really* wanted to be there to cheer you up. He even mentioned he was bringing something that was sure to make you smile."

"Huh," he grunted. "Now you have me intrigued, *radost moya*." Taking out his phone, he asked, "Do you mind if I make the call?"

"I think that's an excellent idea," Sir answered, pressing Brie closer to him.

Eavesdropping on the one-sided conversation between Rytsar and Master Anderson was amusing, especially when he asked about the gift Master Anderson had gotten him. "Really? And you think that is funny?"

"What did he get you?" Brie prodded from the backseat, needing to know.

Rytsar turned his head to face her. "A sack of potatoes. He thought I might like some company while I recover." He turned back around, giving Master Anderson grief for being so cheap.

Brie snickered, thinking the gift was hilarious because Rytsar had complained to everyone about the doctors demanding he act like potato and rest, which he refused to do.

Those two men were all kinds of fun when they got together, and listening to them talk now had her reminiscing about the recent escapade she'd had involving the passionate Russian and that sexy cowboy.

"What has you smiling so, babygirl?" Sir asked.

"I was thinking about the break-in."

"Ah…" He laid her head against his shoulder. "You're lucky you two weren't shot that day."

"It was totally worth the risk." Brie laughed, marveling at how boyishly wicked Rytsar could be at times.

"Exactly what kind of detour do you have in mind, *radost moya*?" Rytsar had asked Brie the evening of the break-in.

Brie could tell she'd piqued his curiosity, and she explained, "I have something to give Master Anderson."

The Russian snarled, suddenly disinterested. "*Nyet.*"

"But it's from Shadow."

A mischievous grin suddenly spread across his face. "Well…if that is the case, I would be happy to redirect our course."

"This is what we will be dropping off," Brie told him, holding up a bag of cat food with a large red bow and a tag that read *Kitten Support*.

"What's this for?" Rytsar asked, laughing.

"It actually started with the bet Master Anderson and I made. He bet me twenty bucks on Sir's first words after the coma. I had planned to use my winnings to buy a bunch of whoopee cushions to hide around his house, but when he brought the kittens to the hospital—"

"He did what with kittens?"

"He snuck the entire litter into the hospital. *That's* when I knew how the money really needed to be spent."

"To be honest, *radost moya*, I like the whoopee cushion idea better," Rytsar told her, chuckling to himself. "In fact, I insist on purchasing them since you have already spent the money."

Brie grinned, remembering how much she'd laughed when she placed one under the cushion in her apartment and surprised Master Anderson when he sat down on it. In a time of great sorrow, it was a happy memory she'd held on to.

She squealed with excitement when Rytsar ordered Maxim to hit the gas as they sped to the store to get more.

Brie couldn't stop giggling as the Russian piled every last whoopee cushion the store carried into his basket.

"There is no such thing as too many," he told the curious cashier when she hit total and raised her eyebrows at the size of the bill.

Rytsar nodded to Brie while they were walking back to the vehicle. The mischievous glint in his eyes, along with that boyish grin, gave him such a youthful appearance that it made Brie literally stop in her tracks.

"What?" he asked, turning around and looking at her questioningly.

"I bet that's the way you looked every time your

mother caught you doing something naughty. No wonder she adored you."

Rytsar stared at Brie for a moment, his eyes softening for a second before he made an abrupt about-face and strode briskly to the car. Brie realized she'd caught him off guard and hoped her innocent comment hadn't caused him pain.

Quickening her steps, Brie was able to catch up to him. His expression showed no emotion whatsoever as he loaded the bags of whoopee cushions into the vehicle. She became more concerned when Rytsar let out a long sigh as he stared aimlessly out the window.

"Are you okay, Rytsar?" she asked in a timid voice.

He inclined his head toward her, frowning. "There are times, *radost moya*, when remembering my mother only reminds me of how much I've lost."

"I'm sorry. I didn't mea—"

He shook his head. "Do not apologize. I need to embrace the pain rather than shove away my memories of her." His eyes filled with unshed tears when he confessed, "She deserves to be remembered. I miss *Mamulya* so much it hurts—even though it's been years."

"Sir feels the same about his father. He told me there will always be a part of him missing because Alonzo is gone. It has become even more pronounced and painful for him with the baby coming."

Rytsar reached out and clasped her shoulder, his tone somber, "I am sorry for my brother."

Brie's heart ached for both men, knowing the weight of the pain they carried. She was lucky she had never known that level of loss.

Rytsar broke the silence, his lips slowly curving into a grin. "Let's head over to Anderson's so we can deliver your package…and mine." The seriousness of the moment seemed to evaporate as Rytsar sat back against the seat, his arms folded, that mischievous look returning to his face.

Brie still found it remarkable that this respected sadist, who was so intimidating during a scene, had this playful side to him.

He turned his head and asked, "So what exactly was your plan for the cat food?"

"I'm simply going to ring the doorbell and dash."

"*Nyet.* I want to see the expression on his face."

Brie bit her lip nervously, aware that Rytsar was still cross with Master Anderson. "You're not planning to cause trouble, are you?"

"I simply want to observe his reaction…and take pleasure from it," he answered with a wicked smirk.

When they arrived, she bounded up to the porch and pushed the doorbell. She grinned excitedly at Rytsar while the two of them waited for Master Anderson to answer.

After a minute, Rytsar pushed the doorbell again.

"He's not home," Brie groaned, noticing that all the lights were off in the house. "But why is his truck still here?" she asked, making a sweeping motion toward the new Chevy. Brie set the cat food down on the welcome mat. "I guess Shey must have picked him up for a hot date or something. At least, when they get back, they'll have a good laugh together."

Rytsar wasn't listening to her as he moved toward the door and fished something out of his pocket. In a matter of seconds, he had the door unlocked and opened.

"Oh my goodness, Rytsar! What are you doing?"

He shrugged, wearing a mischievous grin. "Why not take advantage of this rare opportunity?"

"Wait…are you thinking what I'm thinking?"

"*Da*. Every possible place he might sit that ass down will have a whoopee cushion hidden, just waiting for him."

Brie giggled but hesitated at the doorway. "You know this is considered breaking and entering, even if he is our friend."

"*Nyet*," he scoffed. "Not when it is done for amusement."

"I'm pretty sure Sir would not approve."

"I will gladly face his wrath for both of us. You can tell him I commanded it."

Brie shook her head, laughing. "No, I'm not going to start lying to him now. If I'm doing this, I'm doing it of my own free will, and I will even accept the rice punishment, if I must."

"Excellent," Rytsar said, slapping her on the back like a comrade. He stepped over the bag of cat food and strode into Master Anderson's house as if he owned the place.

"*Radost moya*, you start with the couches. Put one under every cushion. I will head to his bedroom. It's time to get creative…"

Brie felt extremely naughty as she stepped over the

cat food and walked into his house, quietly shutting the door behind her. There was something wicked about being in someone's house uninvited, but the allure of the whoopees made her throw caution to the wind.

After blowing up the first one and slipping it under a cushion of his large leather sectional, her nervousness lessened. She could just imagine the look on his face when he went to sit down and that humorous sound escaped from underneath him.

With glee, she blew up the next one, and the next. While she was positive he would find all of the whoopee cushions she'd hidden in the couch after sitting on the first one, he would never suspect there were more waiting for him other places in the house.

After hiding as many whoopee cushions as she could in his great room, Brie went to see what Rytsar was up to and found him placing a less inflated one in Master Anderson's boot.

"Oh, that's a great idea! I never thought about leaving them partially inflated. That gives us so many more options!"

"Don't hold back," he encouraged her.

She glanced around Master Anderson's bedroom, trying to figure out the best place to put the one she had in her hand. Her eyes rested on his bed. Although his head was not heavy enough to force the air out, just having it under his pillow would let him know she was thinking of him.

Giggling like a loon, she slipped it under his pillow and decided to put one under the other pillow, too. She then left Rytsar to finish as she headed for the next room.

"Oh, my goodness!" she cried when she opened the door.

Rytsar was beside her in an instant, asking what was wrong.

She cooed. "I've found Cayenne and the kittens!" Brie knelt on the floor as the orange tabby walked up to her with the passel of kittens following behind.

Brie was in cat heaven, the whoopee cushions completely forgotten.

She stroked the tabby, telling Cayenne with remorse, "I wish Shadow was here to see this little family you've created. They're adorable."

Cayenne brushed up against her briefly before lying down on the floor. Immediately, three of the kittens ran up and started suckling.

Rytsar snorted, pointing at the hungry little fluff balls. "I bet you're glad you are only having one. That's a lot of mouths to feed."

The black male with the crystal blue eyes was the only one brave enough to walk over to Rytsar and sniff his boot. The kitten let out a sad meow as if he recognized his father's scent and was protesting Shadow's absence.

Rytsar stared down at him and grumbled, "While you do remind me of your father, *kot*, there is no point in trying to get on my good side. I only have room in my heart for one feline, and he had to save my life to get it. Cuteness has zero pull with me."

Brie picked up the kitten for Rytsar to get a better look. "But just look how adorably adorable he is,

Rytsar. How can you resist that cute wittle face?"

Rytsar stared at Brie, unmoved. "There are enough crazy *kot* people in the world. I do not need to be converted."

Brie kissed the kitten on his little nose and set him back down. She suspected it wouldn't take much convincing to get Rytsar to change his mind. Despite his gruff exterior, that sadist had a soft heart.

One just had to look at how he treated Little Sparrow, and the extravagant gift of caviar he'd given Shadow as a thank-you, to know he was secretly a pet person—no matter how much he tried to deny it.

She glanced over at the window and cried, "Oh look, Rytsar! Master Anderson has built an outdoor pen for Shadow's family so they can go in and out whenever they want." Brie pushed on the plastic flap in the window, sticking her head through to look at the large, screened-in pen he'd constructed. It was full of cat ramps, cat cubbies, and scratching posts.

"I think he's serious about keeping them all," she said, turning around to face Rytsar.

"Foolish man. That's why you don't let the creatures into your heart. Before you know it, you've become a pathetic loser. He might as well stamp a big 'L' on his forehead."

"But you're wrong, Rytsar. Lots of women find men who love animals attractive."

He gave her a lustful grin. "Well, I'm enough *animal* for my women."

Brie giggled, loving his manly confidence.

"Now, back to work, *radost moya*. We still have

twenty of these to hide."

"Yes, Rytsar," she answered obediently, kissing each kitten on the head and giving Cayenne one more scratch under her chin before closing the door and heading toward the basement. She knew that was where Master Anderson had set up his adult playroom in his new house.

Oh, what kind of mischief could she cause down there? Brie could just imagine him in the middle of an intense scene, and then the sound of a lone fart cutting through the air at the worst possible moment...

She laughed out loud as she turned the doorknob leading to the basement.

"Just what are you up to, young Brie?" a low, charming voice asked behind her.

She turned around, blushing profusely even as she hid the whoopee cushions behind her back. "I...ah..."

Master Anderson held up the bag of cat food. "I was coming back from my jog and found this on the doorstep. I take it this is from you?"

She stared at the cat food and smiled. "Actually, it's from Shad—"

Rytsar came waltzing into the hallway, oblivious to Master Anderson standing there. "We can't forget the kitchen. That man lives in his k—"

As soon as Rytsar saw Master Anderson in the hallway, he nonchalantly put the incriminating evidence behind his back.

"*You* are trespassing," Master Anderson stated somberly, pointing at Rytsar.

"I am," Rytsar answered, not even bothering to

deny it.

"Why are you here, Durov?"

"Truthfully? I came to get even."

"Even for what? If I remember correctly, you said I was forgiven."

"And I have forgiven you."

"Then why am I still picking up on resentment from you?"

"While I believe it was not your fault that I failed to be contacted right after the plane crash, the fact remains that Nosaka was the one you called to care for *radost moya* after you broke your leg—not me. I still cannot fathom why. It makes no sense to me."

Master Anderson glanced at Brie and shrugged. "I felt Nosaka was the better choice."

"Why?" Rytsar demanded again.

"This may not be the best time to discuss it," Master Anderson stated, glancing over at Brie and motioning his head for emphasis.

"I want to hear it straight from the horse's mouth, and I'm not leaving until I do," Rytsar stated, crossing his arms.

Brie looked at both men nervously. She cared for and respected both of them and did not want the two to be at odds with each other.

"It was a precarious time for everyone," Master Anderson stated.

"Obviously."

Master Anderson glanced at Brie before admitting, "Even I struggled to keep things at a platonic level when she needed help."

She blushed, understanding why he had been reluctant to speak about it in front of her.

Master Anderson continued, admitting to her with a grin of embarrassment, "It was the reason for all the soup."

Brie smiled, chuckling to herself, finally grasping why he'd insisted on making copious amounts of soup at the apartment. "Well, you were always the gentleman to me, Master Anderson," she told him, rubbing her stomach lovingly. "And you made sure my little girl got the nutrients she needed."

Brie told Rytsar with sadness in her voice, "When my world was falling apart, he helped me to keep my path straight, even when I was riddled with doubt. And he made me laugh—I really needed that."

She glanced back at Master Anderson. "I remember every little thing you did back then, Master Anderson, and I will always be grateful to you for it."

He gave her a charming half-smile. "Think nothing of it, young Brie. The fact you are safe and Thane is recovering is all the thanks I need." He placed his hand over his heart, and for good measure, he flexed his pecs, making the material of his shirt dance.

Brie giggled. "See? You always make me laugh, and I love that about you."

"I, too, appreciate your good humor, but..." Rytsar said, looking at Master Anderson, "your statement insinuates that I would have lost control and crossed that line. To assume that I would fail where you did not is extremely arrogant on your part."

"Look, I know what a passionate man you are."

Rytsar narrowed his eyes. "Thane is my brother. Why would you ever think I would betray him like that?"

"Thane is like a brother to me as well, buddy, and I've known him longer than you. But I'm telling you…the struggle was real. Even Nosaka felt it."

Brie's eyes widened. Tono had seemed so calm and in control when he was with her. It broke her heart to know he'd secretly suffered, too. At the time, she'd been so focused on Sir that she hadn't given a thought to anyone else.

Master Anderson pointed at Brie. "See? Look what you've done by forcing me to discuss it. Young Brie feels badly now, and that was never my intent."

Rytsar glanced at Brie, saying nothing for several moments. Finally, he broke the silence, telling Master Anderson, "The truth—I was the *only* one to be trusted."

Master Anderson shook his head in disagreement.

"*Da*, you know it is true. And, yet, I was kept in the dark. You must have realized something was wrong when I didn't show up for weeks after."

"As I told you before, I was barely hanging on, myself. If things had been normal, I would have eventually figured that out."

Rytsar snarled. "I think it boils down to jealousy."

"Jealousy of what?" Master Anderson cried indignantly.

"My relationship with Thane. To be honest, I have wondered if keeping me in the dark was a form of payback."

Master Anderson looked at Brie, brushing his hair back angrily. "Can you believe this guy?"

"Do you deny it?" Rytsar demanded.

"I sure as hell do!" Master Anderson took a step closer to him, physically stating his dominance. "I never once felt jealous of you. Why would I? Thane and I were friends long before you." He squared his jaw and looked Rytsar in the eye. "The fact you even think so is insulting."

"Hah," Rytsar replied, a smirk on his lips. "I said the same thing to you after you dared to question the scars that *radost moya* and I share."

Master Anderson cocked his head to one side, his voice hinting at his growing annoyance. "Yeah…I'm still not sure about your decision to bond with her by blood without Thane's permission. At the very least, it was a rash thing to do."

"But necessary," Rytsar stated firmly.

"Since Thane has not spoken against it, I cannot argue the point with you. However, I would have strongly cautioned you against it, had you asked."

"That's the difference between you and me," Rytsar declared. "You've become overly cautious as you've gotten older."

"And you are still controlled by your passions."

Rytsar crossed his arms.

Brie finally spoke up, the truth being very clear to her. "That's why Sir loves you both. You are authentic and true. Fighting about your differences is like water arguing with fire. You can't change each other's nature nor should you try. I personally think you're both perfect the way you are, and I wouldn't change a thing."

Rytsar snorted in response, continuing to stare Master Anderson down.

Master Anderson, on the other hand, winked at Brie. "Fire describes Durov to a T." Instead of arguing further, he offered Rytsar a challenge. "How about we settle this like men?"

Rytsar raised an eyebrow. "What do you propose?"

"Let's arm wrestle. If I win, you lose that attitude and raise your hands up in the air, declaring I'm the champion. If you win, I will not only concede that you are the champion, but will kiss Brie's scar as a sign you were right all along."

Rytsar smirked. "Are you sure?" He pumped his right arm, his muscles bulging impressively. "I'm no American pussy."

"Neither am I," Master Anderson replied, rubbing his hands together. "Let the battle begin."

When he turned and started toward the kitchen, Rytsar handed Brie the rest of the whoopee cushions he'd been hiding behind his back and whispered, "Do *not* let him see them."

Brie looked around for a place to hide them as she was heading down the hallway and stepped into the first room she passed. Trying not to giggle, she stuffed them in his washing machine and quickly caught up with the two Doms.

The men were in full competition mode. Before they had even made it to the kitchen table, Master Anderson had ripped off his shirt.

They sat at the corner of the table, facing each other, wearing grim looks of determination.

"Young Brie will do the honors of starting the match," Master Anderson informed them.

Brie was afraid Rytsar might hurt his ribs by doing this and warned him, "I don't think you should do this."

"Begin the match," Rytsar insisted.

Despite her misgivings, Brie placed her hands over their clasped ones, making sure neither started before she officially counted down. She could feel the tension in their fists, their muscles tensed and ready as they waited for the war of muscles to begin.

"I'm going to count down from three and let go. Are you ready?"

"*Da.*"

Master Anderson gave her a charming smile. "I was born ready, darlin'."

"Three...two...one!" She lifted her hands and the battle was on.

Both men stared at each other intensely, looking for weakness in the other as they gritted their teeth and channeled all their strength into beating the other.

Brie squealed with excitement, cheering for both as she circled the table. Master Anderson and Rytsar were both stubborn, neither wanting to lose. After a few minutes, the strain was beginning to show as perspiration showed on Rytsar's forehead.

Brie was afraid of the strain he was putting on his broken ribs and told him, "I think you should stop."

"*Nyet,*" he growled through gritted teeth.

Rytsar continued to grunt and growl, unwilling to relinquish his hold even as his body strained under the pressure. Somehow, he took the lead.

Inch by inch, he forced Master Anderson's hand down to the table, pinning it.

Rytsar gave him a self-satisfied smirk afterward. "You have something to say?"

Master Anderson sat back in his chair, shaking his head. "Well, I guess a bet's a bet."

"*Da.*"

Master Anderson smiled charmingly as he raised his hands in the air. "You, Anton Durov, are the champion—this time." He then held out his hand to Brie. She walked over, and he took her wrist, placing a gentle kiss on the scar left from her bloodbond with Rytsar. It was so sweet, it made her heart flutter.

Master Anderson then tipped an imaginary hat at the Russian. "Since you proved a worthy opponent"—he nodded toward the back of the house—"I will *not* call the cops for trespassing, but I'd still like to know what the hell you were doing in my home."

"That was not part of the deal," Rytsar informed him, getting up slowly. "Let's go, *radost moya*. We need to let this cowboy lick his wounds."

Master Anderson held out his hand to Rytsar. "So, we are friends again—yes?"

Rytsar took his hand. "We were always friends, even when I did not care for you."

Master Anderson chuckled. "Same here, partner."

He turned to Brie and asked, "Did you see what I built for the kittens?"

"I did!" she answered. "It's totally amazing!"

"The little buggers certainly seem to enjoy it."

"So you are really planning to keep all six?"

"To be honest, I couldn't bear breaking up the family."

"I'm thrilled to hear you say that," Brie told him, taking advantage of his timely lead-in. "Because that's the real reason I came here today. Shadow feels the responsibility of his fatherhood and, naturally, he insists on paying child support since he can't be here to care for them himself."

Master Anderson laughed. "So that's what the bag of 'kitten support' was doing on my porch…"

"Yes, it would be wonderful if Shadow could visit his family sometime, don't you think?"

"Oh, hell no! I'm not going to allow that cat anywhere near my Cayenne again. Once was more than enough, thank you."

"But you don't understand. Shadow legitimately misses them, Master Anderson. I can *feel* Shadow's pain." Brie looked at him sadly while pouting her bottom lip, hoping to convince him.

Master Anderson shook his head. "You don't play fair, young lady." He glanced over at Rytsar and asked, "How the heck am I supposed to resist that face?"

Rytsar chuckled at him. "As the winner tonight, I say you grant her wish."

"I wouldn't go abusing that power so soon, *champ*," Master Anderson said with a bite of sarcasm.

Rytsar started walking toward the door, his gate stiffer than before. "My job here is done," he announced, heading out.

Master Anderson stopped Brie before she left. "Make sure the Russian didn't hurt himself. I tried not to tax his ribs too much."

"Wait...did you let him win?"

He chuckled. "What you witnessed was a test of wills, young Brie. We're square now."

Brie left, smiling to herself.

What had started out as a humorous break-in had ended with two old friends making amends. Turned out, making whoopee truly was a beautiful thing.

Secrets to Keep

When the car finally pulled up to the hospital, Sir instantly took charge. He told Brie to stay put while he went to get her a wheelchair. It seemed silly, since she wasn't suffering from labor pains yet and could walk just fine, but Sir insisted. Rather than argue, she acquiesced, grateful that he cared.

While she waited, Maxim got out of the vehicle and wrestled Rytsar's wheelchair out of the back, setting it up next to the passenger door.

"Put that away!" Rytsar insisted through clenched teeth when Maxim opened the door.

"Rytsar, what about the doctor's orders?" Brie reminded him, reaching over the seat to touch his shoulder. "I don't want our baby's *dyadya* injuring himself just before her arrival."

Rytsar grunted. "I promise to sit in a chair like a normal person during the birth, but I am *not* going to be wheeled into that place."

Brie saw the double doors slide open as Sir walked out of the hospital, rolling an empty wheelchair toward

the car. Brie blushed with embarrassment, now understanding Rytsar's reluctance, and did not press him
further.

"No wheelchair?" Sir asked when Rytsar stepped
out of the car.

"Do not concern yourself with my affairs, comrade.
You have your woman to look after."

Rather than argue, Sir opened Brie's door and
helped her into the wheelchair. Rytsar grabbed Maxim's
shoulder and leaned against him for support.

Smiling down at Brie, Sir stated, "Let's go deliver
this baby." He wheeled her to the hospital and her
heart skipped a beat as they passed through the entrance. The next time she went through these doors,
she would be holding their little girl in her arms. Brie
looked back toward Sir, shaking her head in amazement.

"What are you thinking?" he asked.

"That you and I are about to become parents."

Sir smiled, his eyes flashing with excitement. "Yes
we are, little mama."

Brie caught Rytsar watching them with a tender
look in his eye. The miracle of this moment—having
both men with her for delivery—struck her full force,
and she began to cry.

"What's wrong, Brie?" Sir asked, concerned.

Rytsar, however, took a more direct approach.
"Someone get a doctor, now!"

Brie waved away the nurse who responded to
Rytsar's request. "I'm fine, I'm fine. Just feeling a little
emotional."

The nurse smiled and nodded, giving Rytsar an inviting wink as she headed back to her station.

Brie had to admit the Russian was impressive. No matter the situation, he commanded the attention of women who couldn't help but respond to his dominance.

Sir wheeled Brie to the elevator and pressed the button, telling her, "They have a room ready for you upstairs. We'll remain there until this little girl graces the world."

Brie grabbed his hand for reassurance. "And she is going to be perfectly fine."

"Of course," he answered. "Our girl is simply a little early."

"*Moye solntse* is strong," Rytsar stated.

Brie turned to him and, for a brief moment, she saw a vision of his broken body the day he returned to them. "I'm so happy you are here with us, Rytsar."

"I've lived for this day," he said, winking at her.

Brie looked up at Sir again. "I re—" Suddenly, she doubled over as her whole abdomen erupted in pain.

"What is it, Brie?"

"Oh God, it hurts. It hurts!"

As soon as the elevator doors opened, Sir wheeled her out, calmly demanding help from the staff. The nurses immediately directed the three of them to the room she was to give birth in, and Sir lifted her up onto the bed while the nurse set to work.

Brie saw the worried expressions on the men's faces, and heard Rytsar mutter to himself, "I hate hospitals…"

She closed her eyes, whimpering as another wave of pain gripped her.

"Breathe through it, Brie," Sir commanded.

The nurse worked quickly, hooking her up to monitors, before slipping an IV into her vein. The doctor came in shortly after.

"Hello, I'm Dr. Glas. I was told your water broke within the last hour."

"That's correct," Sir answered as Brie worked through the wave of pain.

"I'm going to check your cervix as soon as the contraction passes to assess where we are right now."

Brie was charmed by the doctor's Scottish accent and comfortable manner. She nodded her head when the pain had passed.

He slipped his fingers in and smiled as he felt the opening of her cervix. Stripping off his gloves, her told her, "You husband was right to get you here early. It appears the babe is determined to come without delay."

"But isn't it too early?" Brie asked, unable to hide the panic she felt.

"Mrs. Davis, there is no reason for concern. Her vitals are good, as are yours. All you need to concentrate on now is getting this wee one out."

"When can I have the epidural?" Brie pleaded, not wanting to suffer another wave of excruciating pain.

"Unfortunately, you're too dilated for that to be an option now. This wee babe is coming au naturel."

"But that wasn't the plan," she whimpered.

"You can handle this, Brie," Sir said reassuringly, squeezing her hand.

"You don't understand," she told the doctor. "I'm not a masochist."

The doctor smirked, looking at Sir and Rytsar. "Well, today, lass, you are. I can give you medicine that will dull the pain, but it can make you a little woozy."

Brie shook her head. "No, I don't want that." She lay back against the pillow, thoroughly terrified.

Sir squeezed her hand again and commanded in a smooth voice, "Look into my eyes."

Brie did so immediately.

"You are a strong, determined woman. Keep calm and utilize the lessons you've learned and meet this challenge head-on."

Brie swallowed hard. She'd never thought that her training at the Center would prepare her for a moment like this—yet here she was. She glanced over at Rytsar for encouragement.

He gave her a confident smile. "You are strong like your daughter."

Both men had endured incredible physical challenges in their own right. They were the examples she needed to follow. When another labor pain hit, she stifled her whimpers but her courage and conviction seemed to be hanging on by a thread, and she was consumed by one prevailing thought:

I wish my mom was here...

Despite her age, she longed for the comfort of her mother.

A lone tear rolled down her cheek as she remembered the day when her parents had finally had enough of her pushing them away and flew to LA to confront

her.

It broke Brie's heart now, knowing she hadn't even been happy to see them at the time.

Having another early knock at the door surprised Brie. It had been the *second* time in the same day, and she looked at Rytsar in alarm.

"Are you expecting anyone else?" he asked.

Brie frowned, shaking her head. "No, especially not this early in the morning."

She stayed behind while Rytsar approached the door with caution. They had been through too much recently not to be paranoid about unannounced visitors.

Rytsar took a quick look through the peephole and turned to Brie with a smirk. "Things are about to get bumpy for you."

Brie had no idea who could be on the other side of the door, but the glint in Rytsar's eye let her know whoever it was, he expected an entertaining show out of it. Rytsar swung the door wide open and smiled at the couple standing in the doorway.

"Welcome, Mr. and Mrs. Bennett. How nice to see you again."

Brie's stomach twisted in a knot when her parents walked through the door. She'd avoided all contact after the crash because of Lilly. It had been a cruel but necessary decision, but now, she was going to have to face their wrath because of it.

Wanting to curb her father's hostility, Brie hugged her mother first and asked in a forced, but pleasant, tone, "Why didn't you tell me you were coming?"

"Why would we?" her father replied, huffing in disgust. "You would have just brushed us off again. We're your parents, for Christ's sake."

Brie was hit by the force of his anger. Sadly, she knew it was justified so she tried to make amends by hugging him. She hoped the physical contact would ease some of the tension between them.

Brie's mother pulled her back into her arms, holding her tight. It hurt Brie deeply to see her mother's tears. "It's been too long. Way too long, sweetie," she said, staring at Brie's stomach in shock. "Look how big you've gotten! What are you, six months, now?" The tears started up again as she glanced over at her husband, lamenting, "I can't believe how much I've missed, Bill."

Brie was crushed by a wave of guilt, and it only increased when her father added, "You have been very unkind to your mother, young lady."

She could feel his seething resentment under the surface and pleaded with him, "Daddy, I need your understanding, not your anger."

"What? Are we supposed to simply accept that you cut us out of your life as soon as Thane had the accident? When you needed us the most, you became cold and distant instead of reaching out to us. Maybe I can handle such shoddy treatment by my own child, but it's not fair to your mother. She didn't deserve any of this, and you should be ashamed of yourself."

"Please, Bill," her mother pleaded, looking at Brie with compassion. "Let's not start off on the wrong foot."

Instead of backing down, her father turned his hateful stare on Rytsar for emphasis, asking her, "Brianna, where is your husband right now?"

Brie knew her father disliked Rytsar, and she resented the accusing tone. However, she still needed to defuse his anger, so she kept her voice calm as she explained, "He's in the bedroom doing physical therapy, Daddy. Rytsar arranged it so Thane could come home and recover here."

Her mom took pity on Brie and offered cheerfully, "That's wonderful, honey! I'd be happy to help you in any way I can by cooking, cleaning, running errands…whatever you need."

Brie felt threatened by her mother's simple offer to help, afraid that her parents might try to take over her life.

Hell, she reasoned, *I've handled all of it on my own for how many months?*

Trying to keep a level head, she told her mother, "I'm finally getting my life back to normal. As much as I appreciate—"

"Brie, are those your parents I hear?" Sir called out from the bedroom.

"It is, Sir."

Brie felt her father tense when she called Thane by that title. Just one more reason she didn't want to deal with her parents right now.

"Please, ask them to come join me."

Brie purposely used the title again to rile her dad. "Sir would like to see you both."

"Well, at least *someone* wants to see us," her father mumbled under his breath.

Brie trudged slowly to the room, not wanting to bring this added stress into Sir's life. When she entered, however, she felt butterflies in her stomach. Sir was standing upright, with both men to either side, holding him up as he struggled to take a step.

Her heart raced at the sight of him walking again.

"It's going to be a long road ahead," Sir told her parents, "but I am determined to fully recover as soon as possible."

Her mother's jaw dropped. "Thane, I can't tell you how surprised I am to see you doing so well."

Her father felt the need to offer his wisdom during this extraordinary moment. "I can tell you right now, you will never return to what you once were, but you can create a new standard for normal."

Brie was unhappy he sounded so negative, but Sir nodded to him and actually smiled. "Wise words. Thank you for the honest insight, Dad."

Sir calling her father "Dad" had an immediate effect as Brie could feel the tension in the room beginning to ease.

Brie smiled gratefully at Sir. No matter the situation, he always handled her dad with kindness and respect. Most men would not have been so generous. She doubted her father realized how lucky he was to have Sir as his son-in-law.

When Sir's legs began to tremble from the effort, the two hunky medical workers helped him back onto the bed and he asked them to leave.

Sir said to her father, "Brie informed me that she kept you both at arm's length after the crash."

"She did." Her father gave Brie a disapproving look that managed to make her feel like a little kid again.

"I want to assure you that that will not be the case now."

Her mom blurted excitedly, "I was just telling Brie I would be happy to help in any way I can. I'm completely at your disposal."

Brie's heart dropped. No matter what her mother's good intentions were, Brie did not want to lose their newfound privacy, especially with Rytsar staying at the apartment with them. After months of living in the hospital, she was just getting used to feeling normal again. Adding two more people to the mix—*especially* her parents—seemed like too much pressure for them to bear right now.

No… She looked at Sir, silently begging him to turn down her mother's offer.

"Mom, although I wish we could have you stay with us, as you can see, our apartment is bursting at the seams at the moment. However, if you're willing to assist with errands, it would be a significant help to Brie and I."

Brie could suddenly breathe again. With a few careful words, Sir had respectfully informed them that they would need to get a hotel and that he would determine how they could be most helpful without interfering.

Leave it to Sir, Brie thought. *I love my husband!*

Sir continued, "Even more important to me, I would appreciate if you could take your daughter out and give her time away from this place. She has been a devoted wife and caregiver almost to a fault, and she could seriously use a little 'me' time."

"Of course, Thane. It would be my joy," her mom answered, smiling at Brie.

While it was a sweet idea, Brie *really* didn't want to go. She decided to speak up, even though it might displease both Sir and her parents. "I don't want to leave your side, Sir."

The look he gave her was tender and kind. "Baby-girl, you have been at my side for months. It's important that you take time for yourself and enjoy this last trimester of pregnancy."

"Oh, honey." Her mother wrapped her arms around Brie's stiff body. "I would love to go shopping with you for some stylish maternity clothes."

"And I would like to spend time talking to my daughter *alone*. I'm tired of the silent treatment you've subjected us to," her father added.

Brie groaned inside. It didn't seem fair that she should be dragged away from the comfort of Sir and Rytsar's company only to be harassed by her father. She looked at Sir sadly, trying to convey her mixed emotions.

He gave her a sympathetic smile as he sealed her fate. "I would love to see my beautiful wife dress up for a change. Show off your baby bump with pride, my dear."

Brie returned his smile but couldn't hold back the heavy sigh that escaped. She understood he'd given her a gentle command.

"Why are you reluctant?" her father demanded angrily, insulted by Brie's obvious reluctance.

Thankfully, Rytsar spoke up. "I believe your daughter has been so busy caring for everyone else that she's forgotten what it is like to be cared for. It will do her good to spend time with the people who raised her."

Although Brie didn't agree with Rytsar that she needed to be cared for, at least his reply put her father at ease. Maybe she would survive this day...

As much as she was dreading it, her mom was bubbling with enthusiasm. "Hon, remember when we went shopping for your wedding dress? Think of all the laughing we did that day, and now it's going to be for maternity clothes." She looked at Brie, beaming with pride. "I can't believe my little girl is having a baby."

The memory of their adventures trying to find the perfect wedding dress was dear to Brie and she realized she was being unfair to them. She had, after all, been the one to close herself off completely after the crash.

Although her motivation had been to protect the tenuous relationship her father had with Sir, her actions had hurt them deeply. Yet, here they were, wanting to help Brie out. She gazed at her mom with new understanding. "Yes, Mom, it would be nice to shop together again."

The smile that spread across her father's face emphasized to Brie that his wife's happiness was his main concern and it softened her heart. When she went to hug him again, she meant it when she said, "It will be good to spend time together, Daddy."

Her mom insisted Brie sit up front with her father on their way to the mall. Although Brie would have preferred sitting with her mother, she agreed, not wanting to cause any more friction between them.

Sir had given her a pep talk just before leaving, reminding Brie to look at the situation from her parents' perspective, especially given that she was about to be a mother herself.

Staring down at her belly, Brie wondered how she would feel if, sometime in the future, her daughter suffered a tragedy but refused any help. It would absolutely break her heart to be cut off like that.

Turning to her dad, she took the first step toward reconciliation. "I'm sorry, Daddy. I know how I handled things after the crash really hurt both of you. I never meant to, but I was a mess and wasn't thinking of anyone else. I couldn't lose Thane. He was my only focus…" Her voice caught, and she stopped for a moment.

"I understand, dear," her mother said from the back, patting her shoulder reassuringly.

"Let her continue," her father insisted.

Brie took a deep breath, steeling herself before she continued. "I would have reached out to you eventually, but when Rytsar disappeared, things got even worse for us."

Her parents had no idea how bad…

"I know about Lilly," her father stated.

Brie stared at him in disbelief. "What do you mean?"

"I shared that email with your father," her mother informed Brie. "I couldn't stand there being any secrets between the three of us."

Brie sat there in shock. He knew about the black-mail attempt…

"What do you have to say for yourself?" her father demanded.

Still in shock, she faced him. "If you know what Lilly was accusing Thane of, then you must understand why I wanted it kept secret. I appreciated how hard it was for you to accept Thane because of our lifestyle, and I couldn't take the chance you might believe Lilly's accusation."

She looked down at her hands, wringing them nervously. "I couldn't bear it if you ended up hating him, especially if…" Her voice caught again, but she forced herself to finish. "Especially if Thane had died and never gotten the chance to defend himself."

"Did you really think I'm that stupid?" her father demanded.

"Stupid? No, of course not…" Brie faltered, feeling the conversation already heading south.

Her mom reached over the seat and squeezed her shoulder gently. "Your father has a keen mind, honey. Initially, he was as shocked as I was when he read what Lilly was claiming. But, after poring over the anonymous message and the photos, he was able to deduce that she had set Thane up and sent the email to us, hoping to discredit him and to hurt you."

Brie glanced at her father, now wondering if she had trusted him back then, if she might have had her parents' support the entire time.

"I'm not an idiot, Brianna."

"I know, Daddy. But even I was questioning my own husband when she first made those accusations. How could I expect you to react any differently?"

"Your lack of trust hurt, little girl. Are we not family?"

Brie swallowed hard, nodding.

What her father failed to acknowledge was that Brie had reasons to fear what his reaction would be. It had started that first day, when she announced she was dating Sir and he had reacted badly. Things became even more complicated when her documentary came out and both of her parents began struggling with her lifestyle becoming public. All along, her father had wanted to blame Sir for the direction her life had taken, not accepting that everything she'd done had been her decision alone.

Truly, it hadn't been until the premiere of her film, when she had been attacked, that Brie had seen a glimmer of hope around her father's changing feelings toward Sir—it was the first time her father acknowledged that Sir might truly love her.

Being a man of principles, Sir always treated her father with the respect his position deserved, no matter how disrespectful her father was in return. Sir's actions eventually won him over—enough to bless their marriage and walk his little girl down the aisle in Italy.

Despite having solid reasons for her caution, one thing was clear from their conversation: Her parents genuinely loved her and supported Thane, and she had hurt them more than she knew by her continued silence.

"I'm sorry... *so* sorry for hurting both of you."

Her father surprised her by pulling off to the side of the road and turning to face her. "Look at me, Brianna."

Brie braved meeting his gaze.

"What you did was wrong, but your mom and I love you. Our hearts are big enough to forgive you for this. While we will choose to forget and put it in the past, I want you to remember it. Not because I need you to feel guilty, but because I want it to serve as a reminder of our loyalty to you...and to Thane."

She nodded, speechless, his words having touched her so deeply.

"Brie," her mother added, "I understand why you thought you needed to keep things from us. But from now on, we can't have secrets between us."

Brie smiled, but it was with a heavy heart. She wanted to be open with her parents, but there were certain events that would always remain a secret between them, including the attempted kidnapping. Brie knew her parents would never stop worrying if they heard what Lilly had done.

Heck, even now, they might insist on her moving back to Nebraska in a misguided attempt to keep her safe. As their only child, they had everything to lose, but Brie didn't want to live her life that way.

So, even if she knew then what she knew now, Brie would have made the same decision to pull away to protect them—and herself.

Sadly, her parents would have to remain in the dark, but she would do everything within her power not to cause them that kind of pain again. Her parents had done nothing to deserve it.

"While I can't change what happened, I promise not to hurt you guys again. I love you both too much."

Her father chuckled. "Sorry, Brianna, you can't make that promise."

"What do you mean?"

"Parents are always affected by their kids. If you are happy, we're happy. If you are suffering, we're suffering. You are going to hurt us again. It is the way things are, no way around it."

Brie had a better understanding of what he meant, knowing how much she cared about the baby growing inside her. Rubbing her stomach, she told him, "I'm beginning to get what you mean, Daddy." Amending her promise, she vowed, "I will keep in touch with you both no matter what is going on in my life."

"Now, that is a promise I can live with," he stated, holding his arms out to her.

Brie leaned over to hug him. It was an awkward embrace because of the divider in the middle, but it was one of the warmest hugs he'd ever given her.

When she pulled away, she took her mother's hand and squeezed it, smiling with tears in her eyes.

"We will always love and support you, darling," her mother assured her.

"Thank you, Mom."

Her father pulled back onto the road and announced, "First, we get a good lunch down you, a nice Reuben sandwich for old time's sake."

Brie laughed. "It's been forever since I've had one of those."

"No one makes the original like a Nebraskan, but we'll see what we can find in this tinsel town."

"And, after that, we're going to shop our little hearts out," her mother added excitedly.

"Yes, when we return you to my son-in-law, I want him to agree that you are the most stylish pregnant woman he's ever seen," her father announced.

Brie smiled, her heart overflowing with love, yet she still suffered from lingering guilt. She should have trusted Sir when he'd insisted she join her parents for the day.

He knew the profound feeling of having lost both of his parents, and he had simply wanted to ensure Brie took full advantage of the love her parents showered upon her. Brie pulled out her cell phone and sent him a text.

Thank you for this, Sir. I love you!

A short time later, she received a text back.

Make the most of it, babygirl.

A few seconds later, he sent a second.

This man loves you.

She quietly slipped her phone back into her purse and closed her eyes, soaking up the sheer brilliance of his love.

Too Hot to Handle

Weary, Brie looked over at Rytsar, sweat rolling down her face from the pain and the effort. "I can do this…"

"Yes, you can, *radost moya*. You must." Giving her a wink, he added, "I am ready to finally be a *dyadya*."

His words filled her with renewed energy.

Every push was a step closer to meeting her daughter. Brie tilted her head back to look at Sir, who was standing behind her and smiled weakly as she readied herself for another contraction.

"You're doing good, babygirl. The doctor said you only have a couple of centimeters to go."

She laughed tiredly. "Who knew that childbirth was really an extreme version of BDSM?" Brie started breathing more rapidly as another contraction gripped her body.

"You need to slow your breathing," Sir reminded her.

Brie heard him and understood what he wanted, but she was in pure agony. She shook her head, still resisting it as she lay there, gasping for breath after the contraction ended.

Sir wiped away the tears that had formed during her struggle. "They're getting stronger and closer together, which is good."

Brie nodded, knowing he was right, but she honestly didn't feel that way. If she could make them stop in order to give her a breather, she totally would. But nature was a sadist, and the onslaught of contractions just kept coming...

"I demand a safeword."

Rytsar chuckled. "This is your ultimate challenge, is it not? Knowing that there is no end until the task is complete."

Brie sighed as she laid her head on the pillow.

No safewords...

The doctor came back in to check her. "We seem to have stalled out a bit. If we don't start seeing more progress, I'll give you Pitocin to make the contractions stronger."

Brie's eyes widened in fear.

When the doctor left the room, Brie whimpered, legitimately terrified.

"I know what will open you up," Rytsar said with confidence.

"What?" she squeaked.

"Sexy thoughts."

Brie frowned. "Rytsar, you shouldn't joke at a time like this."

"No, I think he's right, babygirl. I want you to think of one of your fantasies. Make it a challenging one to complement the pain you are feeling."

She tilted her head back. "Are you serious?"

"Yes, I think it will help." Sir leaned forward from behind her so he could play with her breasts through the material of her gown. "Close your eyes and let that imagination of yours run wild."

Brie took a deep breath. Already, her body was responding to Sir's touch as he tugged and squeezed her nipples.

She closed her eyes, wondering what fantasy she should play out in her mind. Something challenging and kinky...a smile suddenly came to her lips.

"Have you got one in mind?" Sir asked.

She nodded.

"Does it involve me, *radost moya*?"

"It does, Rytsar...along with Sir, Master Anderson, and Boa."

Sir's chuckle was low and alluring as he whispered in her ear, "Indulge yourself..."

I was nervous. I knew Sir was planning to play out the fantasy I had written in my journal—the one about Sir, Rytsar, and the two hunky men who visited our home daily to help Sir in his recovery.

Unfortunately, I'd already been informed that the two men were strictly vanilla and would not be joining us. Instead, he'd invited men I knew and had scened with before but he refused to tell me which ones.

The only hint was that I would find the scene challenging.

Normally, I would have been intimidated by that, but Sir had a way of taking my fantasies and making them even more delicious than I ever imagined.

I trust him completely, but my curiosity is killing me.

He takes me to a private home, explaining on the way that the owners are off traveling in Europe and have offered their place to him. I like the idea of an unfamiliar environment. It adds to the sense of the unknown and increases my excitement.

We pull up to a mansion in Beverly Hills. It is impressive with its marble path leading up to the house and the giant water fountains on either side, surrounded by lush greenery. There's no doubt important people live here.

Sir leads me inside and I am blown away by the size and opulence of the foyer alone. A small house could fit in that space. I look up at the tall ceiling and muse over what it would look like to have a ballet of submissives flying in jute above me.

I am guided down a flight of stairs and taken through the hallway to a set of grand double doors.

The doors open up to a luxurious, multi-roomed suite with an impossibly large canopy bed next to a window overlooking a manicured garden. Everything about this place is over the top.

To contrast against the luxurious surroundings, Sir asks me to strip. I look to my left and see a wall covered in mirrors. As I take off my clothes, I catch a glimpse of my naked body. I bow before him, turned on by the fact he still wears an expensive Italian suit.

I am his, to be used according to his will, and I know from personal experience that his will is kinky and ravenous.

"I will not be the only one you please tonight."

Rytsar enters the room from one of the adjoining areas. The wicked grin on his face and the erection outlined in his pants alerts me to the fact he is aroused by what Sir has planned for me.

I have enjoyed quite a few scenes with these two and look forward to them putting me through my paces—but we are not alone.

Master Anderson walks in, dressed only in blue jeans and his black Stetson. I bite my lip as I gaze up at his manly chest. He tips his hat to me. He, too, appears to be excited about the evening's events based on the rigid cock trapped in his jeans.

So it is to be three on one tonight. I am curious how it will play out, considering the impressive size of Master Anderson's shaft. I start to feel tingles of fear and excitement, wondering how much my body will be pushed.

That's when a fourth man enters the room. I let out a gasp when I see who it is.

I am very familiar with Boa and his shaft, having studied it closely during class at the Submissive Training Center, and then later having been claimed by it during one of my practicums.

Boa is every bit as challenging as Master Anderson.

I brave a glance up at Sir, wondering how much he

will demand of me.

"Téa, there will be no safeword tonight."

My heart skips a beat. We have never played out a scene without a safeword before.

"Do you understand and consent?" he asks.

As always, I have control over what happens next. My curiosity outweighs my fear and I answer confidently, "Yes, Master."

"Very well."

I feel the sexual tension rise in the room, now that the four men know there are no limits hindering them. However, this will not be a free-for-all because my Master orchestrates the scene.

First, I am taken to a room on the left where a pole in the center of the room dominates the space. Sir binds my wrists as Master Anderson takes out his bullwhip and begins warming up his arm. With no safewords, I am left totally to his mercy.

I glance nervously at Master Anderson, knowing well the bite of his whip, and he winks at me. I understand that he will be delivering pain, but take comfort in the knowledge I will be kept safe under his Dominance.

The other Doms stand on either side of me and at a distance, so they can watch.

Like the other room, one of the walls is covered in mirrors so I can experience the bullwhip as I watch it strike. This adds a whole new element to the scene, and I tremble with anticipation.

"Get ready, darlin'. This is going to sting."

I whimper before the first lash even makes contact

with my skin. The moment of impact, I cry out with the pain I knew was coming, my back on fire with the strength of his first stroke. This initial lash lets me know he is not warming my skin before diving into play.

My focus is now riveted on that whip and the next stroke coming.

Unlike times before, he does not stop or slow down. It is a continuous volley of strokes that leave me no room to breathe. I scream loudly when it becomes too much, but Master Anderson continues to challenge me, enjoying the limit he has crossed.

When the lashes finally stop, I am left panting and shaking in my bonds, my body numb from the on-slaught. I almost feel as if I am an outside participant to my own body, except I still feel the sting when his hands touch the lash marks he has left on my back.

"I love watching your body respond to my bull-whip."

I moan, mesmerized by his voice. He turns my head, kissing me deeply, his tongue unleashing the need and passion produced by our scene. I become caught up in his erotic energy and surrender to his ardent kisses, inviting him to consume me.

He groans in response, pressing his hard cock against my body.

I want him to claim me…to ravage this vessel he has primed for his use. But I am left needy and desperate when he pulls away.

Rytsar joins me next. After taking off his jacket and rolling up his sleeves, he tightens my bonds and whispers in my ear that he is going to make me orgasm.

Claiming my submission, he bites my neck. His teeth sink into my skin, not hard enough to draw blood, but enough to leave a mark.

He kneels behind me and begins strapping a device I know well onto my trembling thigh. Settling the head of it against my clit, he places it at just the right angle to leave me helpless to its vibration. Rytsar backs away without turning it on. He picks up his cat o' nines and I whimper when I hear it cut through the air, knowing the intense pain it will cause.

He smiles as he walks around me slowly, feeding off my fear and obviously relishing it.

Without a safeword, I know he may be the greatest challenge I face tonight. The first time I scened with him and his nines, I'd only taken three strokes before I had cried "red"—and my back still burns with Master Anderson's recent attention.

I have no safety net now…it both terrifies and arouses me.

Rytsar returns to my side, tracing his finger over my lips. "You will count out each strike," he commands before reaching down and turning on the Magic Wand. My whole body stiffens as my clit is rocked by the strong vibration.

Because of the priming done by Master Anderson, I am not surprised when the first orgasm builds at lightning speed.

"Permission to come?" I gasp, having no idea what I will do if he says no, since I have no control at this point.

"Of course," he replies smoothly. "I want you to come often while you scream."

His words frighten me but do not hinder that first orgasm. My whole body shudders in pleasure.

"Good…" he purrs in that sexy Russian accent.

My senses suddenly come back into sharp focus as he stands behind me, swinging the nines lazily, making me wait for that first strike.

I have never been so scared. Out of nowhere, I start to cry.

He chuckles. "I take pleasure in your tears, *radost moya.*"

I whimper softly, glancing in the mirror when he releases that first stroke. Fire erupts on my back as I cry out a painful, "One…" He crisscrosses the next stroke with the same intensity, and I scream, "Two…" His strokes are focused, dragging a beast-like shriek from me when I try to voice the next number.

He growls lustfully, turned on by my agony, and commands, "Come for me."

I shake my head in disbelief. Not because I want to disobey him, but because I think it's impossible while his fiery strokes continue. But it's as if my body is connected to him now, desiring his pleasure. I shift my focus to that buzzing tool between my legs.

I cannot drown out the fierce pain his nines incite, but it becomes melded with the stimulation of the wand. With concentration, I am able to build on it until my next climax hovers on the edge.

"*Da,*" he purrs behind me just as the nines cut through the air, landing on my back.

His verbal encouragement, coupled with the stroke of his nines, sets off a chain reaction in both my mind and body. My entire being shudders as I am taken over by an intense orgasm born of unbearable pain and intense pleasure.

Rytsar pauses for a moment, letting me savor it. But, just as it ends, the nines start up again, and I howl in pain.

"*Radost moya...*" Rytsar says my name with a dangerously lustful tone that calls to the submissive in me.

My next orgasm follows, rocking my body with painful flames of desire. It is like the spiciest of foods in its addictiveness. As much as it hurts, I want more, even though it might hurt me. Before I know it, my thoughts, feelings, and the physical stimuli meld into one. I am no longer aware, lost to where I am and what is happening...

"Come back to me."

The voice of my Master pulls me back from subspace. With great effort, I open my eyes and I gaze into his. I feel his warm hand caressing my cheek, and I sigh in contentment.

"You are not done, my dear."

I let out a small gasp as he lifts me over his shoulder and carries me to a new room where the other Doms are waiting for me. This one has mirrors on all four walls.

Sir sets me down but holds me steady because I am still groggy.

Boa stands naked before me, his enormously large cock proudly announcing its need for my body.

"You will be taking him," Sir informs me.

"Yes, Master."

I know the challenge Boa's cock presents, but I am eager to give in to its girth and length.

Master Anderson surprises me when he takes off his cowboy hat and tosses it to the side before unbuttoning his jeans. His shaft, which is equally impressive in its massive size, escapes the confines of his jeans and points straight at me as if seeking me out.

"You will be taking both of us, darlin'."

Luckily, Sir is still supporting me when my knees buckle. Both men at once? This is DP on an impossible level.

I watch, speechless, as Master Anderson finishes undressing and holds out his hand to me.

No safeword.

Sir gently pushes me forward. I step toward Master Anderson, my heart beating out of my chest.

My stomach does a flip when he takes my hand and squeezes it.

There's no turning back for me.

Boa lies down on an ivory tantra chair set in the middle of the room and begins stroking his cock as he stares lustfully at my body.

I glance over at Rytsar, who is now fully dressed again. The look on his face is like that of a hungry animal. He is eager to watch this impossible coupling.

I swallow hard as Master Anderson guides me over to Boa and helps position me.

"Take all of him, téa," Sir commands.

This I can do. I press my pussy against the head of

Boa's huge cock and moan in pleasure as it breaches my opening, stretching me wide. Because of his length and girth, it requires a period of concentrated effort to take his entire shaft. I let out little cries of discomfort as I force my body to take all of him. By the time my pussy is pressing against his balls, I am sweaty and panting from the sheer strain his cock demands of my pussy.

He stares at his massive cock buried inside my wet mound and tells me in a husky voice, "There's nothing sexier than a woman taking the full length of my shaft."

Boa grabs my hips with both hands and lifts me up. I cry out as he slowly forces me back down on his cock. I am now focused on his substantial shaft, unable to think of anything or anyone else as I mentally force my body to relax and surrender to him.

Eventually, the two of us find a pleasurable rhythm, my body molding around him. My swollen G-spot is helpless against the constant friction his cock provides. I stiffen just before release, moaning loudly as I orgasm.

I hear the other men watching, make sounds of sexual excitement—a grunt, a quiet groan, a low, lustful growl. Their masculine utterances turn me on even more.

Boa gives me a sexy smack, when Sir commands that he make me come again. With strong arms, Boa begins pumping me up and down on his shaft again, faster and faster, stealing my breath away as my body struggles to conform to his energetic rhythm.

Once again, I find myself surrendering to the painful girth of his cock and relishing it as I come again. I make little whimpering sounds, the intense pulses caused by the constant stimulation driving me wild. I throw back my head, gasping as I come.

"Hold her," Sir commands.

Boa wraps his arms around me and pulls me to his chest, holding me still while my pussy milks his giant cock. As I lay there with my cheek against his sweaty chest, I am surrounded by his masculine scent and find it intoxicating. His scent permeates my senses, adding to the erotic dynamic of this encounter.

We are both subs at the mercy of Sir's whims and desires, taking pleasure in our mutual submission to my Master's will. It is an entirely new experience, and I revel in it.

As I lay there, slowly coming down from the ecstasy of my last orgasm, I hear the distinct sound of lubricant being massaged on taut skin.

The fear returns. I tense in Boa's arms, realizing that the time has come for their double penetration. My pussy is already stretched past capacity. I cannot imagine taking Master Anderson's cock in my ass, much less doing so with Boa's buried deep inside me.

This is the greatest challenge I have ever faced, and I am unsure if I will survive it.

Master Anderson moves beside me so I can watch as he liberally coats his impressive shaft with the lubricant. It seems to grow even bigger with his manual stimulation.

My eyes widen, staring in terrified fascination at his massive shaft, wondering how much I will be forced to take.

Rytsar sniffs the air and smiles. "I smell your fear, *radost moya.*"

I glance over at Sir. His eyes locked on me, a look of avarice in his expression that I haven't seen before. My body shivers under his intense gaze, and I am aroused by it.

I hear the unbuckling of a belt and watch as Rytsar removes his dress pants and pulls out his rigid cock. His lustful expression as he stares at me makes my body tingle with anticipation.

Both Sir and Rytsar walk toward me.

As they approach, I feel as if I am about to faint, not knowing how much they will expect of me. My imagination is running wild.

Sir orders Boa to let me go.

Sir reaches out and lifts my chin. I tremble at the feel of his touch, responding to the electricity of it. I look up at him with fear and adoration.

"My goddess, I am well pleased."

I smile, basking in his praise.

"But I want more."

"Yes, Master," I answer, silently wondering if this will be my undoing.

"We are going to dominate not only your body, but also your will, téa."

My pussy instinctually constricts in pleasure hearing this. The submissive in me longs for the level of domination these men offer, but I have never truly sacrificed my will before. Always, I have had the power to walk away if things go past my endurance.

The session with the bullwhip and the cat o' nines was only the prelude to this ultimate sacrifice of will. I hope to experience the greatest of submissive ecstasy.

I am standing on a precipice, about to freefall with no net to save me. I gaze at Sir, drawn to his lustful need. The love and devotion I have for him remains unfaltering. I long to please him—no matter the cost.

My bottom lip trembles. "If it pleases you, Master."

Those simple but powerful words seal my fate.

The four men grunt their approval, their eyes flashing with excitement now that I have officially laid my will down at their feet.

Sir caresses my cheek, and the pride I see in his eyes fortifies my heart, infusing me with courage.

"Anderson will claim your ass while Durov lays claim to your mouth."

I nod in understanding.

"You will keep your eyes locked on mine the entire time. I want to see every emotion play out on your face."

By commanding that my eyes remain open, he has taken away my one escape. Now I must be fully present and aware through the entire scene.

I'm finding it hard to swallow, to breathe, to even think.

Sir kneels down beside the chair and cradles my face with both hands. He leans in and kisses me. His kiss is tender and sweet—like a blessing.

The ache of my devotion cannot be satisfied.

When he pulls away, I know he has taken my will from me. I am theirs—all barriers stripped away.

Master Anderson positions himself behind me and I feel his finger, slippery with lubricant, slip inside my tight opening. He liberally coats the inner walls of my ass to ready it for penetration. I then feel the pressure of his cock press against my taut hole, but he stills himself, waiting.

I whimper, the anticipation of his penetration driving me wild.

Rytsar straddles the tantra chair, his cock level with my mouth.

"Ride Boa's cock," Sir tells me.

I start rocking my hips, and my body is instantly reminded of Boa's generous girth. While looking at Sir, I mentally force my body to relax and hear Boa's appreciative groan as I coat his shaft with my excitement.

It is true…I desire this—to be used for pleasure.

"Open your mouth," Sir commands huskily. "But keep those beautiful eyes on me."

I rest one hand on Boa's muscular chest, grasping Rytsar's hard cock with the other. I wrap my lips around the smooth head of his shaft while keeping my gaze locked on Sir. I know the Russian's cock well and purr when I taste his precome.

My eyes are on my Master, and I see that he is pleased. For a brief second, I forget everything but Sir.

"Claim her," Sir commands, his eyes gleaming with that look of avarice I'd seen before.

Master Anderson grabs my waist and holds me as he forcefully presses the head of his cock against my resistant pink rosette.

A cold chill rushes through me, but I override the primal instinct to resist and allow Master Anderson inside.

"That's it, darlin'. Let me in."

He presses harder and my cries are muffled by Rytsar's cock as Master Anderson begins to breach my opening.

I freeze up, my body overwhelmed by the intense sensation.

Sir can see that my body is fighting against this. In a velvety voice, he tells me, "I want to see the expression on your face when the head of his cock slips in."

The command has been given.

"Suck my cock, *radost moya*," Rytsar growls seductively, pushing his cock deep into my throat. I concentrate on his cock and moan in pleasure as Boa begins playing with my breasts.

The tugging and squeezing of my nipples primes my body for deeper penetration, not only coating Boa with my wetness, but also naturally relaxing my muscles. I suddenly recall that Boa's Mistress had played with my nipples during my practicum with Boa when I became personally acquainted with his mighty shaft that first time.

I realize that both men are helping me, so I suck harder on Rytsar's cock, moving in rhythm with Boa's tugging of my nipples.

It relaxes my clenched muscles enough that Master Anderson is able to push in. I scream against Rytsar's shaft in discomfort and excitement as I feel the head of his massive cock enter my ass.

"Oh, shit…" Boa groans passionately as his hands squeeze my breasts roughly. I can only imagine what this must feel like for him.

I am left gasping and panting, unsure how I can survive having two giant cocks pumping inside me but wanting to try.

The look in Sir's eyes lets me know he is extremely aroused, which excites me even more.

I feel the butterflies take over when I hear him say, "Claim her."

My body is about to be taken beyond its limit and I'm tempted to close my eyes to prepare for this fucking, but I obey my Master and keep my eyes locked on his as Boa grabs my waist and Master Anderson grabs my hips.

Together they begin moving inside me and I can't even breathe. I can feel it coming for me, the elusive gift of subspace coming to take me away…

"Brie, open your eyes."

Candles & Kinbaku

S he looked up into Sir's eyes and her reality suddenly shifted as the very real pain of childbirth took
over the remnants of her sexy fantasy.

"*Radost moya*, you must tell me what had you moaning so?" Rytsar insisted, staring at her lustfully.

She forced a smile as a strong contraction ripped
through her abdomen. She was grateful to have had at
least a momentary escape from it.

"I assume your imagination helped, based on the
noises and the hardness of your nipples," Sir commented with a hint of amusement in his voice.

Brie blushed, wondering just how loud she'd been.
"It did give me a much needed escape."

Sir kissed the top of her head. "You always are
good at putting yourself fully into a scene…"

Brie sighed, still buzzing from the unresolved
arousal caused by her fantasy of the four men. "And
what a scene it was, Sir…"

Another contraction took hold of her, demanding
Brie's full attention. The labor pains made it feel as if

her body was trying to tear itself apart from the inside out. She had experienced a variety of pain exploring BDSM, but this was completely different.

This pain had purpose beyond the experience itself. It was a rite of passage. One that was required for her to enter the world of parenthood and see her child.

Having Sir with her through this meant everything and gave her courage. At the height of one of her worst contractions yet, Sir's steady voice carried her through the pain to the other side. He became her rock to cling to whenever the unrelenting tempest crashed over her.

Rytsar, on the other hand, provided a different kind of encouragement. He remained in his chair as he had promised, watching her intently as she worked through each powerful contraction. "You are beautiful when you embrace the pain," he told her.

The warmth of his compliment spread through her like fine vodka, giving her the confidence she needed to face this ever-increasing challenge.

"Thank you," she told him, grateful for his unique influence in her life.

She tried not to gasp in pain when the next one hit, but she could tell right away that this one would be much worse than the others.

"Breathe, babygirl," Sir instructed her in his soothing voice.

She instantly thought of Tono and clung to the memory of their last scene together to get her through.

Brie heard the doorbell ring and hurried to answer it, shocked to find Tono and Autumn standing in the hallway. Her heart leapt with joy at the sight of the beloved Kinbaku master, and she immediately hugged him and Autumn.

"What the heck are you two doing in LA?"

Stepping aside, she ushered them both in, telling Sir, "Look who decided to surprise us today!"

Tono went to shake Sir's hand while Autumn hugged Brie again, gushing, "You look positively radiant with motherhood, Brie."

Looking down at her huge belly, Brie told her jokingly, "Radiant and *huge*."

Tono turned to her, a tender smile on his lips as he gazed at her. "Durov flew us in to capture your motherhood for all eternity."

Knowing Rytsar's wicked sense of humor, Brie asked hesitantly, "What do you mean?" She glanced at Thane, assuming he knew what was going on. Sir shook his head at her unvoiced question, looking as surprised as she was.

She refocused her attention on Tono, noting that the Asian Dom looked relaxed and happy—his hand casually wrapped around Autumn's waist.

"I'll be taking pictures of you, as well as creating a decorative wax mold of your stomach." He turned to Thane. "With your permission, of course."

"You not only have my permission, but also my gratitude, Nosaka."

"Wonderful," he replied, smiling at Brie.

He nodded to Autumn and explained, "We will get

the equipment out of our rental car and set things up. Mr. Davis, you are going to be part of the shoot, as well, so please dress formally."

Brie was tickled beyond words. It felt like a lifetime ago since she'd last seen Tono and, in some ways, it was. She looked forward to spending the day catching up with them both. "What would you like me to wear?" she asked him.

"A favorite outfit…and a flattering bra and panty set. I will be taking both traditional shots and ones that show off your bare stomach."

"Nosaka."

Tono turned to answer Sir. "Yes, Sir Davis?"

"I would also like photos of Brie completely nude with nothing to distract from her natural beauty."

Brie put her hands to her lips, trying to contain her excitement—totally enchanted by his request. But, knowing how shy Autumn was, Brie asked her friend, "Would you be okay with that?"

The genuine smile that spread across Autumn's face was answer enough. "I have no issues at all. I think these photos will be stunning."

Studying Autumn, Brie realized how much her friend had changed since the last time she'd seen her. This was *not* the shy girl who'd wanted to hide behind a veil. This woman radiated an easy confidence. Brie noticed she now wore makeup and had styled her hair, bringing focus to her face rather than trying to distract the eye from her facial scars. It actually made the scars less noticeable because her captivating eyes, high cheekbones, and lips were now the main focus.

It seemed as if Autumn had transformed into a new woman, much as Brie had after her training at the Center. It was exciting, and Brie couldn't wait to ask her about it.

What an incredible gift Rytsar had given her...

Brie glanced at Sir, shaking her head in wonder. "I can't believe Rytsar did this for me! We should invite him over so he can watch." She rummaged through her purse for her phone so she could call him.

Tono stopped her, saying, "Actually, he told me that he wanted to be surprised by the photos we take. I'm to make two sets of photos. One for you and one for him."

Brie shrugged, looking at Sir. "Well, there's no harm in thanking him, at least." She was disappointed when Rytsar didn't pick up and she was forced to leave a message. Wanting him to know how grateful she was, Brie promised in her message, "We'll be sure to take a photo especially for you."

While Tono and Autumn left to get the equipment and set up for the photo shoot, Brie followed Sir to their bedroom to get ready. She was still buzzing with excitement and cried, "I can't believe this, Sir. What a perfect surprise!"

"Durov is certainly full of surprises," he replied, buttoning up his white shirt.

Wanting to look perfect for him, she asked how he would like her to wear her hair.

He stared at her for a moment before answering. "I would like you to keep your curls, but sweep it back and use this to secure it." Thane walked into the closet and came back with the white orchid comb Nosaka had given her as a gift.

Brie's face lit up. "That's beyond perfect."

She quickly freshened up her makeup before starting on her hair. She was acutely aware that Sir was watching her as she added extra curls to enhance the look. It made the task much more enjoyable knowing he was taking satisfaction in observing her. It reminded Brie of the days when he would set her in an artful pose and sit back, watching her for hours.

There was something exceedingly sensual about being someone's entire focus. In a world that moved at a lightning pace, such encounters were a rare and coveted treat.

"Very nice," Thane complimented her as she modeled for him after she was done.

Brie blushed, pleased by his praise. A girl could never get enough of that, especially being a subbie.

"While you finish getting dressed, I'll discuss a few ideas I have with Nosaka. Don't feel that you need to rush, babygirl. We have plenty of time."

Brie watched him with pure adoration as he slipped on his jacket and buttoned it up. Whether Sir wore a formal suit, dressed casually, or was completely naked, he was always devastatingly handsome. She was thrilled they would be capturing him on film today. In fact, she wanted a whole wall covered in photos of him.

She thought of Rytsar and silently thanked him again before she set about the task of getting dressed for the shoot. She glanced at her reflection in the full-length mirror and caressed her stomach lovingly.

Although her pregnancy had been riddled with pain and suffering, she had enjoyed the pregnancy itself. Feeling the baby move inside her felt like a miracle each day. It seemed extraordinary that her body could create and support human life.

As she stared at her belly, Brie realized that she would miss this part of her life. Being pregnant had actually been a beautiful experience for her, despite feeling constantly uncomfortable.

She walked out of the bedroom, her heart bursting with joy again thinking about what lay ahead for the day. "I'm so excited about this!" she confessed to Tono and Autumn. "Not only do I get pictures and wax, but I also get to spend the whole day with you two. It's been far too long."

"It is an honor to be here for such a happy occasion," Tono told her in his soothing voice, sending pleasant waves of peace through her soul.

Memories of their last time together flashed through her mind, including that terrifying moment when Tono had saved her from the kidnapping attempt. She could not hide the emotion in her voice when she told him, "Thank you, Tono—for everything."

He graced her with a gentle smile.

Tono turned to Sir and said with conviction, "I always remained confident you would recover. You have a strong spirit and a devoted heart."

"I am grateful Durov thought to call you. It gives me a chance to formally thank you for what you did for Brie while I was indisposed."

Tono picked up his camera and pointed the lens at Sir while he adjusted it. "What I did, I considered a privilege because I think so highly of you two. It fortifies my heart to see you both now, whole and content."

He then asked Autumn, "Could you adjust the angle of that light for me, *kohana*?"

It warmed Brie's heart to hear the pet name he had for Autumn. It spoke to the level of comfort the two shared, now that Autumn was training under Tono as his submissive.

Autumn smiled at Tono as she corrected the angle. Meanwhile, Tono guided Brie to the spot where he wanted her to stand. He took his time to pose her, making little adjustments until he was satisfied.

Brie looked at Sir, her cheeks hurting from smiling so much.

"Sir Davis," Tono asked, "would you stand behind Brie and wrap your arms around her, placing your hands on her stomach?"

When Sir stood behind her, Brie felt like she would melt from the tenderness of the pose when he placed his hands on her belly. She stared into the camera lens, riding high on a state of emotional bliss.

Sir was extremely patient and amenable, allowing Tono complete freedom to pose the two of them in various positions so Tono could realize his artistic vision. Afterward, he took the reins, directing their photo for Rytsar.

Brie giggled as she sat on the floor completely naked, the vodka bottle, which sported the homemade label with the red line through it, sitting between her legs—artfully hiding her pubic area as she gave the camera a humorous smirk.

When Sir felt satisfied they had enough shots, Tono handed Brie her silk robe so she could join them as they previewed the final shots.

"Perfection, babygirl," Sir whispered, wrapping his arm around her.

"I think Rytsar will love it," she told him.

Sir surprised Brie when he led her away to speak privately. "I have an important errand I'm obligated to run, but I've requested that Nosaka take additional pictures of you in his jute."

Her heart fluttered at the thought of being bound in Tono's rope, and she enthusiastically agreed.

"Don't forget, you will also be enjoying the session of wax that Durov arranged."

"Wax, too!" she squeaked.

Sir smiled. "And, in gratitude for their time and kindness in coming today, I've ordered a home catered meal. Nosaka will let the cook in if I am not back by then."

She looked at him with concern. "How long do you think you'll be gone, Sir?"

He stroked her cheek. "I need to check in with a friend, but I'll be back as soon as I can. Who knows, you may still be flying in subspace by that time and won't even notice my return."

"I doubt that," she giggled. However, the idea of experiencing subspace again bound in Tono's jute had Brie more than a little excited. However, she hated that

Sir had to leave and begged, "Are you sure you can't stay?"

"No, my dear. But on my return, I will expect a full accounting of your day as we look over your pictures together."

Brie tried to pout, but it didn't last long before she broke into a smile. "Thank you, Sir."

"For what?"

"For being so wonderful."

He leaned down and kissed her tenderly on the lips. "I can see you're giddy already, just thinking about the jute."

She blushed. "You know me too well."

"Enjoy this, babygirl. It will make Durov exceedingly happy."

"Sir, if he ends up calling you first, would you tell him how happy I am?"

"Of course," he replied, kissing her again.

Sir said goodbye to Tono and Autumn, giving Brie a private wink before he headed out the door. Brie hated to see him go but was immediately distracted when Tono's favorite flute music filled the room.

"Close your eyes," Tono ordered softly.

Brie obeyed his command, letting the music carry her as she waited. When he told her to open them again, Tono stood before her, dressed in his black kimono, a length of colored jute in his hand.

"Your Master has requested that his beautiful wife be bound in my decorative jute."

Brie nodded, biting her lip in excitement.

"Let Autumn help you into your lingerie," Tono

instructed.

She glanced at Autumn, who was holding up the panty set Brie had picked out. Although she and Autumn had never worked together in a scene, she felt completely comfortable with her here.

"I have a confession," Autumn told Brie. "When Tono invited me to join him for this shoot, I actually squealed."

"I can attest to that," Tono replied, chuckling.

Brie was grateful to hear it. "So you weren't weirded out that it would be with me?"

Autumn shook her head, smiling. "Now that I've had time to get to know Tono, training as his submissive, I see things much more clearly." She glanced at Tono proudly. "Ren Nosaka is the most honorable man I've ever met. I am completely and utterly in love with him." Autumn smiled self-consciously, looking to the ground as a smile played on her lips.

Tono blushed slightly, but Brie saw in his eyes that the love Autumn had for him was returned.

Reveling in the feeling of peace and love that surrounded her, Brie quickly shed her robe and slipped into the lingerie Autumn held out for her, sincerely grateful for the help.

"Come," Tono told Brie, holding out his hand when she was done.

She glided over to him, feeling as if she were walking on clouds. When he took her hand, Brie blushed, feeling a sense of déjà vu as he helped her onto the jute mat he'd laid out.

"Sit comfortably. I will act as your support."

Brie felt awkward as she tried to find a position that was comfortable for her and the baby. But once she found it, Tono moved behind her and sat down, pulling her back against him. "I want you to close your eyes so you can concentrate on my breath."

"Breathe with me..." she murmured, a smile on her lips.

"*Hai*," he answered softly.

Brie imagined her tiny child safe within her womb, hearing the muffled but soothing sound of the flute as she was flooded with the overwhelming peace of her mother. Brie unconsciously caressed her stomach.

"Yes, I feel her, too," Tono replied quietly.

Brie smiled. Tono had always had a special connection with her, so it seemed only natural that it extend to her child, as well.

That, my little girl, is my dear friend, Tono Nosaka, she said silently.

"I will not be binding you tightly today," Tono explained. "I do not want to cause any stress for you or the baby."

Brie felt the length of the rope trail across her skin, causing delightful tingles wherever it touched. She opened her eyes and smiled up at Autumn, surprised to see her holding a camera, the lens pointed at Brie, while Autumn silently took photos of them.

It was the same role she had played at Brie's wedding—taking candid photos of the wedding party. Brie was grateful for the unique perspective Autumn would bring to recording this experience.

Closing her eyes again, Brie relaxed, doing just as

Sir had asked, losing herself in the moment—there were no cameras, no audience, only the sound of the solo flute, the feel of jute, and Tono.

Giving in to the sensations, Brie felt as if she was floating effortlessly in the ocean, and a soft peal of laughter escaped her lips.

"Yes," Tono encouraged her quietly, reaching around Brie as he tied incredibly intricate knots with skilled effort. The pull of the jute, the grazing of it against her skin, and the sound of his steady breathing filled her senses, leading her to nirvana.

When he was done, Tono stood away from her briefly to take pictures of his own. He moved around Brie, getting different angles and perspectives, smiling at her the entire time.

When he returned to her, he told her, "And now the pictures for your husband." Tono slowly unhooked her bra and pulled it through the bindings in time with the music, leaving her breasts exposed. He gently moved her long curls to the side before taking the camera from Autumn.

"When you look into the lens, I want you to speak to your husband," he instructed her.

Brie stared at the camera, the emotional high of being constricted in rope playing into her feelings for Sir and mixing with the miracle of their love growing inside her. A lone tear formed, and there was nothing she could do about it as it slowly rolled down her cheek.

"Could you wipe it away?" she asked Autumn.

"No," Tono told Brie. "Do not erase your feelings—embrace them. Look at the camera again and let your eyes reflect the depth of what you are feeling."

Brie nodded, looking at the lens as if she were staring into Sir's eyes. She felt jubilant, the joy of the rope lifting her spirits, but it melded with her profound love for Sir. Rytsar suddenly invaded her thoughts, and she felt a seed of panic.

Tono lowered his camera. "What is it?"

"Rytsar."

His expression changed to one of concern. "What about him, Brie?"

She closed her eyes, seeking to understand the reason behind her fear, but as quickly as the feeling had come, it disappeared. In its wake came a flood of warmth like the sun's rays, bringing with it a sense of bliss.

She shook her head. "I don't know what that was, but it's gone now."

Tono's eyes softened. "I am glad to hear it. Would you still like to continue?"

Brie smiled up at him, her heart light again. "Please."

"Match my breath again," he instructed.

Brie closed her eyes, reconnecting with Tono's beautiful spirit as she slowed her breathing to match his. It didn't take long before she was riding the emotional high of being bound in jute. Tears pricked her eyes when the baby moved, adding to her overall sense of euphoria.

"That's it..." he encouraged, taking several pictures in rapid succession.

She glanced over at Autumn and caught her smiling.

"You look so beautiful, Brie...like a goddess," Autumn said with a hint of awe in her voice.

Brie blushed at her compliment, but she knew Sir would love that.

Refocusing her attention on Tono, Brie appreciated how serene he seemed. Tono had always had a calming nature, but it was an outer peace he released into the world. Now, Brie could feel an inner peace that was new.

She understood.

Tono had finally found the key to his soul in Autumn—just as she had with Sir. A love that profoundly challenged a person, but also brought about positive change. She had instantly recognized those outward changes in Autumn but, as she studied Tono now, she realized the significance of the change in him. His entire aura was one of light and anticipation. It was as if he knew some wondrous secret of the universe and it made him that much more attractive.

The loving glances Autumn kept shooting his way highlighted how close they'd become during her training, and it left Brie to wonder if an official collaring was in the near future.

After a few more clicks of the camera, Tono handed it to Autumn and returned to Brie's side to begin the unbinding process. She loved that every bit as much as the binding itself, and sighed in sheer pleasure when she felt his arms around her, the warmth of his breath caressing her neck as he slowly untied the knots he'd created.

Once again, the world disappeared as she focused on Tono and the magic of his jute.

It seemed much too soon when she heard him call to her, "Brie…"

It wasn't until she opened her eyes that Brie realized she had drifted away. She looked up at him, feeling slightly dazed when she realized her head was resting in Tono's lap.

He looked down at her and smiled. "The call of the rope."

Brie answered in a wistful tone, "I call it nirvana."

Tono helped her sit up and went to the kitchen, returning with two cups of hot tea. Brie took one from him, enjoying the warmth of the cup in her hands.

Looking around, she asked, "Where's Autumn?"

"She left so you would have no distractions during the next scene."

"Autumn didn't need to do that. I enjoy having her here."

"As do I, but she mentioned wanting to visit Lea while we're here."

Brie nodded, waiting until Tono took a sip of his tea before she took hers. She couldn't help purring as the warm liquid traveled down her throat. "Still the best tea in the world."

His smile was tender, with no of hint of sadness behind it.

"You have changed," she said.

"I have."

The two continued to sip their tea in easy silence.

With Tono, it always seemed that words were unnecessary. She stared at him, conveying in their pleasant silence the joy she was feeling because of Sir's recovery, Rytsar's rescue, and the baby's upcoming birth.

"I celebrate with you, *toriko*."

Brie reached out and squeezed his hand. "I feel the same, Tono. I have never seen you so settled in your soul."

He nodded. "Autumn and I are on a path of empowerment. I hope our journey will inspire others."

"In every fiber of my being, I believe it will."

He finished his tea, placing the cup on the floor. "I will be forever grateful that you brought her and me together."

She remembered when she'd asked Autumn to watch her film a scene of Tono and Lea together. That was the beginning of it all…

Upon meeting Autumn, the gentle Dom had pulled her veil away without asking. Looking back on it now, Brie thought it was the perfect metaphor for their relationship—Tono exposing Autumn's beauty to the world—and to herself.

"It's time we begin," Tono stated, transitioning from sitting cross-legged to standing in one graceful move. He held out his hand to her.

Brie's movements were the opposite of his as she struggled to her feet, laughing as she did so. "Pregnancy is a real trip," she confessed.

He led her to the tantra chair, saying, "I believe this will be the most comfortable place for you."

She looked down at the sexy chaise lounge and

smiled, recalling the first time she had lain on this piece of furniture, having no idea what its purpose was.

"An excellent choice," she agreed.

Tono covered the entire chair, as well as the surrounding floor, in a light plastic sheet that had a cloth lining on one side. Brie appreciated his thoughtfulness as she lay against the soft material.

"A little jute," he said, holding up a length of natural jute to her nose so she could take in its alluring scent.

Tono bound only her wrists this time, lifting them over her head and securing them in that position. He then pulled out a white strip of cloth. "Your experience will be enhanced with the blindfold."

Brie's heart fluttered, grateful that Tono knew her preferences well. The blindfold would add an extra level of connection between them as her other senses were forced to take over. She lifted her head and purred as he placed the cloth over her eyes, tying it tight.

"I am going to paint your torso in a thin layer of wax made with a blend of botanical oils to begin. It will aid in the removal of your cast," he informed her.

Her heart began beating more rapidly in anticipation as she listened to him gathering the materials and smelled the odor of the match as he lit each candle.

It had been a long time since she'd felt wax against her skin, and her body longed for its warm caress.

Tono turned off the soothing flute music before he began, and the room suddenly became heavy with silence. He commanded in a tender voice, "Concentrate on the experience. Don't let any detail go unnoticed."

"Yes, Tono," she answered, eager to consume every morsel of this scene with him.

Brie giggled when she felt the first light stroke of warm wax on her skin. "It tickles."

"Shh…"

She bit her lip, trying to stay silent while he applied the second stroke of wax. The touch of it was light enough to cause a tingling sensation that made her toes curl. Tono had chosen a wax that melted at a temperature that felt warm and did not burn.

With time, Brie grew used to the ticklish feel of the brush as he coated her entire stomach in a thin layer of wax. Once completely covered, she heard him set the brush down and pick up something new.

Brie squeaked and then giggled when the first drop of wax made contact. It was much hotter, but the initial layer protected her skin.

"Color?" he asked.

"Green. Oh, I like the challenge of it."

"Good," he replied warmly.

Soon, he had Brie's heart racing, not knowing where the next drop would fall, her whole body anticipating it. Tono played with her, alternating candles and temperatures, so she never knew what to expect.

She loved his play!

Brie was grateful that Tono continued, building layer upon layer—the hot wax rolling down from her stomach, making ticklish trails on her skin as it dripped onto the cloth.

When he set the candle down on the tray and didn't return to her, she wondered if he was done and called out to him.

Tono chuckled. "Patience. I'm not finished yet."

"Good, because I don't want it to ever end," she confessed.

He returned to her side and began painting with the wax again. With a thick layer of wax covering her entire stomach, there was little she could feel, so she concentrated instead on the sound of his breathing as he created his art.

It was an intimate connection, being a canvas for his masterpiece, and was something she cherished.

When he was done, she heard the paintbrush handle clank against pottery.

"May I see it?" she asked breathlessly.

Brie could actually hear the smile in his voice when he answered. "Not yet."

She lay there, acutely aware that he was staring at her. "What is it you painted?"

"Something that has deep meaning in my culture but is also significant to you and me."

"An orchid?" she offered as a guess.

"No." Tono's light laughter filled the room.

He knelt beside her and unbound her wrists before lifting her from the chair and placing her on her feet, careful not to disturb his work. With his hands on her bare shoulders, Tono guided her down the hallway and into the bedroom. Once he had her positioned, he removed her blindfold, but told her, "Do not open your eyes yet."

Brie kept them closed, smiling as she waited for his command.

He whispered in her ear, "Open."

What she saw when she opened her eyes took her breath away. On a black background of wax, he had painted a cherry tree in full bloom, individual pink flowers painted with meticulous precision. A red bridge with a stream running under it completed the scene.

"Tono, it looks like a real painting," Brie said in awe. "No wonder it took hours."

"I wanted to create something worthy of the canvas it was painted on."

Tears filled her eyes.

"No need to cry," he softly chided her.

Brie smiled through her tears and nodded.

Tono looked at her in the reflection of the mirror. "As I told you, this has great significance."

"This is the tree you visited after your father died."

"*Hai.* It is important and connects you and me to it. In my culture, the cherry blossom has profound meaning." He placed her hand on her belly so she was touching the painted tree covered in flowers. "The cherry blossom represents the fleeting beauty of life, but also renewal and hope."

Brie nodded, too moved to speak.

He placed her hand on the bridge. "This symbolizes us transitioning from the physical world into the realm of the spirit."

"The death of your father…"

He nodded. "That is part of it, yes. However, the bridge also references the journey you take whenever you answer the call of the rope."

She looked at him, grinning. "I like that symbolism very much, Tono."

He returned her smile, continuing, "And as far as the color red, it denotes that which is sacred, as well as representing wisdom and metamorphosis. To me it speaks to Sir Davis's transition from death back to the living world."

She looked at her reflection in the mirror in awed silence.

Tono placed his hand over hers. "The fact that the canvas for this is your pregnant belly has the greatest meaning of all. Your love and fearless determination has brought new life into the world. Renewal and hope personified."

Brie leaned her head against his shoulder, completely captivated by this gift and the many layers of meaning behind it.

"Tono, this is truly a masterpiece."

"I am honored you like it."

Brie looked down at her belly, still in awe. "No, Tono. I absolutely *love* this."

I'm Not a Masochist!

Brie whimpered softly, trying to keep up a brave face when the doctor walked into the room. "Let's see how much you've progressed, shall we?"

He slipped on a pair of gloves and slipped his fingers inside. Brie felt a sense of hope when she saw him smile this time.

"I don't know what you did, but you are fully dilated, lass. Are you ready to push the wee one out?"

Brie nodded vigorously. She had no idea how painful it would be, but no matter what happened, she knew she could do this and make both men proud.

The nurse instructed Sir to lift her leg and cup her heel, holding it up and out to help with delivery. When she took the position on the other side to support Brie's other leg, Rytsar stood up.

"*Nyet*, that is my job."

"You can't. Please sit," Brie protested.

"*Radost moya*, it is important that I be the one."

Brie looked to Sir.

Sir answered her silent question, "It is his decision."

She looked at Rytsar with concern, but nodded in understanding.

The nurse stepped back and explained to her, "They are here to support you. Don't push against them, but allow the angle to aid you when you push."

"Okay," Brie answered, looking to Dr. Glas for further guidance.

"Now, Mrs. Davis, we are going to be working with your contractions, not against them. When you feel one coming, I want you to push as hard as you can down here." He put pressure on the area he wanted her to concentrate on when she pushed.

There was an excitement in knowing the time had finally come. In a couple of minutes, if she pushed hard enough, not only would the pain end, but her little girl would be in her arms.

Brie looked at Sir and Rytsar, fortified by their strength and love.

When the next contraction hit, Dr. Glas encouraged her, "Push, push, push."

Brie closed her eyes, holding her breath as the pain invaded her every thought. She tried her best to push through it.

When the contraction finally ended, Dr. Glas ordered her to rest.

They followed the same routine for the next several contractions, but Brie could tell that, despite her best efforts, her pushing was ineffective. She laid her head back, exhausted and disappointed with herself.

"This is your first time, lass. It takes a bit of practice," Dr. Glas assured her.

Brie nodded, ready to give it another try. When the next powerful contraction hit, she closed her eyes and imagined her entire body pushing the baby out, but this pain was on a different level than before, and she screamed at the top of her lungs, "I'm not a masochist. I'm not a masochist!"

Afterward, she lay back, feeling discouraged.

"I think the entire hospital now knows your limit," Rytsar teased.

She covered her eyes with her arm, completely embarrassed.

"Think nothing of it, babygirl," Sir told her. "With this next contraction, I want you to transform the pain into action. Harness it."

Brie took a deep breath, wanting to have control over the pain. When the gut-ripping contraction started up again, she focused on it, inviting it to hurt her. The progress was slow, but at least there was progress.

"That's it, lass. Now we're getting somewhere."

That small success gave her courage, and she readied herself for the next one.

"Push," the doctor commanded.

Her body shook from the effort, but she felt something give and pushed even harder. Suddenly, the room filled with the sound of an alarm.

"What's wrong?" Sir yelled.

"The baby isn't getting oxygen. I'm going to reach inside and try to relieve the pressure around her neck."

Brie cried out in pain as he tried to manipulate the baby from the inside, but the alarm kept sounding. She felt a cold chill run through her when she saw the look of fear on Rytsar's face.

"Mrs. Davis," Dr. Glas stated calmly, breaking through her growing panic. "We're going to rush you to the operating room. We need to do an emergency C-section."

Both Sir and Rytsar let go of her and stood back as nurses rushed around them, disconnecting tubes and wires, before releasing the brakes on the bed. They pushed her out of the room with Brie crying in fear, "My baby…"

"She's going to be fine, Brie," Sir shouted from behind her.

"*Moye solntse* is strong like her mother!"

Brie closed her eyes as she was pushed down the hallway, shutting everything out, including her fear, as she tried to connect with her baby.

I'm here, little girl…

To keep her mind focused and calm for her child, Brie replayed a memory that brought her hope now.

"Sir," she giggled, "I don't know if it's the whole nesting instinct kicking in or not, but I'm seriously feeling the urge to get the baby's room ready."

"I suppose now is as good a time as any."

"There are just so many things to get."

"Such as?"

"Oh, you know…decorations for the baby's room,

all the tons of equipment and cute little baby doodads."

Sir smiled, pulling out his wallet and handing her cash. "Shop to your heart's content, my dear. Have fun with it."

Brie hesitated before taking the money from him. "But…"

"Yes?"

"I was hoping to do it with you. I'd like everything to reflect both of us—as a couple. From the way her room is decorated and the type of baby carriage we buy to the music she'll fall asleep to."

He sounded amused when he told her, "Actually, I'd planned on leaving that up to you. Wouldn't you have more fun calling one of your friends, or even your mother, to help with that?"

Brie shook her head, feeling it was too important. "I want her to have the kind of environment that will encourage her growth and happiness. Your input will help to ensure that."

He smiled but did not seem convinced.

"Sir, it weighs on me knowing our baby has been through so much stress during the pregnancy. I really want her first months to be peaceful and calm, yet stimulating for her growing brain."

It was obvious by the look on Sir's face that he felt responsible for the stress the baby had endured. She heard the sorrow in his voice when he said, "You *both* have suffered far too much."

Brie looked at him with compassion. "This isn't about what's happened, but her future will be. One that I want us to create together."

He nodded thoughtfully. "Then understand I will not have an opinion about everything but, if I do, I will express it."

"Great! Let's start with the baby's room first."

Sir chuckled as Brie ran down the hallway to get her tablet. When she returned, she showed him the different rooms she'd already picked out. "The baby's room is a place we both need to feel comfortable in since we'll be visiting it so much. So, I have three examples here to kind of guide us along. What strikes your fancy?"

He looked them over with a critical eye.

Brie had never forgotten how Sir had felt about having a Christmas tree cluttering the aesthetics of his apartment, so her money was on the stylish brown one she'd chosen. She pointed to the screen and said, "What do you think of this first one with the chocolate brown theme? The stripes on the walls and brown rug give it a more adult feel…"

He surprised her by saying, "Much too formal. Looks like a dining room, not a baby's room."

Curious, she immediately cued up the next one. "Okay, how about this? The fun, playful animal theme?"

"I don't care for anything cartoonish."

"Are you leaning more toward the whole 'You Are My Sunshine' theme then?"

Sir's tone became serious. "While the *moye solntse* theme makes sense, the song itself has a negative connotation, considering Lilly is now associated with it."

Since she had shown him her top three choices, she asked, "Do you have any suggestions, Sir?"

"Yes. I think melding the animal theme with the sunshine might work. More of a nature-themed decor. More realistic than what you showed me, but still colorful to stimulate her senses."

"It's perfect, Sir."

Brie adored the idea and was grateful she'd asked for his input.

"As far as larger items such as the crib, car seat, stroller, etc., I can research those, if you would like, while you take care of the smaller things. But it would help me to know if you are more concerned with quality and functionality or general aesthetics."

"Hmmm...actually all three," she answered with a giggle. "I want something that will last, is easy to use, but still looks good."

"Like you, babygirl."

She smiled at his unexpected compliment and gave him a peck on the lips.

He let out a low, seductive growl that sent shivers down her spine as he grabbed the back of her neck and planted a long, drawn-out kiss on her lips.

"Had I known planning for the baby could be romantic and sexy, I would have started this long ago."

Sir laughed, looking back over her long list of baby items. "As far as the other incidentals, make a day of it with your friends. Personally, I don't care what diaper pail you get as long as it keeps the odor sufficiently contained."

Brie was suddenly struck by the oddness of their

conversation. She stared at him with a wistful expression. "You and I are in for some major changes—a life full of dirty diapers and burp rags."

"It will be interesting to see how it all plays out."

"In some ways, I can't wait, but I'm also terrified," she confessed. "I have no idea what I am doing. I really wish there was a six-week training course on being the best parent."

Sir chuckled. "We're no different than any other couple starting a family. Luckily, you have your mother to turn to for advice when needed. Her wisdom will prove invaluable to us." Sir placed her tablet on the table and opened his arms to her.

Brie settled into them, sighing with contentment. Nothing felt better than being here in Sir's arms.

"It's important we enjoy the journey ahead," he told her.

Pulling away to gaze into his soulful eyes, she said, "It's also important that we don't lose ourselves as a couple…"

"I won't let that happen, babygirl."

"But how can I serve you as a submissive without involving her, especially as she gets older and begins to notice things?"

"It will simply take thoughtful planning. We'll make it a point not to pressure our daughter into living and participating in the lifestyle until she is old enough to make that decision herself."

"I agree with you completely, but on a practical level, how will that work in our apartment? Even if I wear a ball gag, our little girl will hear everything."

"I've actually been thinking about that. As much as I enjoy our place, I feel a move is in order. One that allows us the space to grow as a family, but also gives you and me the privacy we require."

"I should have guessed you'd be planning ahead."

He kissed her forehead. "While it's true we have numerous changes ahead of us, I'm confident we can meet them."

She settled back in his arms, a feeling of serenity washing over her.

Whenever she scened, she trusted Sir completely, and that was true in their vanilla lives as well. He was a good partner, always looking ahead, anticipating obstacles and planning for ways around them.

"I feel confidence because I have you with me," she stated.

"So…" he began, pausing for a moment. "Have you given any thought to having another child?"

Brie laughed, assuming he was joking. "No, I'm not even done cooking the first one yet."

"I realize that," he replied, chuckling. "However, once she's born, we will need to make that decision fairly quickly. As I mentioned before we started this endeavor, I'm not getting any younger, Brie. It's important my offspring have an active, involved father."

Brie imagined Sir on the floor, playing with his children, and her heart about melted.

Children…

Without really needing to think about it, Brie felt they were meant to have more than one. Being an only child had given Brie the advantage of receiving one hundred percent of her parents' devotion and attention, but it had also left her alone. There had been many times she'd felt jealous of her friends when they talked about their siblings. That kind of bond was something she would never know.

"If I am honest, Sir, I *do* want our daughter to have a brother or sister. How do you feel?"

"I'm in agreement. I would like our daughter to have the intimate connection only siblings can experience."

She stared at him in shock. "And, just like that, we're planning for another." Brie shook her head, giddy at the thought. "Our children…"

The baby pushed against Brie's stomach, making herself known. "Come now, little girl, don't go abusing your mama so," Brie chided.

Sir placed his hand on the protruding area and smiled when the baby kicked again. "She seems eager to join us."

"I do find it amazing that my body is giving her everything she needs right now but, soon, I will be responsible for feeding her, burping her, changing her diaper, making sure she's warm enough…"

"You're not the only one responsible for her."

"Really?"

Sir stroked her cheek. "While I obviously can't breastfeed the baby, I will be happy to burp her and change my fair share of diapers."

She couldn't hide her stunned expression. "You'll change dirty diapers?"

He seemed surprised by the question. "Naturally."

"I just assumed...."

"Assumed what?"

Brie shrugged, blushing. "You're my Master."

"So you thought, as your Master, I would shy away from taking care of my child? Did I not tell you that I would never expect you to do anything that I wasn't willing to do myself?"

"I didn't think you meant in *all* aspects of our lives, Sir." She threw her arms around him, leaving trails of kisses down his manly jaw. "How amazing to think our little girl will know the love and care of both parents. That's more than my dad ever did. My mom said he stayed at least ten feet from any diaper and never once burped me."

"His loss, then. I remember my dad sharing some of the humorous situations he found himself in while caring for me as an infant. He wanted that extra time with his boy because of his constant traveling, and I am forever grateful for it."

"Our daughter is a lucky girl."

"I'm not entirely convinced of that. You've felt the wrath of my demons before. How can a child, who knows no better, handle such a thing if it should happen again?"

Brie smiled tenderly. "We've become different people since that day you first collared me. You're working through those demons and are not the same man you were then."

"True, I am not."

"And I'm totally convinced every parent struggles.

My parents are good examples of that. Sure, bad things happened while I was growing up, but I knew I was loved and cherished even when my dad had to leave us behind. It's not what happened to you as a kid that defines your childhood, but how our parents handled it. That's what stays with you and shapes you as an adult."

Sir looked at Brie, his gazed still haunted with lingering doubt. "I fear my good intentions will not be enough."

"It will be, Sir."

Brie laid her head on his chest, watching her stomach jump because of their active child. "In just a few more months, we won't be talking about how to care for her. We'll be living it day by day."

Sir's voice suddenly became more somber. "There was a time when I didn't think I would have that chance. So, long nights awake with the baby seems like a small price to pay for such a miracle."

Tilting her head up, Brie was overwhelmed with love for him.

"I couldn't agree more, Sir."

Hello

B rie was jolted back to reality when they lifted her and placed her on the operating table. The nurse reconnected her to all the monitors while Dr. Glas scrubbed up. When he returned, he checked the position of the baby and announced, "Her vitals are back to normal for now. We can try delivering her vaginally if you can push her out in the next few contractions."

Brie felt a hand on her shoulder and felt a flood of relief when she looked up to see Sir dressed in scrubs. She was not alone, and that gave her the encouragement she needed to face this. She had been uniquely prepared for this moment, and she would not fail.

"I want to try," she told him.

"Good," Dr. Glas stated, explaining, "When the next contraction comes, I want you to push with everything you've got, and I don't want you to stop until I tell you."

Brie braced herself, readying for the greatest challenge of her life.

As soon as the contraction hit and Brie started pushing, the alarm started sounding again, letting her know her baby was in distress. She redoubled her efforts, roaring like a primal animal.

"That's it, that's it. I see the head. We're almost there. Don't stop!" Dr. Glas ordered.

From deep within, Brie harnessed the last of her strength, gritting her teeth and pushing with everything she had, knowing her daughter's life hung in the balance. Another primal scream escaped her lips, with Sir's words of encouragement filling her ears.

Brie's whole body shook from sheer effort as she forced the baby out and her child slipped into the ready hands of the doctor.

Brie collapsed onto the bed immediately afterward, thoroughly spent. She felt Sir's reassuring touch stroking her cheek. "Is she okay?" she croaked.

Instead of crying, which Brie was waiting to hear, there was only silence.

"Is something wrong?" Brie cried out.

"Nothing is wrong," Dr. Glas assured her. "Your little girl seems to be quietly taking it all in." Brie watched as he began rubbing her tiny back. Suddenly, the reassuring sound of her healthy cry filled the room.

Brie closed her eyes and let the tears fall as relief flooded through her. She opened them again when she felt Sir's hand on her cheek. "Well done, little mama."

Instead of placing the baby in Brie's arms, the nurse took her from the doctor, whisked her away, and began quickly working on their child.

"Dr. Glas?" Brie questioned him, concerned.

He lowered his mask. "You did well, Mrs. Davis. She may be a wee one, but she is healthy. While my nurses take care of her, I'll go ahead and stitch up your small tear."

"Can't I hold her?"

"Since she surprised us with an early arrival, it's important we check her over first," he explained. Putting the mask back on, he prepared to begin the procedure.

Before he began, Brie bravely voiced her request, "Could you make it a little tighter?"

"No," Sir stated beside her. "Tighter would not be an improvement. I'd like you just the way you were."

The doctor smiled behind the mask. "Spoken like a true gentleman." Dr. Glas winked at Brie, assuring her, "I will do my best to restore you to your previous state, Mrs. Davis."

Brie stared up at Sir, suddenly exhausted to the core of her being.

"I'm so proud of you, babygirl. You were amazing."

Brie smiled, but then the tears started up when she imagined how hard this birth would have been if he had died in the plane crash.

Sir leaned down and whispered, "There's no need to cry, my love. This is a happy day."

Brie stared intently at the nurse's back while she handled their baby. Once the doctor was done with Brie, he walked over to assess the child himself.

"A healthy girl at six pounds on the dot," he announced.

The nurse turned around with the tiny baby in her

arms. "Would you like to hold her now?"

"Please!" Brie begged.

Walking over to her, the nurse laid the baby on Brie's chest.

She looked at her daughter in awe. Her skin was a warm olive tone, a testament to her father's Italian heritage. Her soulful eyes also reminded Brie of Sir, but that pert little nose and arched lips came from Brie's side of the family.

This little miracle was the perfect combination of the two of them. With tentative fingers, Brie caressed her soft head, covered in brown peach fuzz.

You're perfect.

Brie smiled as tears of joy ran down her cheeks when her daughter squirmed, making cute little baby noises.

"Isn't she perfect, Sir?"

"She certainly is," he agreed with pride in his voice. Sir leaned down, inches from her tiny face, and smiled at his daughter. "Welcome to the world, little one. I have been waiting a long time to meet you."

The nurse apologized, informing them, "We need to monitor her due to the early delivery."

Brie gave Sir a worried look.

The nurse noticed and smiled reassuringly at Brie. "Your daughter appears to be doing fine. If her vitals remain good, we'll bring her to your room so you can begin feeding her."

Brie gave her daughter one last kiss before relinquishing her to the nurse. She watched as the tiny bundle that had just become her whole world was whisked away.

Sir leaned down and whispered huskily, "Mrs. Davis, it appears you make beautiful babies."

Brie smiled up at him. "*We* make beautiful babies."

She was wheeled into a recovery room where Rytsar was waiting for them.

"The babe?" he asked with concern as soon as he saw her.

"She's healthy, but they are monitoring her now to make sure everything's okay because she was early," Brie told him.

Sir clasped Rytsar's shoulder. "I'm sorry you could not be there."

"The only thing that matters is that *moye solntse* is well."

"She is," Brie assured him.

"Are you, *radost moya?*"

"I am now, but it was so scary, Rytsar."

He nodded, a pained expression on his face. "I thought I would go mad, waiting to hear news of you both."

"She is safe and Brie is well, brother. There is reason to celebrate,"

Brie reached out to Rytsar, and he took her hand, kissing it gently. "If I were healed enough, I would be doing the Cossack dance in celebration right now."

"Oh goodness, no!" Brie laughed, a vision of Rytsar

doing the strenuous Russian dance in the recovery room flashing through her mind. "You must rest."

Rytsar stared at her as if he was trying to convince himself she was really there. It was easy to tell he was still a bundle of nerves after being left behind.

"Are you doing okay?" Sir asked when Rytsar started pacing.

Rytsar stopped and stared at them both. After several moments, he confessed, "I am anxious to hold her."

"Soon, brother."

After Brie was released from recovery, the three of them waited impatiently for her daughter's return. They sat in the private hospital room, counting the minutes. To pass the time, Rytsar began reminiscing about Brie's first visit to Russia.

Brie shook her head, laughing when he brought it up. "I remember how shocked I was when I found out you were a sadist."

"I don't think she actually believed me until we visited your dungeon," Sir told him.

Brie's eyes widened, thinking back on it. "Oh, that was a real education."

Rytsar looked at Brie with a wicked smile. "That trip was the first time you experienced my nines."

"And that was a humbling experience," Brie confessed, remembering just how little she could take of the leather whip. "I sure was quick to use my safe-word."

"*Da*, you were," Rytsar agreed, "but you were courageous enough to try. I knew I would win you over eventually."

"Your nines still scare me, Rytsar."

"As they should," he said with a smirk.

A shiver went through her just thinking about his nines. She glanced at Sir and smiled. "I remember scening with you in front of his Russian colleagues. Now, that was intimidating, but delicious fun..."

"You made me proud that night, babygirl," Sir told her.

Brie remembered how scared she'd been to scene in front of Rytsar's BDSM friends, all well-respected Doms who had come to watch the Americans scene together. Even though she had still been relatively new to submission at the time, Sir had artfully guided her through that scene, and even surprised her with fire play at the end.

"That's not all I remember about that first trip," Rytsar growled.

Brie sighed happily, remembering the snowy cabin. That was where they'd had their first encounter as a threesome. Memories of that scene still made her hot to this day. "I will always cherish our time at your cabin in Russia."

"You mean *your* cabin," Rytsar corrected.

Brie giggled. "Oh, yes. My special birthday gift from you."

"That cabin holds many good memories," Sir

agreed huskily.

"So many memories…" Brie echoed.

"We should visit there and make more," Rytsar suggested.

"And I can show off the swing set you bought for our little girl."

He raised an eyebrow. "I have added to it since."

Brie shook her head in amusement.

"Did I not tell you I would be the best *dyadya* in the world? I mean to live up to that claim."

"It was that swing set that started the whole discussion that led to this day," Sir stated.

Brie nodded, realizing that Sir was right. Rytsar's desire to be an uncle had prodded him to discuss the possibility of children with Brie. In a sense, that simple swing set had changed all their lives.

When the nurse walked into the room, they became silent, all eyes on the baby she carried in her arms.

"It's time for her first feeding," she told them, smiling at Brie.

Rytsar's eyes were riveted on the child as the nurse walked past him, and he said in awe, "She is so *krasivaya…*"

Sir leaned down and whispered in Brie's ear. "Do you mind if I make the formal introduction now?"

"Please, Sir," Brie answered, smiling over at Rytsar.

Sir gently took the child from the nurse's arms and said, "Please give us a moment."

He stared down at his little girl as he cradled her in his arms. The tiny baby looked up into his eyes, transfixed by her father's gaze. "I will protect and love you all the days of my life. It is my solemn vow to you as your father." Sir kissed her lightly on the forehead, and then walked over to Rytsar.

The burly Russian already had his arms out to receive her.

"Anton Durov," Sir said in a formal voice. "I would like to introduce you to Hope Antonia Davis."

Rytsar looked at him in surprise. "She carries my name?"

"We wanted you to be a part of her," Brie told him from the bed.

Rytsar shook his head, almost losing himself to the emotions coursing through him. He closed his eyes and steeled his jaw, visibly struggling to rein them back in.

Sir waited patiently, keenly aware of how important this moment was to his friend.

When Rytsar was ready, he opened his eyes and smiled at Brie. "Thank you, *radost moya*. I am truly honored."

He held out his arms again, and Sir carefully placed the tiny infant in his muscular embrace.

"Hello, *moya solntse*," he said in a soothing voice, grinning down at her. "May I have this dance with you?"

Cradling her tiny form against his chest, Rytsar began to sway to a tune only he could hear as he moved slowly in a circle.

Brie had to hold back the tears as she watched Rytsar keep his promise to her.

Sir returned to Brie's side and took her hand, squeezing it tightly as they both watched.

Rytsar looked down at Hope while he danced, stating with wonder in his voice, "I knew you would be beautiful...but you take your *dyadya's* breath away."

Gift of Memories

Brie was trying to feed the baby, still learning how to help Hope attach to her breast correctly so she could suckle. Brie had always assumed it happened naturally, having had no idea it was a process mother and child had to practice together.

Thane was standing beside her, giving her encouragement when the babe slipped off again. He got a phone call and excused himself while the lactation nurse assisted Brie in getting her to reattach.

He came back smiling. "I have good news for you, babygirl. Your parents have just landed and should be here soon."

She looked up at him, beaming. "I can't wait for them to meet their grandchild." She looked down at little Hope, completely and utterly in love with her. "They're going to be so proud...."

"I wonder if your father will be wearing the mouse ears," Thane joked.

Brie started laughing, causing the poor baby to slip off again. Brie's giggles wouldn't stop and she had to take several deep breaths before she could begin nursing again. "Forgive me, Hope. Your grandpa has an interesting relationship with your father."

She had to squelch more laughter for the baby's sake as she thought back on how that had all played out.

Brie was wrapping up the Bambi music box to set it into the shipping box, along with the Mickey Mouse ears and the bottle of catsup.

"No," Sir told her. "I think they should be sent separately. Your father's first, and then your mother's gift the day after. It's the only way for it to have the correct impact."

Brie wondered what he was up to and shook her head, grinning.

Sir explained as he handed her another box. "Your father will open this box without the return address to find only the ears and the catsup bottle inside with no explanation. While he thinks about who could have possibly sent it, your mother's gift will arrive the following day with a sweet note from you telling them we hope they enjoy the gifts."

"You've thought this all out, haven't you?"

Sir stroked his chin. "Yes, I have, as a matter of fact. After your father realizes the gifts came from us, he will look at the items in a new light. If we are lucky, he will make the connection to the diner those many years ago. As to what he will think of it, well…that's what makes this interesting for me."

Brie pulled the music box out and replaced it with more paper so the items were well cushioned for the trip. "So no note to Dad?"

"Correct."

Brie giggled as she taped the box shut. "You're so naughty, Sir."

"Hopefully, he will receive it in the spirit it's been given," he replied with a smirk.

While Brie was readying the second box, Sir walked over and handed her a blank card. She took it from him, admiring the delicate artwork of flowers.

"For your mother. It reminds me of her. She seems fragile like a flower but, in truth, she is strong—strong enough to counterbalance your father and do it with grace."

Brie smiled, running her fingers over one of the flowers on the front of the card. "You're right, Sir. My mother has a silent strength. They make a perfect team, I think." She smiled at him. "They're like us in some ways—but totally vanilla."

"And he's stubborn," Sir added with a chuckle. "However, the fact that your father invited me into your family means a great deal to me. I am indebted to him."

Brie wrote a short note and was about to lick the envelope when Sir stopped her. "I would like to write something, as well."

In his perfect penmanship, he wrote:

Mom,

Brie saw this music box and said you would enjoy
it. Naturally, we had to get it for you.

I am honored to be a part of this family. Here's
to adding to the ranks in a few months.

Please give Dad our best.

Love, Thane

"She'll love this note, Sir," Brie commented after
reading it. "I think they both will, once my dad gets
over the shock."

At five minutes after six, exactly three days after
mailing her mother's gift, her cell phone rang.

Glancing at the clock, Brie grinned at Sir. "It's Dad.
He's just gotten the mail. He does it right after he gets
home. My dad is all about keeping to his routines, and
he goes to the mailbox exactly at six every evening."

"This phone call should prove interesting, then," he
chuckled. "Would you like me to answer it?"

"Oh, no, Sir. Let me do the honors." Brie answered
with an innocent, "Hello?"

"What is the meaning of this?" her father growled
on the other end of the line.

"Oh, hi, Daddy! Did Mom like the gift?"

"I'm not calling about your *mother's* gift."

Brie held her hand over the receiver and mouthed
the words, *He sounds mad* to Thane.

"I would like to speak to your husband," he demanded.

"Certainly, Daddy. Let me put you on speaker-phone." Before she did, she rubbed her tummy, telling him, "The baby must know her grandpa is on the phone because I just felt her kick."

She then hit the button for the speaker, handing it over to Thane as she looked down at her belly, whispering, "That was perfect timing, little girl."

"Thane," her father barked.

"Yes, Dad?" Sir answered in a calm voice.

"Are you trying to provoke me?"

"How so?"

"This package I received. It must have come from you."

"I'm glad you got it, Dad."

"I don't understand, and I don't appreciate being played for a fool."

"That was not our intention, I assure you."

"Then why send it anonymously, *son*?"

Brie spoke up. "We were hoping it would jog your memory, Daddy."

"What?" her father growled in irritation. "Brianna, what has one thing got to do with the other? It makes no sense."

"Brie and I made a connection we hadn't realized before," Sir explained. "We were wondering if you might remember it, too. That's why we sent you the two items."

"Wouldn't it be easier just to ask?" he grumbled.

"It would but, Daddy, it wouldn't be nearly as much fun."

"You're testing my patience, little girl."

Hearing the anger rising in his voice, Sir encouraged him to ponder the meaning behind the gifts. "Take a moment to think back on a past vacation. I'm positive it will come to you."

He winked at Brie.

After several moments, Bill started mumbling to himself and then called out to his wife. "Marcy, do you remember how old Brianna was when we took her to Disneyland?"

"I think she was seven, dear?"

"Oh hell…"

"What is it?" her mom asked in the background.

"Are you seriously telling me that it was *you* at the diner?" Bill demanded.

"It was."

"I don't believe it."

Her mother begged him to put them on speaker-phone too, and asked, "What's this all about? I want in on the joke."

"It's not a joke, Mom," Brie told her. "Actually, it's quite amazing."

Her father replied harshly, "That's certainly one way to spin it."

"Please, someone take mercy on me and tell me what this is all about," her mother begged.

Sir detailed how they'd come to discover their past history. "Your daughter and I were at a café, and she happened to notice a little girl wearing mouse ears. Naturally, it caused her to reminisce about her trip to Disneyland as a child. A momentous occasion for any child, I'm sure. A quick calculation in my head led me to ask her what her favorite Disney character was. I met a little girl once who loved Pluto."

"Wait. What does this have to do with catsup?" her mother asked, clearly still not understanding.

"Marcy, do you remember that college boy who wanted to molest our daughter?"

"No! It can't be..." she laughed. "Do you mean that nice young man who handed Brie the catsup?"

"That's not how I remember it," he muttered.

"How do you remember it, Daddy?" Brie asked, having way too much fun with this.

"A man his age had no business interacting with you."

"He was only trying to pass me the catsup."

"Well, you shouldn't have been talking to him in the first place, Brianna," her father huffed. "You don't know what kind of perverts are out there."

The line grew silent.

"Bill isn't trying to imply you're a pervert, Thane," her mother quickly added.

"Maybe I am," her father stated abrasively.

"Is that really how you felt at the time?" Sir asked.

"I didn't trust you. I know that much."

"Was your distrust specifically toward me, or was it a general mistrust of men around your daughter?"

"Both."

"Really, and why was that?"

"You were too smooth. I could tell you were trouble."

Sir laughed. "All I did was hand her a bottle she couldn't reach."

"But she trusted you enough to talk to you. I taught

Brianna better than that."

Brie thought back on that encounter and realized her dad was right. She had trusted Thane, even back then.

"So, how do you feel about it, knowing I would eventually marry your daughter?"

"How do I feel *now*?"

"It was Fate, Bill!" Brie's mother exclaimed excitedly. "It's obvious these two were meant for each other."

"To be honest, I'm in shock," he replied. "If I had postponed the trip to Disneyland, would you two still have hooked up years later?"

"It certainly begs the question," Sir agreed. He pushed it one step further. "If you could change the past, would you?"

There was a long pause on the phone.

The longer the silence dragged on, the more nervous Brie became. "Daddy?"

"In answer to your question, Thane, I guess I would have to say no. Even if I had the ability to change the past, I would choose to sit there and allow you to interact with my little girl. Despite everything."

Brie felt a surge of relief.

"I am glad to know that," Sir said, his voice tinged with emotion.

"You are good to my daughter, and I trust you will be the same to our granddaughter. However, I can't stand the thought of her being a part of your kinky lifestyle."

"I assure you that our child will be encouraged to think for herself and lead a life that is of her own design, not ours."

"I trust you to do just that," Bill stated firmly.

"So, did you like the ears, Daddy?" Brie prodded.

"It certainly was a surprise, and to find out that the four of us have met before is disconcerting, to say the least."

"It was a surprise to us, as well—once we put two and two together," she giggled.

"Whether Marcy is right about it being Fate or not, the simple fact is that we love you, little girl. We did then when we made your childhood dreams come true with a trip to Disneyland, and we do now as you are about to become a mother yourself."

Brie felt her throat constrict, touched by her father's heartfelt words.

"I'll make you this promise, Brianna."

Brie cleared her throat. "What's that, Daddy?"

"I will wear these ears when we take our little granddaughter to Disneyland. How does that sound?"

"Like a dream come true," Brie told him, tears filling her eyes.

After the phone call, Sir gathered Brie into his arms. "Well, that went even better than expected."

"I agree." She pressed herself against him. "Just when I thought I knew my dad, he completely surprises me."

"I could say the same about my own family, I suppose. However, my surprises never ended up being good ones where they were concerned."

"We are your family now, Sir. And you are accepted by my dad just the way you are."

"It was an unexpected revelation to come from this little stunt, I must admit."

"And well deserved, Sir. You are a gentleman through and through."

"You, my dear," he said, grasping a fistful of her hair and pulling her head back, "inspire me to be a better man."

She smiled up at him. "You have always been a good man. I'm just the lucky girl who gets to inspire your kinky domination."

He pressed his lips against hers, drawing out her sexual desire with his deep kisses. "And you *do* inspire me, babygirl…"

Hope was peacefully asleep, cradled in Brie's arms, when her parents walked into the hospital room. The instant her mother saw the baby, she stopped in her tracks and started crying.

Her father put his arm on her back and guided her forward, whispering, "Isn't she beautiful, Marcy?"

Brie smiled, thrilled to see them. "Would you like to hold her?"

"Not yet," her mother said, wiping away her tears. "We don't want you to wake the baby."

"She can sleep through anything, Mom. Please…" Brie held Hope out to her. "Say hello to Hope Davis."

"Hope…what a lovely name." Her mother tentatively took the baby from her arms, shaking her head as she stared down at the child. "She's so tiny," she whispered in wonder.

Her father stood beside her, grinning down at Hope like the proud grandfather he was. He looked up at Thane. "You have a beautiful daughter."

"And you have an equally beautiful granddaughter," he replied.

Her father snorted in response, and the baby startled, her hands flailing out momentarily before she settled back to sleep.

"Bill," her mother whispered, "don't go scaring the baby like that."

He looked down at Hope and stroked her cheek softly. "Sorry, munchkin."

Brie's heart swelled with pride, watching her parents with her child. She had never known this level of happiness. It was impossible to explain.

"How was the delivery, honey?" her mother asked softly, not wanting to disturb the baby again.

"As you know, she came sooner than expected, and it got a little scary there at the end. But here she is, a healthy, six-pound girl."

"What happened during delivery?" her father asked, clearly concerned.

"She was struggling for oxygen, so I had to push as hard as I could to avoid a C-section. But I did it, and here's the proof," she said proudly.

"So she's healthy even with the early delivery?" he pressed her.

Brie gestured toward Hope. "As you can see, Daddy, she may be small, but she is strong. Dr. Glas said that avoiding a cesarean was important for her health because she was preterm. We were also lucky that her lungs were mature enough to handle her early entry into the world. Now, I just have to make sure she gains the weight she needs."

"That must have been so frightening for you, sweetheart," her mother said.

"I was freaking out a little, at first." Brie took Sir's hand. "But Thane was a rock through the whole thing."

"Durov had a part to play in that, as well," Sir stated.

Her mother seemed surprised. "Was he there for the birth?"

Brie nodded, smiling at the memory of his first dance with Hope. "He was up until I had to go to the operating room, Mom."

"Isn't that a little strange?" she asked.

"No, Mom. Rytsar was actually the reason Thane and I started planning for a family. It seemed only natural to have him there at the birth, especially after all he's suffered to be here. We were lucky to have him with us." She reached out to her mother. "But I really wanted you there, too. I can't tell you how much."

Her mother frowned. "I wanted to be here, Brianna. Your father can attest to how frantic I was when we couldn't find a sooner flight."

Her dad nodded. "It was a real shame she didn't get the chance."

Brie looked at Sir questioningly, wondering if it would be okay to tell her parents about their future plans. She smiled when he nodded.

"Mom, Dad...you'll get your chance. We're planning to have another baby so Hope can be a big sister."

Her mother's mouth dropped. "Another one?" she asked, her voice trembling with joy.

Brie nodded, smiling at her.

"Oh, Bill, isn't that wonderful news?"

"Yes," he agreed. "As you know, Brianna, I wasn't thrilled to see you tie yourself down with a family so early in life. But the fact is, Marcy was right. We had you soon after we got married and have never regretted that decision. I am happy for you."

Her mother told Thane, "I would give you a hug right now if I wasn't holding your precious daughter."

"Consider the hug received, Mom," he said tenderly.

Her father looked at Brie with a glint in his eye. "That reminds me..." He patted his pockets, looking for something, then pulled out a small, wrapped gift. He handed it to Brie, saying, "It's from the both of us."

Brie looked at Sir excitedly, ripping at the paper. She burst into giggles when she held it up for Sir to see. It was a tiny headband with miniature mouse ears and a red polka dot bow. "That's the cutest thing ever, Daddy!"

He smiled modestly. "I'm glad you like it, little girl."

"I'm not so little anymore," she laughed.

"You will *always* be my little girl."

"Oh, yikes," she muttered when her eyes started to water. "I don't want to cry. I've been doing that all day today."

"No need to hold back your emotions," Sir reassured her.

She nodded, smiling at him before turning back to her father with tears running down her cheeks. "I want a hug."

"Oh, little girl…" he croaked, close to tears himself as he took Brie in his arms. "I love you."

The Sheik

B rie insisted that Sir get one last night of uninterrupted sleep before she came home with the baby,
officially making a good night's rest a thing of the past
for them both.

He was reluctant at first, but then reasoned that he
could better care for Hope on their first day home by
giving Brie the rest she needed.

"You certainly won't be getting uninterrupted sleep
in the hospital," he chuckled.

"I know! Which is all the more reason I want you
to head home, Sir. At least one of us should have sweet
dreams tonight."

He raised an eyebrow. "That gives me an idea,
babygirl."

Sir left for a couple of hours, returning with her
favorite take-out and an even more exciting treat—her
fantasy journal.

"Tonight, I want you to write a new fantasy for
me."

Her heart fluttered when she heard his command.

Her journal was like a blueprint for Sir, giving him inspiration whenever he wanted to surprise her with a special scene. And, lucky for her, the man was *exceedingly* creative with his interpretation of her words.

"It's been a while since I've written one of these," she mused as she took the journal from him.

"I enjoy the challenge of them, téa."

Hearing him calling her by her sub name made Brie feel all warm inside.

He gave Brie a chaste kiss on the forehead. "I look forward to reading it while you lie sleeping in my bed."

Brie settled in for the evening after feeding Hope. The nurse had taken the baby to monitor her overnight since they both were being released in the morning.

It meant Brie was alone for the first time in the hospital. It would have been depressing, if it hadn't been for Sir's assignment.

She got out her beloved journal and picked up the special pen the Submissive Training Center had given her. Sifting through the pages to find the first blank one, Brie opened the book wide, laying it in her lap. She smiled as she stared down at the lines that begged to be filled.

Brie unconsciously nibbled on her pen as she contemplated what fantasy she wanted to see played out. Her recent daydream of not having a safeword had been alluring, so she decided to go with that and a variation of her Warrior Fantasy...

I hear them coming and know we are in trouble. The marauders are without mercy, taking whatever they want—supplies, weapons, food...and women.

I run, knowing my life depends on it, but I am smaller than the others, and my short strides keep me from catching up.

I hear the hard breathing of an approaching horse and the shrill cry of its rider just before my feet become entangled in bindings and I fall hard to the ground. The impact is so great, it knocks the air out of me. I struggle to breathe as the dark shadow of a marauder hovers over me. He grabs my feet, undoing the bindings he has so skillfully wrapped around my ankles with his throw. Before I have time to break away, he forces my wrists together and binds them quickly, dragging me to his horse.

I know if I cannot escape now, I will never see my village again. I scream and thrash as he tries to throw me onto the horse. When I won't cooperate, he chooses to tie me on the back of the beast like a sack of goods. He jumps onto his horse and heads north, toward the Sheik's territory.

I try to scream for my father, but the bouncing hindquarters of the beast continuously knocks the wind from me. I leave my home with only muffled cries, watching the village burn down behind me.

My future is lost...

The journey is long, and those of us who have been captured are given little to drink. One of the younger girls dies along the way, but I do not know the cause. We are nothing now. Slaves to the Sheik—without status or names. Forced to work until our dying breath.

I weep in the dark of the night, knowing my life is over be-

fore it has really begun.

When we finally arrive, I am confronted by a sea of tents. The sheer number is as amazing as it is horrifying. The Sheik is a very wealthy man.

We are taken off the horses, tied together, and led away. I glance around desperately, hoping to see a kind face in the crowd of strangers. These people are nothing like mine. They are nomads, dressed in expensive robes and turbans, flaunting the wealth they've gained off the backs of those they have plundered.

I know the Sheik is a powerful man, feared by all who are unfortunate enough to cross his path. His reputation is the stuff of nightmares. He is ruthless and cruel—terrorizing the land with his merciless bandits.

I think of Dabir and tears come to my eyes as we are presented to a group of men. Dabir will never be my husband, our young love one more casualty of the Sheik's marauders. In the blink of an eye, I go from having a future with a husband, to the bleakness of being a slave with none.

The men before us appear to be important, based on their ornamental attire. The marauders separate me from the group and bring me before them. The two men talk amongst themselves as they look me over critically. One touches my hair and then nods.

Rather than being returned to the others, I scream in terror as I am dragged away.

A large stranger covers my mouth with his hand, lifting me up over his shoulder to carry me to a nearby tent.

I understand now what is happening to me and thrash in terror. I've heard horror stories about young girls being used by the bandits—it is the worst fate imaginable.

I realize now that being made a slave would be a gift com-

pared to this. Although I have been silenced, tears run down my cheeks as I struggle for my life.

Death would be preferable to this...

A woman opens the flap, and I am carried inside. I instantly relax when I see there are only three women standing before me. No men.

Once I stop struggling, the man sets me down and immediately leaves the tent.

I stare at the women in silence, wondering what they have in store for me. Two walk over and begin ripping at my clothes. But the other one holds up her hand, a smile on her lips as she shows me a piece of fruit.

My stomach growls, not having eaten for days.

The other two move away after stripping me bare. Despite my fear, I cannot resist the alluring smell of the fruit and walk toward the woman, taking it from her and stuffing it into my mouth.

Sweet heaven fills my mouth and the tears I cry are of joy.

She speaks to me in a soothing voice as she directs me to sit. I do so, hoping for more food if I am compliant.

My body is thoroughly washed, the sweat and dirt of travel cleansed from it before I am shaven, including my mound. They then wash and comb out my hair. The women seem to marvel at it, stroking my mane of hair—a gift of my lineage.

They dress me in a simple gown, the material see-through and light. An opulent veil, adorned with exquisite jewels, covers my face.

I feel like a princess as the women stand back to admire their work.

Such fancy dress can only mean one thing: I am to become part of the Sheik's harem, one of many women held prisoner and used for his pleasure. To be committed to a man who will treat me as if I am a faceless commodity, a slave to his perverted desires, is little better than what I first feared.

I start crying.

The women hush me, trying to console me with words I do not understand as they dry my tears. A plate of food is brought out and the women proceed to feed me fresh fruits, dates, and cheese. I momentarily forget my fear as I indulge in the abundance of delectable foods.

Always, for as long as I can remember, I have been hungry. This is the first time I am allowed to eat until I am full. I smile at the woman who wipes away the juices that have dribbled down my chin.

I reconsider my fate and can understand why these women seem happy for me. However, I will be the property of the Sheik, a man known for his heartless cruelty.

I wait fearfully after the three women leave the tent, laying my head against a soft pillow on the floor. I mourn for the loss of my family and the life I have known. I will never experience the love of a loyal man or the joy of having children with him.

I am only property now.

Late in the afternoon, they come for me. One of the eunuchs sticks his head into the tent and gestures that I follow him.

I suck in my breath, frozen for a moment, but force myself to stand up and leave with him.

My heart is racing as he leads me to a large tent in the center of the camp. I hesitate for a moment before I enter. The inside is lined with fine textiles, and the floor covered in soft Persian rugs. I stop for a moment, overwhelmed by the colors. Never in my life have I imagined such luxury.

The Sheik stands on the other side of the tent, watching me.

His gaze burns my skin as his eyes slowly travel over my body, the material of my clothing leaving little to the imagination. He does not smile when our eyes meet, and my heart skips.

I am afraid.

He voices a command I do not understand. The eunuch pushes me forward, and I force myself to walk toward him, each step difficult to take.

The Sheik cups my chin and stares into my eyes. His are dark brown, deep, and full of treacherous mystery. He says nothing as his thumb grazes my bottom lip.

He then barks a command to his men. They nod to him in respect before walking out of the tent. All except for one.

I have no idea what is about to happen here. My mother would have told me the ways of men on the day of my wedding, but now that day will never come. I swallow down the sense of cold terror threatening to overwhelm me—wishing I could spirit myself away while my body endures his manly needs.

The Sheik is an older man with salt-and-pepper hair. He does have a handsome face, but the fact he does not smile makes him intimidating. He stares at me for a long time, making no move toward me.

A blush warms my cheeks, wondering if something is expected of me.

The Sheik nods to the other man and, suddenly, he pulls my hands behind my back and holds them in a tight grip. My heart starts racing.

Placing his finger under my chin, the Sheik tilts it upward as he leans in to kiss my lips. I am too frightened to respond but, as his kisses continue, I fearfully open my mouth to him.

My body begins to tingle with excitement. His sexual confidence is like an aphrodisiac to someone as inexperienced as me.

I've only known Dabir's boyish fumbling, and this man oozes a confidence and erotic desire my body can't help but respond to.

He presses himself against me, grabbing the back of my neck as he kisses me again. His tongue invades my mouth, and my nether regions seem to explode with fiery need.

When he lets go, I am left breathless and weak.

The Sheik stares intently at my breasts.

I hold my breath, unable to move as I watch him reach out and touch my nipple through the thin material. My insides contract and I begin to tremble as he caresses it.

He looks at me, his eyes now filled with passionate fire. I am like a frightened rabbit, frozen in place as he pushes the material off my shoulder, exposing my naked breast to him.

Letting out a low grunt, he grasps my hardening nipple and rolls it between his fingers. A feeling like a bolt of lightning shoots to my loins, and I gasp.

He is encouraged by my response and pulls the material down off my other shoulder so it falls to my waist. His strong hands begin caressing and squeezing my breasts as his tongue plunders my mouth again.

I am lost in his taste and the new sensations he evokes with his touch. I want more of him.

With no warning, the other man releases me, and I cry out in surprise as the Sheik picks me up, carrying me to an area shielded by a canopy of silks. Once inside, I find the floor is covered in luxurious pillows. He lays me down and promptly begins ripping at my thin gown, leaving me naked and on display under his gaze.

I close my eyes, embarrassed to be naked in front of this stranger.

The Sheik takes a hold of my chin and barks a command.

When I open my eyes, he forces me to watch as his lips descend on my nipple and he begins sucking on it. I have never known such a feeling, and my whole body tingles in pleasure.

Is this man a sorcerer? I do not know, but I am totally captivated by him as goosebumps of pleasure rise on my skin.

His kisses begin to trail lower, and I tense. My mound is completely bare. Although Dabir has snuck his hand under my clothes several times in the past, I have never been kissed there. I think I may burst into flames if he tries it.

I whimper when the Sheik's lips land on that sensitive area between my legs, and then his tongue grazes the entire length of it. Moaning softly, I twist and squirm, unused to such stimulation and unable to process the mounting sensations it creates.

He chuckles to himself and stills me with his strong hands. I am forced to take the sensual attention of his tongue, and I whimper helplessly as his hands play with my body.

Spreading my thighs wide, he stares at my sex and then snaps his fingers. The other man appears. He has a leather satchel with him. The man lays it down and unrolls it, exposing a number of items I have never seen before.

I whimper when the Sheik picks up one of the items, a thin glass rod, and rubs it against my sex. Chills course through me as he slowly inserts the tool into my virginal opening. It is strange and unnatural, but as he begins to stroke my inner walls with it, I feel a new tingling take over. I close my eyes, gasping as the tension in my loins begins to build. My body tenses, and then an explosion of pleasure bursts from between my legs and my whole body pulses in ecstasy.

Both men chuckle in approval.

The Sheik removes the thin rod, now covered in my wetness, and places it to the side. I have not torn and am still a virgin, but something miraculous has happened, and I want more.

I open my legs wider, hoping for his attention.

This time, the other man, whom he calls Raja, picks up two delicate, small, beaded items. They look so pretty, like hanging jewels. He hands one to the Sheik, then moves beside me. I watch with trepidation as he places it on my nipple. He tightens it and soon the pressure becomes pain, and I whimper.

The Sheik hands him the other one to repeat the process. I grab Raja's wrist to stop him. He only smiles as he moves my hand away before continuing.

Tears run down my cheeks as I lay there, both nipples adorned with their cruel decorations. The two men sit back and watch as my chest moves up and down rapidly.

At first, it is terribly uncomfortable, but my nipples become numb and I stop crying. Raja begins to play with my breasts, and I find the attention uniquely pleasurable.

I blush, embarrassed that I am so aroused by it.

The Sheik grunts his approval and spreads my outer lips wide, as both men stare boldly at my sex. He begins stroking my clit with his finger. I hold my breath, uncertain what he will do. His touch creates a fire between my legs and I quiver with excitement.

He suddenly stands up and begins to undress before me. The ravenous look in his eye is dangerously captivating. There is a primal part of me that longs to satisfy his craving.

I am shocked when the other man begins to undress, too. I look from one to the other, my body tensing.

The second man speaks to me in a soothing tone. His charming smile is a stark contrast to the Sheik, whose lips remain firm and serious. I silently pray the other man's alluring smile means he will not hurt me.

My eyes widen when I see the Sheik standing above me, fully undressed. He has a toned physique with beautiful bronze skin and a chest covered in fine hair. His manhood is long and erect.

It demands my attention.

I glance at the other man and see his shaft is rigid as well.

Chills run through my body as the Sheik lies down beside me and I feel the warmth of his naked body next to mine. He wastes no time, kissing me as his hard cock presses against my thigh, announcing its intention. I cannot help it, I close my eyes again to concentrate on his kissing and distract myself from what is to come.

His kisses are electric, sending pleasurable jolts through my body, convincing me that I need to fulfill his desire. But I can't help it. When he climbs on top of me and settles between my legs, I cry out in fear.

That feeling is only increased when Raja takes my wrists, pinning me down.

"Shh...shh...." my handsome Sheik whispers in my ear as he presses his shaft against my virginal opening. I hold my breath. Tilting my head back, I look into Raja's eyes as he holds my wrists.

My mouth is covered by his warm lips as the Sheik claims my virginity. He begins to thrust his cock inside me, my body willingly taking his manly invasion.

Raja frees my wrists. I feel his warm lips begin to explore my body while he continues to watch the Sheik push deeper inside me.

It is obvious by the man's erection that he finds watching us stimulating.

When the Sheik begins rolling his hips, I come to know what it is to be possessed. I turn my head and moan into the pillow—the Sheik my only reality.

My body accepts his deeper penetration when I feel teeth against my neck. It causes a seductive chill to course through me as Raja claims my throat with a bite.

I am like a young animal, instantly relaxing, allowing the Sheik to take more of me. I cry out in pain and pleasure as he begins pumping his seed deep into my virginal depths.

Afterward, he pulls out and collapses beside me, panting heavily. The two of us lie there, his spent shaft resting against my thigh. I glance at Raja stroking his cock and realize this encounter is not over.

However, I know that the Sheik would never allow another man to impregnate me. The bloodline must remain pure. It is the reason eunuchs are the only males allowed to care for his harem.

I tentatively reach down and touch my ravaged sex to see the blood on my fingers, announcing that my innocence has been claimed.

With tenderness I did not expect, the Sheik begins to cleanse the area, wiping away all evidence of his claiming. Afterward, he leans down and gently kisses my sex, that sly smile returning to his lips.

My heart melts a little bit when I realize there is more behind his daunting exterior.

My heart begins racing when he removes the clamps on my nipples, causing a painful ache. With gentle attention, the Sheik rubs my breasts before kissing each tender nipple.

I close my eyes and sigh, amazed at this man's power over my body.

The Sheik slowly turns me over onto my stomach, and places a pillow beneath my stomach, propping my pelvis up. He then lies beside me, stroking my soft hair. Nothing more happens, and I begin to relax as I enjoy the delightful tingling he creates that travels from my head all the way to my toes.

I remain in this relaxed state, watching Raja take something from the leather satchel, but I cannot see what it is. I look into the Sheik's eyes, needing his reassurance.

I notice the ravenous glint in his gaze has returned and he barks a command to the man. Raja positions himself behind me and I feel the hardness of his cock resting in the valley of my buttocks.

I hold my breath as the slippery head of his manhood presses against my ass. When I struggle, the Sheik stills me.

"Shh…shh…"

He hushes me, letting me know this is what he hungers for. Goosebumps rise on my skin as I still myself and feel Raja's hard shaft slowly entering me.

The Sheik begins kissing me again, his kisses becoming more passionate as his tongue ravages my mouth. He is clearly excited by my acceptance and grunts in pleasure as Raja starts pumping my virginal ass with his cock.

I whimper between kisses, both frightened and excited by what is happening. As we sync into a sensual rhythm, the three of us become one. I respond to the Sheik's deep kisses as I accept the fullness of Raja's cock.

Even though both men are strangers, I have never felt such a connection. I had no idea such a thing was possible between three people. When Raja fists my hair and pulls my head back, the Sheik takes advantage of my exposed breasts and plays with my nipples.

I feel the tension building again.

They have taught me the pleasure my body is capable of. So, instead of fighting it, I give in to the mounting tension, letting it crash over me as I cry out in pure pleasure. Raja joins me with his own groans of passion, and I am filled with his warm seed. There is no threat to the bloodline—a wicked way to ensure it.

Afterward, the three of us lie there in silence. I am completely spent, but take comfort being between these two men. I wonder if this is how it will always be or if this is a one-time encounter.

I turn my head to look at the Sheik. He's staring at me, his hand moving leisurely up and down his shaft.

It seems this is just the beginning…

Brie looked through the pages she had just written, realizing it was longer than her other fantasies. She giggled as she set her journal on the tray and laid the pen down. She couldn't wait to see how Sir would play this one out.

Lea for the Win

With the baby arriving three weeks early, the baby shower her friends had planned was cancelled. Instead, all the gifts were shipped to their apartment so they could use the baby items when they returned from the hospital.

Brie enjoyed unwrapping the adorable gifts from their friends like Master Anderson's miniature fairy garden and pink cowboy boots; the *matryoshka* nesting dolls Rytsar had custom-made of intricately hand-painted woodland animals to match the baby's room; a monthly subscription of baby books from Marquis and Celestia; Tono's beautiful Japanese doll made of porcelain, dressed in an intricate silk kimono of pink; Lea's black onesie with stylish ruffles and "My little black dress" in rhinestones; Faelan's case of Mommy's Time Out wine; Mary's swaddling blanket with the words "Shit just got real"; and Master Coen's cute stuffed kangaroo sent all the way from Australia.

Brie was extremely touched by all the presents, but she was sad that she never got the chance to hang with her friends. However, she needn't have worried.

Brie picked up her phone when it started ringing, and saw that Mary was calling.

"Hey Brie, I need to talk. Stat."

"What's up, Mary?"

"This isn't something I can talk about over the phone. Mind if I come over?"

"Everything okay?"

Mary snorted. "Is that your roundabout way of saying no?"

Brie laughed. "Not at all, but let me ask Sir if he minds having a visitor. He's been busy today."

Pressing the mute button, she asked, "Sir, something's up with Mary. Do you mind if she comes over for a bit?"

He stopped what he was doing and turned from his desk to answer her. "I could use a little break. I'll leave so you can have some privacy."

"Oh, no. No need for that."

He stood up and stretched. "Actually, it would do me some good."

"Are you sure?"

Sir asked her, "How often does Miss Wilson ask to talk?"

"Never."

"Then I think she should come."

Brie nodded, unmuting her phone and putting it back up to her ear. "It's a go. Come on over."

"Good. I just need to pick up one item before I head to your place. Hopefully, it won't take long."

"What do you need? Maybe we have it."

"Nah, don't worry. I'll see you when I get there."

As Sir was getting ready to leave, he told her, "I think you should wear your pearls."

She laughed. "Why? It's just Mary."

He gave her a seductive smile as he was heading out the door, "There is a high probability that you may be molested when I return home."

Brie grinned, throwing him a kiss as he shut the door. Not only did she get out her long strand of pearls, but she also dressed in something a little more stylish and sexy, wanting to impress Sir when he came back home.

Once she was dressed, Brie checked on Hope and saw that she was just beginning to wake. Picking her up, she sat down in the nursing chair, wanting to feed her before Mary arrived.

As Brie rocked slowly and Hope suckled, she hummed a lullaby. Nursing was her favorite time of the day. Having that intimate connection with her daughter, a stolen moment between just the two of them, was something she deeply cherished.

By the time Mary knocked on the door, Hope was already asleep again in the bassinet Brie had placed next to the couch. She wanted Hope close, so she could give Mary her full attention without needing to check on the baby.

She went to answer the door, wondering what had Mary concerned enough to stop by. She hoped it wasn't anything serious.

"Surprise!"

Brie just about jumped out of her skin, then began

laughing as Lea, Candy, and Autumn shook cheerleading pompoms, shouting, "Hope, Hope, Hope…"

"It's your After Baby Baby Shower!" Lea cried.

"Oh, my goodness, you guys almost gave me a heart attack," Brie cried, giggling as she ushered them inside. Mary followed behind them with a heavy bag. "What, no pompoms?" Brie teased.

"Not my thing, Stinky Cheese."

Mary went to the kitchen to unload her bag while the other girls headed straight to the bassinet. "Oh, my gosh, she's so dang cute," Lea cooed.

Brie looked at Autumn in surprise. "I can't believe you came from Denver for this."

"Shh…we haven't said anything yet, but Tono came with me to scope out the housing situation. He's considering moving back here."

"With you?"

She blushed. "That's the plan."

"Whoo-ee!" Lea cried. "That's the best news I've heard all day."

Hope made a noise from the bassinet and Lea instantly covered her mouth. "Sorry, Brie," she whispered.

"I've found that newborns sleep a lot," Brie said, laughing. "And it's hard to wake this little one after she's been fed."

Lea stared at Brie's boobs. "Wow, girl, yours are looking almost as impressive as mine these days."

Brie looked down at her breasts and grinned. "Yeah, I must admit, it's a nice perk of breastfeeding."

Candy looked at her own smaller ones and joked,

"Maybe I should look into it."

"No way, girl," Mary called from the kitchen. "You know how Captain feels about your nips."

"Yeah, you're right." She giggled, blushing a deep shade of pink.

Brie started toward the kitchen to see if she could help, but Mary stopped her. "Don't come any closer."

"But, I—"

"Look, Stinky Cheese, I didn't go to all this trouble for nothing. You just head on back there and stay there."

Lea came up beside Brie. "Mary, what can I do to help?"

"You could start by making the drinks."

"What about us?" Candy and Autumn asked.

"You guys can set out the food."

Brie shook her head. "I can't believe you guys did this."

"We didn't," Lea answered. "This was all Mary's doing."

Brie turned to Mary in surprise. "You did this for me?"

"Hey, I figured somebody needed to throw you a party since you got gypped, popping out the kid too early."

"You're right. I was feeling sad I missed out."

Mary gave her a wink before telling Lea, "Get drinks made already. I'm dying of thirst here."

"Yeah, yeah...Blondie."

"Enough with the sass, big boobs. Get the lead out."

Brie grinned, loving the familiar banter between the two.

Mary tore open a bag of miniature colored clothespins, explaining to Brie, "Lea *insisted* I had to have games for this party. Well, I googled baby shower games and they were all too damn stupid. So this is all you get." She handed each person three clothespins. "Pin these on yourself where everyone can see them. Once I say go, if you catch someone saying the word 'baby,' you get all their clothespins. The woman who wins them all gets to keep them and utilize them however her kinky heart desires." She opened and closed the purple one in her hand. "And, let me tell you, these puppies aren't just good for the ol' nipple…"

Brie giggled. "Only a bunch of subbies would look at a simple clothespin and, instead of thinking laundry, immediately think pervertibles."

"You got that right," Candy said, giving Autumn a friendly elbow in the ribs. "I hear you're one of us now."

Autumn blushed. "Actually, I'm just training under Tono. I'm not official like you guys."

"Nonsense," Lea said.

Brie agreed. "Doesn't matter if you train with one Dom or a school of them."

"*Especially* if you're training with Tono," Lea said. "You got yourself a dreamboat there, Autumn."

"And 'Go', the game has officially started," Mary announced to the group as she pinned her purple pins on. Looking at Brie, she added, "So, rather than waste time with these lame-ass games, I thought it would be more fun to sit and chat like we used to. It's been a long time since we've been able to do that as a group."

"I love me some Girl-Time," Brie agreed.

"Nice pearls, Brie," Lea said as she walked over to give Brie her glass of coconut milk. "I was expecting you to be in sweats with your hair up when we got here."

Brie laughed, but Lea's comment started her thinking. She pulled out her phone and texted Sir:

Baby Shower. But I bet you already knew that.

Enjoy, little mama.

She suddenly realized that had been the reason he'd insisted on pearls.

Am I still going to be molested, Sir?

Of course.

She smiled to herself.

Looking forward to it!

Setting her phone down, Brie took the middle seat on the couch and put an arm around Lea. "You remember when I would record you and Mary after our lessons at the Center, and then we'd stay up all hours of the night talking about it?"

"Absolutely. I still think about those days."

"We were idiots back then," Mary commented, sitting down with her drink.

"Actually, only one of us was an idiot. And, to be clear, it wasn't Lea or me," Brie teased.

"Right…"

"But it *is* funny to think how naïve I was back then," she told them.

"I have to say, girlfriend, you were always true to your heart," Lea said. "I loved that about you."

"Well, I loved your goofball ways, and it all began for us with that MasterCard joke."

Lea giggled. "That one *is* a classic!"

"I sure wish I could have been a part of it," Autumn mused.

Brie wrapped her other arm around her. "Well, you are now." She looked at Mary. "Thanks for including Autumn and Candy."

Mary snorted. "Sure thing, Stinks. I figured I'd keep it small and intimate."

"I feel honored to be invited," Autumn confessed, "and I kind of hate that we have to head back to Denver tomorrow."

"Hey, if you don't mind me asking, how is your training with Tono going?" Lea asked.

Autumn blushed. "I love everything about that man, and the more we work together, the closer I feel to him."

"The jute does create an incredibly personal encounter," Brie agreed. "Especially in Tono's hands."

Autumn look at Brie and Lea shyly. "You both know I've never thought of myself as beautiful but, with Tono, I'm beginning to believe it. And we've been practicing…" She trailed off, suddenly looking anxious.

"What?" Brie encouraged. "Unless, of course, it's supposed to be a secret and you can't tell us."

Autumn shook her head, laughing nervously. "No, it's not a secret. It's just that I'm embarrassed to say."

"Okay, now you have to spill, girl," Lea insisted.

"Absolutely," Candy said.

"Well…" Autumn's blush grew deeper as the seconds ticked by. "You see, Tono has a whole show he's been creating, and it revolves around…"

"Yes?" Lea prompted.

"Me," she answered softly, looking extremely uncomfortable.

"Autumn, that's amazing!" Brie cried, feeling tingles on her skin. She knew whatever Tono was planning, it was going to be big.

"I thought Tono was crazy when he first suggested it. But, after some time and a lot of practice, I see his vision, and it's really exciting."

"Dang, girl!" Lea said. "You *are* the lucky damn sub. I adore Tono's rope."

"That's what makes this even more wonderful. The fact that I'm his sub-in-training makes every practice session meaningful to me. It never feels like work. It's just…well, wonderful."

"I have to admit, I am a tad jealous," Brie admitted. "Spending all that time in Tono's jute would be a dream come true."

"I don't get it," Mary stated. "How is he making a show around just you?"

"The theme is transformation. At first, I was totally against the idea of anyone seeing me without my prosthetic. I've always been self-conscious about it and the scars on my face. However, he has convinced me that taking the audience on my personal journey, by removing each barrier I wear one by one until it is just me in lace panties and jute, will be empowering for others. Oh, and the music he has chosen is amazing."

"Oh, Autumn, I can just imagine it!" Brie said excitedly. "You flying in rope, completely free by the end of the performance...that would be truly incredible to watch. Not only sexy, but profoundly inspiring."

Autumn gave her a pleased smile. "You and Tono must share a similar vision, then. I couldn't embrace it when he first approached me with the idea, but now? When we practice that last scene together, I get a glimpse of the way he sees me..."

Brie was so moved, tears came to her eyes and she was left speechless, nodding her head in amazement.

Lea decided in the ensuing silence that a joke was in order. "Did you hear about the flasher who was thinking of retiring?"

Mary held up her finger. "This is number one."

Lea nodded, and then told everyone, "He decided to stick it out for one more year."

Groans and giggles followed, but Mary's response had piqued Brie's interest, so she asked, "What's with the counting?"

"I told Lea the Lame that she is only allowed three jokes at the party."

Brie looked at Lea. "And you are okay with that?"

She shrugged. "I think Mary secretly loves my jokes. That's why she insisted I tell three."

"Well, that's one way to look at it," Mary mumbled sarcastically.

There was a little hiccup sound from the bassinet, and Candy peeked inside to check. "Looks like the baby's still sleeping."

Lea let out a peal of laughter as she grabbed the clothespins from Candy's shirt. "Sorry, missy, but you just said the magic word."

Brie laughed as she watched Lea pin the three next to hers. "Wow, I didn't even notice."

"I didn't either!" Autumn cried. "Something tells me I am going to suck at this game."

"But I bet you suck *real* good," Lea teased.

"Actually, of all the people I've met, Mary is the best at sucking," Brie said.

Mary wiped her lips as if she had just finished off and smiled. "You know it, Stinky Cheese."

Candy laughed. "You guys are great."

"So, Candy, how is it going with your new endeavor?" Brie asked.

Candy's eyes lit up. "I seriously can't tell you how fulfilling it is to help other subs. When you handed me that business card, you literally changed my life. Now, I get to do the same for other subs who are hurting like I was. I'm so grateful that Baron asked Captain and me to join him."

"And how is Captain?" Mary asked her.

"He has found his second calling, I think. It's like he's a kid again. There was a time when he was considering un-collaring me because of the difference in our ages. He didn't feel it was right to hold me back. But now? Captain is so passionate about what we are doing he couldn't imagine doing it with anyone else. And he's gotten so frisky!"

"I'm glad to hear that." Mary nodded her head to herself, muttering, "Yeah, that makes me happy."

"So, Lea," Autumn said, "how are you handling things since moving back to LA?"

"Actually..." Her eyes shone with excitement. "I just met a guy."

"Really?" Brie asked, excited to hear that Lea seemed to be moving on after the difficult breakup with Ms. Clark.

"Yeah, it's pretty new, so I don't want to say anything and jinx it. But things are finally looking up for me."

"That's great news, girlfriend." Brie gave Lea a hug. "I'll admit, though, I kinda wondered if you and Rytsar might hook up."

Lea grinned. "Oh, that sexy Russian will always have a special place in my heart."

Mary frowned, grumbling. "Wish I could say the same...I still haven't had a scene with that man."

"Okay, you girls have me curious. What's so special about Rytsar Durov?" Autumn asked.

Brie sighed dreamily. "He's passionate on a level most men aren't. He seems all intimidating and, believe me, he *will* challenge you. But he has a way of making you want it and...his aftercare is enlightening."

Lea piped up. "Yeah, that's when his guard goes down. It's truly delicious. I've never met anyone like him."

"He sounds divine," Candy stated. "Although, I'm so not into sadists. Still, there's something about him that makes you curious to try, isn't there?"

"I hear what you guys are saying, but I know my limits, and he is *way* past mine," Autumn stated.

Mary sighed in frustration. "Well, the Russian is still on my bucket list."

Lea perked up, "Hey, Mary, what's up with that Holloway guy you're dating? I've heard rumors that he knew you as a kid."

Mary's face suddenly seemed to lose color. She immediately got to her feet and headed into the kitchen. "I've been a shitty hostess. Anyone want another drink?"

The girls looked at each other in concern, but Brie was the only one brave enough to acknowledge the elephant that had suddenly appeared in the room.

"Is something going on with Holloway? You know, whatever you say is safe with us."

Mary came waltzing out of the kitchen with a rum and Coke in her hand.

"Mary…"

"Nope, Stinky Cheese," Mary stated firmly. "This topic is not open for discussion. Next…"

A cold silence fell over them. In an attempt to lighten things up, Lea threw out another joke. "So what did the bra say to the hat?" After a pregnant pause, she answered, "You go on ahead, and I'll pick up these two."

The room remained silent.

"That's number two," Mary stated. "Too bad nobody laughed. Better luck next time, Lames."

Lea looked at her with sympathy, which Brie could tell Mary didn't appreciate.

To stave off any arguments, Brie asked a general question to the group. "What are you guys doing for fun these days? My fun is pretty much limited to taking care of the baby."

Autumn perked up, pointing to her. "You said 'baby'!"

Mary deftly grabbed Autumn and Brie's pins. "Two for the price of one. Thanks, Autumn."

Autumn shook her head, stunned. "I told you guys I suck at this game."

Brie shrugged. "I haven't caught anyone yet, so don't feel bad."

Mary surprised Brie when she actually responded to the question Brie had asked everyone. "I've started a new hobby."

"Do tell," Candy said. "I can't wait to hear what it is."

"I suppose it's not really a hobby, but a new passion of sorts."

Brie assumed it was something dark and dirty, but what came out of Mary's mouth left her speechless.

"I'm volunteering at the Tatianna Center."

"What's that?" Autumn asked.

"It's for girls who were victims of human trafficking. Even though I'm the one volunteering my time, it's really those girls who are helping me. I've never seen such courage. They've inspired me to try to be a better person. I figure if they can remain positive after everything that's happened to them, it gives me hope that I can too."

"How did you find out about the place?" Candy asked her.

Brie held her breath. Mary was playing a dangerous game, associating herself with the Center after acting as the informant for Lilly there. If anything bad happened to Mary, it would devastate Brie.

"I saw it on the news, I think. After what my dad did to me as a kid, I felt a connection with the victims on a profound level. So, one day, out of the blue, I just decided to go to the Center, and that's where I met Stephanie. The woman runs the place, and she is a powerhouse of positivity. Normally, I can't stomach that crap, but Stephanie is a dynamo. And what she is doing for these girls will echo down through generations."

Mary looked at Brie. "I think that's part of the reason I volunteer there. It's the one thing I can do that has the potential of bettering these girls' lives, and the lives of their children and grandchildren. The cycle of victimization stops with them."

Candy smiled at her. "That sounds similar to what we do."

"Yes," Mary agreed, nodding her head.

"That's wonderful, Mary." Her conviction astounded Brie. Faelan had shared with Brie that he'd seen a real change in Mary, but this went far deeper than Brie realized. She actually admired the woman now.

Mary smiled smugly, taking a sip of her drink. "I think so."

That typical Mary smugness gave Brie an idea. "I may have too much time on my hands, but I can't help thinking about kinky ways we could use those walkie-talkie things people put by the crib—"

"Baby monitors," Mary instantly corrected.

Brie squealed with joy, snapping up all of Mary's clothespins.

Mary's look of surprise quickly returned to that smug look when she said, "Well played, Stinky Cheese. Well played."

"I didn't even see that one coming," Lea laughed. "You were so sneaky, Brie! Was I right or was I right that games are totally necessary?" She stuck her tongue out playfully at Mary.

"Yes, it was slightly amusing, Lame Girl," Mary said, taking another sip of her drink. "And you've got one more joke left to tell. Today appears to be your lucky day."

Lea turned to Brie and asked, "So, I have a question for you, Brie. Why did you keep Hope's name a secret for so long?"

"We were waiting to announce it after she was born."

"Why?"

"Rytsar asked us not to tell him the baby's name until he could hold her for the first time."

There was a collective "Aww…" in the group just before Lea snagged all of Brie's clothespins.

"What the heck?" Brie cried. It took her a moment to realize she'd used the forbidden word. "That was very sneaky, Lea."

"Hey, I learn from the best! To make up for beating you all, here is my last joke for the day, in honor of our Russian friend's cold motherland."

"Give it to me."

"If you're cold, you should sit in a corner. Do you know why?"

Brie shook her head.

"It's 90 degrees!"

Mary was the first to laugh.

"Isn't it *acute* joke?" Lea finished.

"Oh, Lord, you're making a math joke," Candy laughed.

Autumn looked at them, confused. "Sorry, guys. I was never good at math and I'm the only one here who doesn't seem to get it.

"You will," Brie said, drawing on a napkin. She handed it over to her. "See? A corner is at a 90-degree angle."

Autumn put her hands to her mouth, laughing. "Oh, Lea, you really do have the best jokes."

"Don't believe her, Lea," Mary protested.

"Come on, you laughed, Mary. Don't even pretend you didn't," Lea scolded.

"Okay, I'll admit it was slightly better than your norm."

"I personally loved the 'acute' part," Candy said. "It was the icing on the cake."

"Oh, oh, oh…" Autumn said. "I have one for you."

"We're all ears, girlfriend," Lea told her enthusiastically.

"Wait!" Mary complained. "I said only three jokes allowed."

Lea grinned. "Your limit was for me, not for Autumn."

Mary looked at Autumn and sighed in defeat. "Fine, but you only get one."

Autumn giggled, looking over at Lea. "Okay! Well, anyone who knows me *knows* I hate clowns. But the other day a clown held the door open for me. I thought it was a nice jester."

Her joke was met with unanimous groans, except for Lea, who clapped her hands, shouting, "Bravo, Autumn!"

"And *that* is why I limit jokes with you two," Mary exclaimed.

Brie was laughing so hard it hurt, *and* she woke the baby, but O-M-G, it felt so good to be together again! Getting to let your hair down and just laugh was a coveted treat.

Me Too

Lea came to visit a few days later, wanting just to hang out. She was playing a mindless game on her phone while Brie put the baby down for a nap.

Shadow jumped onto the dresser beside the crib. It had become his favorite place since Hope had come home. The cat would sit there for hours watching the baby as she slept. Brie thought of him as Hope's guardian angel. Initially, Sir had been worried about how the old tomcat would act around the baby, but it was clear he understood that she was a part of Brie.

Brie petted his head, after tucking Hope in. "You're a good friend, Shadow."

He brushed his cheek against her hand, a look of contentment in those yellow eyes.

As Brie headed out of the baby's room, she thought about how lucky she was to have her best friend, Lea, back in her life after years of separation and turmoil. They were close again, as if no time had passed between them at all.

"Can you imagine if your life consisted of sleeping

as much as a baby?" Brie asked Lea.

"Why *do* babies sleep so much?"

Brie shrugged. "Guess all that growing makes them exhausted."

"And all that warm milk," Lea added, staring at Brie's boobs. "I had no clue how much those suckers eat."

Brie clutched her breasts. "Sucker is right. My nipples are getting quite the workout these days."

"Hey, what did the baby say to its mother after breastfeeding?" Lea beamed a smile. "Thanks for the mammaries."

Brie giggled…man, she loved this girl and all her bad jokes.

Lea winked at her as she began scrolling through the newsfeed on her phone. Brie took the opportunity to sit down and close her eyes to chill for a bit. She liked the ease of their friendship. It didn't require needless energy because they knew each other so well.

When Brie opened her eyes again, she noticed Lea staring hard at her screen. She glanced up and asked Brie, "Girlfriend, is this Darius? I didn't realize he was hot."

Just the sound of Darius's name gave Brie chills down her spine. She took the phone from Lea and stared at the photo of him in shock. Seeing those familiar brown eyes literally made Brie sick to the stomach. It felt as if he was reaching through the screen to torment her again. She quickly handed the phone back to Lea, shuddering. "Yeah, that's him."

Lea frowned. "I'm so sorry, Brie. I was just scrolling through and found this article about some new local talent. I didn't realize he was connected to you until I read the name. He's the guy who bullied you as a kid, right?"

"What did he have to say in the article?"

Lea looked back at her phone, reading it over. "The article is just a brief introduction. Says he's a model and actor, and mentions that he knew you in elementary school."

Brie felt queasy. She hadn't thought about Darius since the birth of Hope, but now the old fears associated with him came rushing back. "That asshole tormented me in elementary school. Why in the hell would he say anything about it now?"

"I don't know, Brie." Lea reached out to comfort her.

"He was so cruel, Lea," Brie said with tears in her eyes. "I can't tell you the number of times he beat me up after school. Hell, he was the reason my mom and I were homeless while my dad looked for a new job. They were determined to get me far from that place. It's how we ended up in Nebraska."

"I remember you telling me about being homeless for a while…"

Brie shuddered again. "I have tried to push every memory I have of him from my life, and I almost had. Why would he dredge it all up now?"

Lea squeezed Brie. "I don't know, my friend. Maybe he wants to make amends?"

"I don't believe that for a second." Brie pulled away, wrapping her arms around herself, feeling shaky and out of control.

Seeing how upset she was, Lea asked her, "Do you want to cancel going to lunch?"

Brie took a deep breath and held her head up in defiance. "No. I'm not the scared little girl he tormented all those years ago, and that bastard is *not* going to ruin my life now."

She moved through the day, having lunch with Lea and window shopping afterward just as they had planned, but those memories of Darius kept replaying in her head. It pissed her off that he had reentered her life by simply stating that he knew her.

That night, when she had a moment alone with Sir, Brie crawled into his lap. She rested her head against his strong shoulder, needing the connection. He began stroking her hair.

"What's wrong, babygirl?"

Brie buried her face against his chest, taking in his masculine scent as he continued to hold her. She felt safe and protected. It gave her the courage to tell him, "Darius was in the news."

Sir stiffen beneath her. "In what capacity?"

"Lea saw a short article that had a picture of him. He mentioned knowing me growing up."

"Nothing else?"

"I guess he's a model and actor now." She laid her head back on his shoulder. "My memories of him won't stop. Every time I think about him, I get all anxious inside and feel like I need to run."

Sir held her tighter and continued to stroke her hair. "I will have someone look into it. I find it odd that he would mention knowing you."

Brie pulled away and frowned. "I do, too. Lea thinks he wants to make amends."

Sir pressed her head back against him. "Whatever his motives, he has no power over you now."

Brie nodded, wanting that to be true even though her memories said differently.

"Until we know more, I don't want you to dwell on it. Concentrate on constructive things."

"I will try, Sir." As soon as those words left her lips, Brie expected a correction. "Trying" was not enough in their household.

But he didn't. Instead, Sir continued to stroke her hair in silence. She took comfort in his quiet support and was able to fall asleep later that night, in his safe embrace.

In the middle of the night, she woke up with a start, her heart pounding in her chest. She thrashed violently trying to scramble out of the bed and ran to the bathroom.

"What's wrong, Brie?" Sir called out to her.

Brie retched in the toilet, her whole body numb with fear.

Sir got out of bed and went to reach out to her, but Brie flinched at his touch and instinctively pushed him away.

"What's going on, Brie?" he demanded gently, cutting through the fear that surrounded her.

Brie looked up at him, her voice trembling when she answered. "I don't know…"

He held out his arms and she moved into his embrace. She was crying but didn't understand why.

Once Sir had her cleaned up and settled back in bed, he asked, "Were you dreaming?"

"Yes, I...I think so," she answered hesitantly.

"What about?"

She looked at him with concern, shaking her head. "I don't remember, but I woke up feeling like I was choking to death."

Sir squeezed her tighter.

Brie looked at him sadly. "I'm sorry I pushed you away."

"No need to apologize," he assured her.

Brie settled back against him and closed her eyes, trying to fall back asleep, but knowing there was no hope. The unsettling feeling of choking had released a flood of memories centering on Darius and, in the darkness of the night, she was unable to keep them at bay.

There had been one incident in particular that she had never shared with a soul—not her parents, not her friends, and not even Sir. Reliving it now, even with the passage of time, filled her with a deep sense of shame and humiliation.

That secret had held her captive and tortured her for years. It wasn't until the Submissive Training Center and her encounter with Baron that she'd been able to move beyond it.

Darius had been the sole reason she'd been so afraid of the kind-hearted Dom on that first day of training, and why she had to look into his eyes every time they scened together, even though Ms. Clark had punished her severely for it.

Baron's gentle hazel eyes had been the anchor she needed when their scenes triggered old memories. Eventually, she stopped thinking about Darius when she was with the Dom, and eventually came to believe she'd overcome the trauma of the past.

However, today had sparked those memories she had kept hidden.

Darius had not only bullied her relentlessly—which her parents found out about the day he stabbed her with the needle—but just days after the incident, his actions managed to infiltrate the very core of her soul.

She had suffered in silence with the terrible secret ever since, and she knew it was the reason he still held power over her now. Her parents were not aware that their decision to move had saved her life back then.

At the tender age of twelve, Darius stole a piece of her innocence she could never get back, and it had almost destroyed her.

Getting out from under his brutal influence had allowed Brie to bury all memories of it. The small town in Nebraska proved to be what her spirit needed because *nothing* happened there. Bored to distraction, Brie often visited the theater house that played the classics in the afternoon. It was in that small, run-down theater that Brie discovered her love of film. She devoured the best of the best, never tiring of watching films like *Dances with Wolves, Braveheart, Titanic,* and *Avatar.* Luckily, the owner of the theater was a true lover of film and he introduced her to the classics, including *Gone with the Wind*—which became one of her favorites.

The small theater became her safe haven. There, she could completely lose herself in the worlds created on the big screen. What started out as a source of entertainment eventually became her inspiration.

On her fourteenth birthday, she asked for her first movie camera. Her parents, encouraged by her newfound confidence, indulged her in whatever used equipment they could find. Her father soon became a regular in the pawnshops in the surrounding towns.

To their credit, her parents never complained about her filming them on a daily basis. They put up with their privacy being invaded because every Sunday night, they would gather in the living room to watch the week's events documented in film.

Her father would close the curtains while Brie got the projector ready and her mother made a bowl of popcorn. Brie called her clips "My Hilarious Life" as a joke, since living in Nebraska was anything but hilarious—being the snooze-fest that it was.

However, each week, along with the clips of her parents moving through their daily routines, she captured something simple and unique that other people often missed: a lone dandelion blowing in the wind in the middle of an abandoned parking lot; an adorable colony of prairie dogs popping their heads in and out of their holes; a hawk circling in the sky making its lonely call; or a determined ant on the ground dragging its impossibly large piece of food back to its colony.

Brie found that hidden beauty existed all around

her whenever she looked through the lens of her camera. That was the magic of film for her—the ability to expose rare beauty in the ordinary.

By making weekly films, Brie caught those silly moments when her parents' guards were down. There were even times when she caught raw emotion like the time she filmed her father answering the phone. The look on his face when he got the news that his grandmother had died in a car accident was something she would never forget. It was horrible, but that moment showed a side of her father that Brie had never seen. She replayed it in private, mourning along with the devastated little boy revealed in his face.

Brie believed there were times her movies made reality even more real. It was a gift, this ability to show a different perspective of the world and be able to share it with others.

On her sixteenth birthday, she wrote in her diary in the style of Scarlett O'Hara:

As God is my witness, I will become a filmmaker...

She had kept that promise to herself, knowing her father would consider it an impractical profession with an uncertain future. To prove that she had a true gift that needed his financial support, she continued to make her weekly films well into high school, even recruiting friends to play out her first attempts at movies. It was her hope that her father would agree this was what she was meant to do and allow her go to college to follow that dream.

Yes, Nebraska turned out to be a huge blessing to her...

Brie sighed in contentment remembering those days and finally drifted back to sleep again beside Sir.

"Where are you going?"

Brie pretended not to hear Darius as she picked up her pace, her fear making it hard for her to breathe. She'd hoped after the needle incident he would leave her alone, but the tone in his voice let her know that it had only made things worse.

Head down, keep walking, she told herself.

She heard his shoes on the gravel as he ran up behind her. Brie had learned in the past not to run from Darius. It only made things worse for her when she did. Fighting that natural instinct, she continued to walk, knowing he was catching up.

Brie was surprised he did not have his usual entourage with him. Was it possible they had abandoned him after they were sent to the principal's office a few days ago?

She desperately hoped so. Maybe she could take him on in a one-on-one fight.

Brie cried out when he grabbed her by the shoulder, spinning her around to face him. "I asked you a question, girl."

She slowly dragged her gaze up to look him in the eyes, taking note of the position of his crotch. She planned to kick hard and run fast, but she knew she only had one chance, and she would pay dearly if she missed.

Darius grabbed her chin and forced her to look up at him. "Well...?" His eyes held a dangerous look, one she hadn't seen before, and her stomach twisted in fear.

His smile was cruel, his white teeth gleaming against the darkness of his skin. Brie suddenly realized that his entourage had actually been a blessing for her. Even though they held her down, at least they were witnesses. Without an audience acting as a deterrent, who knew what he was capable of?

Brie glanced around, realizing they were alone here. Anything could happen here...

Darius grabbed her wrist and twisted it, forcing her to her knees.

"No..." she cried out piteously.

He frowned. "No?" Twisting a little harder, he made her cry out again. It was obvious he was enjoying his power over her, so she clamped her mouth shut, not wanting to give it to him.

Glancing around desperately, Brie prayed for rescue.

Darius's eyes became dark with rage. "You snitch. You got me in trouble with my old man."

He twisted her arm again, bringing tears to her eyes, but she remained silent.

"And I *hate* my old man," he growled, spitting in her face.

Brie looked down at the ground, wiping her face with her free hand.

Without warning, he slammed his fist into her chest, causing her to fall violently onto her back.

Her chest exploded in pain and she gasped, struggling to catch her breath. He straddled her, holding her wrists down.

"You know the only thing that got me through the beating?"

Brie stared at him, saying nothing.

His smile spread as his eyes flashed with dangerous excitement. "I imagined how I would make you pay."

Brie felt a cold chill, wondering what terrible thing he had in mind as punishment.

He released one of her wrists and wrapped his hand around her throat, squeezing slowly. Brie struggled under him, the blood pounding in her head as her body fought for oxygen.

He let go and laughed when she coughed, desperately gasping for air.

Before she could regain her breath, he wrapped his hand around her neck again, choking her harder. Her eyes grew wide and she saw flashes of light in her peripheral vision. Her body instinctually thrashed, trying to break his hold.

Darius released her before the darkness closed in.

Brie sucked in the air she needed and began coughing violently. Darius only stared at her, no sympathy in his eyes.

Was he planning to kill her?

A force she never knew existed boiled up inside her and suddenly erupted. With an angry howl, she bucked her hips, and he was momentarily thrown off balance. She struggled to get out from under him, growling like a demonic animal.

But Darius was far stronger and wrestled her back down, both hands around her neck this time. The smirk on his face as the darkness closed in around her terrified her. Brie gave a strangled cry, the blood pounding in her skull.

Darius laughed when he finally loosened his grip. "I like seeing your eyes bug out like that."

He looked her over with a cold gaze when she grabbed her throat, coughing uncontrollably. His eyes landed on her open shirt, several buttons having broken off in the life-and-death struggle.

She felt a new level of terror when his expression changed.

Darius took hold of her wrists against, pushing them painfully to the ground as he got uncomfortably close to her face. "I want you to do something for me."

Brie shook her head.

His cruel smile returned. "Show me your titties."

She shook her head more violently.

"Yes…" He released her arms again, resting his full weight on her pelvis as he stared at her chest. "Unbutton your shirt and show them to me."

Again, she shook her head, her bottom lip trembling.

"Show me," he demanded.

Brie was only twelve, her chest still flat like a boy's. There was nothing for him to see, but she couldn't bear being exposed to him like that.

His eyes flashed with malicious anger. "Do it."

Brie looked around, hoping against hope that someone would walk by and save her.

Darius only chuckled. "It's just you and me...Brianna Bennett."

Brie couldn't bring herself to do it even though she knew he would hurt her if she did not. After several moments of waiting, he smiled strangely at her.

She hoped he was having a change of heart, but those hopes died when he wrapped his hands around her throat again.

Brie whimpered as he squeezed even tighter. Her body, having experienced it before, went straight into panic mode. No matter how desperately she clawed at his hands, she could not break his hold. This time, he did not stop—he squeezed until the twinkling lights in her head faded to black and she lost consciousness.

The return was frightening and confusing. She first became aware of a lone dog barking somewhere far off. Her vision seemed blurred—seeing but not seeing—and she found every breath painful. It took several minutes before her brain could process as she slowly came back to reality.

The dark form in front of her slowly crystallized into Darius. He was still straddling her with that smirk on his lips. "Welcome back."

Brie swallowed hard, the pain in her throat causing her to wince.

"You know what I want."

Rescue wasn't coming. She was completely on her own, and she wanted to live. With shaking hands, she fumbled at the remaining buttons, but her fingers refused to cooperate. Darius appeared to take pleasure in watching her struggle and made no move to help

her.

Brie closed her eyes, tears falling, the humiliation she felt threatened to swallow her whole as the first button finally gave and she went to unbutton the next...

She dropped her hands in shame and defeat when she was done.

A cold breeze swirled around her skin when he pulled the material of her shirt away, and a sob escaped her lips.

"Don't make a sound," he warned her. A chill like ice coursed through her veins when he touched her. He said nothing as his hands ran over her flat breasts and the tiny buds of her nipples.

Brie kept swallowing hard, her eyes closed tightly, trying to keep herself from sobbing. She was completely unprepared when she felt his lips on hers.

Brie shook her head violently, breaking the kiss.

He grabbed her chin, holding her still as he did it again. It felt so wrong, like eating poison, and she suddenly felt sick.

Her body froze when she felt one of his hands move lower.

"No," she begged.

His hand did not hesitate as it slipped under the material of her jeans. Her whole body became cold as a terrifying numbness took over.

No...

Bile rose up her tender throat and she started thrashing as she began making retching noises, Darius jumped off her just in time to avoid being covered in her vomit. She rolled over, getting on her hands and knees as she threw up violently, her body expelling the contents of her stomach.

When it was over, she looked up and saw that Darius had fled. Wiping her mouth, she sat on her heels and tried to button up her shirt, but her hands wouldn't stop shaking. She closed up her shirt, hugging herself as she sat there.

The dog continued to bark in the distance.

Daddy...

Why had no one come?

Brie closed her eyes and the tears fell as she began sobbing uncontrollably. She sat there in the dirt for what felt like hours.

Alone.

It felt surreal when she finally buttoned her shirt back up, stood up on shaking legs, and began the long walk home, avoiding people at all costs. Everything around her was the same. Same streets, same houses, nothing had changed—but everything had changed for her.

Brie stumbled into the house. Her mother was singing to the song "Don't Worry, Be Happy," a Bobby McFerrin favorite, as she prepared the night's dinner in the kitchen.

"Brie, is that you?" she called out.

Not wanting to face her, Brie answered in a hoarse voice. "I'm going upstairs to study."

Her mother popped her head out of the kitchen. "You're late. I was starting to get worried."

Brie was barely holding on by a thread emotionally.

She couldn't face her mom—not now. Holding out her backpack to hide behind it, she said, "Gotta head upstairs…" Brie bolted up the stairs, but her mother called from the bottom step.

"Brie, what happened to you? You're cover in dirt from head to toe."

"It's nothing, Mom," she insisted, trying to move up the stairs faster.

"Stop right there, young lady."

Brie stopped on the last step, her heart beating out of her chest, wishing the earth would open up and swallow her.

Knowing her shirt was missing several buttons, and uncertain what her face looked like, Brie couldn't chance turning around to face her. There would be no getting out of this if she did.

"Walk back down here this instant, young lady…"

The terror she felt in the dream woke Brie straight out of her nightmare, and she screamed in the dark. Sir reached out to her, his touch in her current state causing her to scream even louder.

Sir enveloped Brie in his arms, holding her tightly and refusing to let go until she quieted against him. "Darius," he stated rather than asked.

Oh God…how did he know with such certainty? There was no way he would let this go.

"Talk to me, Brie," Sir insisted in a low, comforting

tone.

She had no choice. They had promised to be open with each other about everything. But this...this memory was a long-buried secret she had never wanted to share.

He rolled her over to face him. "Brie."

She couldn't look at him when she finally found the courage to speak. "Hearing about Darius today sparked a memory."

"Of his bullying?"

"Yes..."

"And something more?"

She cuddled against him, needing his physical reassurance.

"You're shaking, Brie." Sir pressed her against him, tucking the blanket around her.

Even though the memory filled her with a deep sense of shame, she finally voiced the secret only she and Darius knew. "He was mad at me for tattling about him stabbing me with the needle..."

"What did he do?" Sir asked, a hint of anger coloring his voice.

Brie found it difficult to speak. "Darius cornered me alone and...choked me."

Sir waited, brushing his hand against her cheek.

"He made me take off my shirt..." she said, a sob escaping her lips. "He did it to humiliate me, but then he touched and kissed me."

"And you were how old?" he asked, his voice strained.

"Twelve."

Brie could feel the heat of his rage building. The anger in his voice was barely contained. "Did he do anything else?"

"He tried to force his hand between my legs, but I threw up."

"Thank God for that," Sir said, gathering her into his arms. He buried his face in her hair and shook his head, saying nothing.

Sir's response surprised Brie. She felt no condemnation, no shame in his arms.

Needing him to know the whole story, she continued. "I headed home afterward because I knew my mom would be worried. Before she was out of the kitchen, I ran up the stairs to hide in my room. Mom tried to stop me, but I was too ashamed and afraid to face her. Thank goodness, too. I ended up having to wear a scarf for weeks to cover up the marks he left on my throat. It was embarrassing because my mom told everyone that I was going through a fashion phase, and she was so proud of my new look. She never knew what happened."

Sir growled under his breath.

"Looking back now, I realize I should have told her. By saying nothing, it's almost as if I was protecting Darius. My silence made it seem like what happened was okay, but I was just a little kid, and it was so weird what he did. I couldn't really understand what had happened, and I was deathly afraid of him."

Sir squeezed her tighter. "No fault lies with you, babygirl."

Brie braved a look up, gazing into his eyes. "Do

you know what eats at my heart?"

"What?"

"I left. We moved out a short time later. Without me there, he moved on to someone else. Because I said nothing..." Her throat closed up, and she had to force the words out. "...some other little girl became my replacement."

Brie buried her head against him and cried.

Sir let her release her pent-up tears but, when she began to quiet again, he lifted her chin, looking at her in the darkness. "Stop holding that little girl hostage for something that should not have been expected of her."

"But—"

"It really is no different than the guilt I carried because I decided not to tell my father about my mother's infidelity when I was a kid. We were young and innocent—the consequences do not lie on our shoulders."

Brie was struck by how sad it was that Sir had blamed himself for his father's death. It made her weepy to think of that young man grieving the loss of his father, believing he was partly to blame for it.

Brie caressed his jaw, speaking to the little boy he once was. "It was not your fault."

"And it was not yours," he replied.

Brie nodded. Although she would still worry about those Darius had hurt after she'd left, the little girl Brie had once been deserved her empathy.

"You might find it helpful if you told your parents what really happened."

"No," Brie said resolutely. "My dad never forgave himself for Darius stabbing me with the dirty needle even though he sacrificed everything to get me out of there. He would feel responsible for this, and he shouldn't have to. My parents saved my life, getting me far away from there. I honestly don't know how long I would have lasted." She smiled sadly at Sir. "It's the reason I never complained about living in a shelter with my mom. I knew I was much better off."

"It's a testament to your strength—the fact he wasn't able to crush your sweet spirit," Sir told her, his voice tinged with pain.

Brie thought back to that first day of submissive training. "If Baron hadn't been so gentle and understanding during the practicum, I would never have made it through the first night."

"I was confident he was the right man to guide you through the scene, but I had no idea of the severity of your past."

"No one knew…until now."

He took her face in both hands, pressing his forehead against hers. "May the voicing of it bring you much deserved peace, my love."

Tears came to her eyes. "Thank you, Sir."

They stayed in that embrace, Brie soaking in the relief of not having to bear that terrible secret in silence any longer. "Sir, I don't know what to do about Darius now."

"You don't have to do a thing, babygirl. It's unfortunate that there is no legal recourse for what he's done because he was a child at the time he assaulted you. However, I plan to check his background to determine the motivation behind this public comment. I suspect he was looking for free publicity, hoping to ride on the coattails of your success. But…" Sir growled harshly, "…if he becomes a threat, I will show him no mercy."

"Lea thought he might be looking for absolution, but even if that is his intention, I'm unsure if I'm capable of forgiving him."

"And you don't have to. It must be a need of yours, not his, before I would encourage it."

It was remarkable how Sir had a way of making her feel empowered. She told him with regret, "All these years I've carried that secret inside like a festering wound. What a fool I was."

"You're not a fool. You were waiting for the right person and situation. That kind of information in the wrong hands had the potential to hurt you."

"What about you, Sir? Was Rytsar the person you turned to?"

Sir nodded. "In part, but I still held on to the guilt. I was not truly free until after I survived the crash. It became clear to me how unfair I'd been to the child I was at thirteen. To expect the wisdom and maturity of an adult is unreasonable and pointless. I *was* a child then, and what happened had nothing to do with me."

"It did not."

"So I ask that you be kind to the little Brianna you carry inside you."

Hope let out a cry from the other room.

"I'll take care of her," he said, immediately getting out of bed. "You lie still and try falling back to sleep for me."

As he was leaving the room, he turned around and added tenderly, "That's a command."

Oh, Rhett…

"Brie, could you come here?"

She gave Hope a kiss before putting her down for a nap, then walked into their bedroom to see what Sir needed.

On the bed she saw a big box decorated with a large bow, with a much smaller box sitting on top. "What's this?" she giggled excitedly.

"Open the smaller box first," Sir answered.

Brie walked over, a smile playing on her lips. Picking up the small box, she lifted the lid and saw Sir's old cell phone nestled inside. He'd been carrying it the day the plane went down.

For Brie, it held only bad memories, and that played across her face now.

"This gives you the reference," he stated. "Now, open the larger box."

Still having no clue what this was about, Brie lifted the lid and let out a gasp of surprise as she opened the folded tissue paper to find the extravagant dress inside. It was an exact replica of the green and white garden dress Scarlett wore at the Wilkes' picnic in *Gone with the Wind*.

She glanced over at Sir, and a smile spread across her face. "Rhett?"

He nodded. "When I listened to the messages, I came across one that mentioned a desire to play out a particular scene together."

Brie shook her head, a myriad of emotions flooding in. "I was watching *Gone with the Wind* when…" Her voice broke. "…I almost lost you." She looked at him sadly. "I can't bear to watch that movie anymore."

"Well, tonight we are going to change that."

"What do you have planned?"

He gave her a mysterious smile. "All you need to concern yourself with is getting ready. I will take care of the rest and meet you downstairs, outside the lobby, at exactly seven."

Brie blushed, excited by the prospect of a night out together. However, other than her parents, no one else had babysat Hope up to this point. "Sir?"

He raised an eyebrow. "Yes?"

"If we are leaving, it means we have to get a babysitter, and I…"

"What?"

"I'm not sure I'm ready to leave our little girl with someone just yet."

"Babysitting arrangements have already been made. It's time for you and me to reconnect as a couple."

Brie understood that he was honoring her request to keep their relationship strong, even as new parents. However, now that she *was* a mother, she felt hesitant to leave Hope with someone else.

"It's time, téa," Sir insisted, reading the uncertainty in her expression.

She blushed, touched that he had set up this romantic role play to ease her back into the world they both loved, and she did long to scene with him, as well—especially as Rhett and Scarlett. Still, she found it more difficult to leave Hope than she had ever imagined and looked at him pensively.

"You are curious about who will be watching our child?"

She nodded.

Sir said with a glint in his eye. "You will have to trust me."

"A little hint?" Brie begged, giving him doe eyes she hoped he could not resist. When he did not respond, she nodded, accepting her responsibility to trust him without question. "It always seems to come down to a matter of trust," she mused.

"That does define the D/s relationship."

"Yes," she agreed, bowing her head as she knelt before him. A feeling of peace washed over her as she took on the formal role again. Brie looked up and gazed into his eyes, fully his submissive.

He placed his hand on her head and said in his velvety smooth voice, "Stand and serve your Master, téa."

Her heart filled with the familiar joy she felt as his submissive. She stood up gracefully before him, head still bowed, waiting for his command.

Sir put his finger under her chin and lifted it. "We are going to scene tonight." She felt her loins contract with pleasure. "But first, you must take care of your hair and makeup. When you're ready, I will help you into your gown."

"Do you want a subtle look, or full-on Scarlett O' Hara?"

He winked at her. "Rhett is looking to meet up with Scarlett."

Brie loved his answer. "Then it may take a little longer, but I promise to be ready by seven."

"I insist you start with a warm bath. I need you relaxed and pliable for tonight."

She took his hand and kissed the palm before placing it against her cheek. "Thank you, Master."

He chuckled. "For what? We haven't even begun."

She gazed over at her dress. "For reminding me of who we are together."

He leaned down to kiss her. "I would never let us forget."

Brie watched as he left the room, her heart rushing with love and excitement.

To do the dress justice, she spent nearly two hours getting herself ready. Wanting to look perfect, she whipped out her phone and studied still shots of Scarlett so she could re-create her look.

Brie curled her hair just right and painted her lips with the pert red arches that had made Scarlett's mouth so kissable.

Standing back afterward, Brie stared at her reflection in the mirror with her cascade of brown curls, wearing those adorable frilly white bloomers, the petticoat adorned with eyelet lace, and the white corset included in the box.

"I'm ready now, Rhett," she called out playfully, excited for him to see her.

Brie was startled when Rytsar walked into the room. "Where's Sir?"

"What, *radost moya*? Am I not enough for you?" he joked.

Brie giggled, giving him a hug. "I've missed you!"

"I have been a good potato so that I could heal." He lifted his arms wide. "And now I am a man once more."

"I'm so happy." She hugged him again, excited to see him looking so well.

"Your man is not here and has left me in charge of helping you with getting dressed. However…" he said with a seductive growl, looking her over, "…I think you look delectable just as you are. Let me help you out of that corset…"

"No, no," she laughed. "But I would appreciate it if you would tighten it a little."

He moved behind her and she felt his warm breath on the back of her neck as he grabbed the ties and yanked them tighter. "Like this…?" he questioned lustfully, his sudden action taking Brie's breath away.

Rytsar quickly adjusted the laces. He then stood back and turned her around to admire his handiwork. She found herself blushing under his scrutiny, his eyes riveted on her cleavage.

He said in admiration, "*Radost moya*, motherhood agrees with you."

Brie glanced at her reflection in the mirror and

grinned. He was right. Her breasts were impressive these days, and the corset totally rocked them out.

"I see you like the look as well," he observed. "Shall we skip the dress, then?"

"Absolutely not," Brie giggled. "The scene *requires* the dress."

"Very well, then," he muttered good-naturedly, "but it is tragic to cover up such beauty."

Brie kissed him lightly on the cheek, leaving a light imprint of her red lips. "Just you wait, Rytsar. When you see me in all my glory, you will understand."

She had him help her into the hoop skirt and waited breathlessly as he slid the dress over her head and let it fall into place. Rytsar tied the sash around her waist, then commanded, "Turn for me."

Brie felt like a true Southern belle as she turned slowly, basking in the joy of it.

Rytsar let out a low whistle. "I'll admit, *radost moya*, while there are far too many layers, you wear it well."

Just then, they heard a little cry come from Hope's room.

As Brie started to leave, Rytsar placed his hand on her bare shoulder. "Stay. I will take care of this."

Rytsar went to attend to the baby, leaving Brie standing in the room alone. Curious, she gave in to the urge to peek. She watched with a sense of pride as Rytsar gently picked Hope up. Cradling the tiny infant against his chest, he spoke to his niece in Russian and then began singing a haunting lullaby in a low, comforting tone.

Hope instantly stopped crying.

Brie was as mesmerized by Rytsar's song as her daughter. He looked up and caught Brie staring. Rather than scold her for her disobedience, he winked while continuing to sing to Hope. It was a tender moment between *dyadya* and child.

Brie finally made the connection. Rytsar was the babysitter for the evening, and she felt totally at peace. "Thank you, Sir," she said quietly as she watched the two together.

Brie left them to make a list of instructions for Rytsar but had to laugh when she found Sir had already written a similar list and left it on the counter. Reading over it, Brie was impressed Sir had not missed a single item.

Rytsar came out of the baby's room, still carrying Hope in his arms. "Do not worry, *radost moya,* I will hold down the fort here."

She smiled at him gratefully. "She couldn't be in better hands."

"*Moye solntse* and I understand each other," he stated, looking down at the babe.

"I see the connection she has with her *dyadya*."

"So there is no reason to concern yourself with us." He held up the tiny babe. "We want you to have a good time with my comrade."

Brie walked over to kiss Hope on the head and left a matching imprint of her lips on her forehead. "I thank you, both. If you need anything, don't forget we're just a phone call—"

"Do not fret," he insisted. "Spending time with her is exactly what my heart desires."

Brie smiled at him tenderly, touched by his devotion. "I love you, Rytsar."

"And I you. Now, go. Do not make your Master wait."

Brie gave Rytsar a formal curtsy with a full view of her impressive cleavage. He whistled in appreciation as she headed out the door.

Sir was waiting outside beside a limo when she exited the building. Brie suddenly felt butterflies. He had slicked back his hair in the style of Rhett's, and he was dressed in the same classic black suit and vest from the movie. He also wore a devilish smirk on his lips.

"You are looking positively radiant this evening, Miss O'Hara."

Brie felt the warmth of a blush on her cheeks. "Mr. Butler, you do know how to turn a girl's head."

Sir held his hand out to her. "Let me give you a real reason to blush, my dear."

Brie sauntered over to him, causing her skirt to make delightful swishing sounds as she walked. She smiled to herself when she caught him staring intently at her cleavage.

"Do you like my new dress?" she asked sweetly, twisting back and forth where she stood.

"It's not the dress that catches my attention," he replied, opening the limo door for her.

Getting into the vehicle proved an amusing challenge with her voluminous dress. Sir chuckled as he helped maneuver the ungainly skirt into the car. Getting the seatbelt around her caused another round of giggles.

Sir kept their destination to himself, leaving Brie to wonder the entire ride. When they pulled up to the theater, she let out an excited gasp.

"Tonight's play happens to be *Gone with the Wind*. I thought you would enjoy it," Sir told her as he helped Brie out of the limo. She smoothed out the material of her dress, pulling down the ruffles on her shoulders to expose more skin for Sir while making a nice frame for her cleavage.

She laughed at herself, suddenly reminded of a scene in the movie where Scarlett had done the exact same thing. Harnessing the Scarlett vibe, Brie embraced her role as she took the arm Sir offered and they walked into the theater.

People couldn't help staring and pointing, some even asking for selfies with the two as they made their way up to the balcony seats. Sir was patient, handling the attention with grace.

When he was finally able to guide her to their private box seats, she squealed in pleasure. "This isn't the exact same balcony, is it?"

"It is, my dear."

Brie grinned as she sat down, remembering the night when Sir had taken her to this theater, acting as her Khan. Naughty things had happened on this very floor, but the night had ended abruptly when she unwittingly said the word "love" out loud, causing him to conclude their evening.

It was astounding how far they had come since then...

While Brie watched the play, Sir made slight advances—lightly grazing his fingers along her bare shoulder, giving her a nibble on the ear or a kiss on the neck. Nothing overly sexual, but all incredibly erotic since she knew he had plans for her later.

"Are you enchanted with the story again?" Sir whispered huskily when Rhett carried Scarlett up the stairs to have his way with her.

She nodded, anxious to experience the same thing herself.

"Shall we leave, then, my dear?"

"Yes, please."

The halls of the theater were quiet as everyone watched the end of the play. Sir took advantage of it, suddenly stopping and pressing her up against a wall with his body. "I can't seem to resist you, Miss O'Hara," he growled hungrily before planting an impassioned kiss on her lips.

Brie melted against him, thoroughly captivated by his heated desire.

Leaving her breathless, he led her out to the limo, and then the driver took them to the Submissive Training Center. Sir produced a black coat from the trunk and held it out to her.

"So we can be discreet," he explained.

Regular business classes were about to end for the evening, and many who attended the regular college at this campus were oblivious to the fact that there was a BDSM Training Center on the lower level.

Although the coat poofed out excessively due to the dress, it did cover her cleavage. After her coat was buttoned up, he led her to the front desk, where

Rachael stood waiting, greeting them with a warm smile.

"It is such a pleasure to see you two again. You look absolutely wonderful, Sir Davis," she said with awe, having seen him in a wheelchair the last time.

"Thank you," he answered.

"And how is the baby?" Rachael asked Brie.

"She's doing well, and Uncle Rytsar is watching her right now."

"That's too adorable," Rachael admitted.

"He's wonderfully sweet with her."

"I can imagine, and I can't wait to see your little girl myself."

"We will be having a gathering as soon as the pediatrician gives us the okay," Sir assured her. He gave Rachael a curt nod, then fell back into his role as Rhett.

Placing his hand on the small of Brie's back, he asked her, "Shall we take our leave, Miss O'Hara?"

She batted her eyes at him as Sir walked her to the elevators leading to the Submissive Training Center. On the way down, he explained, "I'm taking you to a place you have never been." She smiled, assuming he was talking about a new kind of play they hadn't tried.

Brie was surprised to see Master Nosh, the head trainer of the Dominant Training Center, when the doors slid open. The handsome Head Trainer had the distinct facial features and long black hair that spoke to his Native American heritage. Beside him stood another man whom she had never met before.

"Good evening," Sir said, addressing the Head Trainer before holding out his hand and escorting Brie out of the elevator. He then turned to the other man while Master Nosh introduced him.

"Sir Davis, this is my top student, Hunter."

Sir shook his hand firmly. "It is a pleasure to meet you. Such high praise from Nosh is unusual. You must be truly exceptional to have earned it."

The man returned the handshake, nodding humbly in response. The two highly respected Doms standing beside him did not diminished his own aura of dominance. It was impressive for a student.

"It is an honor, Sir Davis," Hunter said with respect. "Your reputation precedes you."

"I look forward to hearing more about your endeavors in the future."

"Thank you, Sir Davis."

The two men entered the elevator, but as the doors were closing, Master Nosh looked directly at Brie and stated, "I would interview with you, should you request it."

Brie sucked in her breath as the doors closed. Master Nosh was well known for his quiet, but uncompromising, nature, as well as his utter devotion to excellence. He was not one to trifle with something he did not feel strongly about. So, the fact that he had made such an offer to Brie was a bit of a shock.

"Did you ask to interview him?" Sir asked.

Brie shook her head. "I wanted to a while ago, but it never panned out."

"Interesting..." Sir murmured, staring at the elevator doors.

Returning to her role, she snuggled against Sir's

arm.

He smiled down at her and said warmly, "Come, Miss O'Hara."

Sir walked her past the Head Trainer's office, and Brie had to quell her excitement as they continued into the wing reserved for the Dominant classes.

Although she knew where the classes were, she'd never been allowed on this side of the building. It felt exclusive and almost naughty for her to be here now.

Lea had been a submissive for the Dominant training course. The fact was, submissives *were* allowed in the Dominant area; they just weren't asked to this side of the Center unless there was a reason for it.

Brie glanced up at Sir, finally understanding what he'd meant in the elevator when he'd mentioned taking her somewhere she'd never been. The man was always surprising her.

As they continued to walk, she wondered what was behind every closed door they passed. Were the Dominants' classrooms and practice areas the same as the submissive side, or were they completely different?

As they were passing by another door, it opened and a student walked out. Brie quickly averted her eyes, looking to the floor, momentarily forgetting she was role playing the confident Scarlett by her Master's side. She quickly snuck a glance, getting the opportunity to peek into the room before he closed the door behind him.

Brie had to laugh when she saw rows of desks similar to Mr. Gallant's classroom. She overheard the instructor's confident voice ringing through the room:

"Safewords protect not only your submissives, but you as a Dominant—" His words were cut short when the door shut.

She smiled to herself as thoughts of those carefree days under Mr. Gallant's instruction came to mind. Her life as a submissive had begun in his classroom…

Brie's reverie ended when Sir stopped in front of a bright red door. Brie stared at it, taking a moment to put herself in Scarlett's shoes. Tonight, she was hoping Rhett Butler would do unspeakable things to her during their clandestine meeting at this underground establishment. She knew it was unwise to be alone with him, but she couldn't resist. The man was impossible and dangerously alluring in his charm.

Holding her breath, she entered the room, anxious to see what secrets it held. The walls were covered in luxurious curtains of burgundy velvet and braided cord. Her gaze drifted to the antique loveseat set in the middle of the room. Over on the right was a polished wooden bar with large, ornate bottles of various liquors displayed behind it. She was thoroughly enchanted and inspired by the romantic feel of this room.

She allowed Sir to take her coat off before she headed toward the bar. Taking on the sassiness of Scarlett, she looked back over her shoulder flirtatiously and said, "You really shouldn't look at a lady that way, Mr. Butler."

Taking a line straight from the movie, he replied, "You, my dear, are no lady."

"And you, sir, are no gentleman!" she retorted, turning to face him. Following the scene in the movie, she raised her hand as if to slap him across the face.

But Sir grabbed her wrist firmly and tsked loudly. "Do you know what I do to spoiled little girls?"

Brie frowned. "I'm no child!"

The charming smirk returned to his lips as he brazenly looked at her breasts. "I can see that—quite clearly."

Brie tried to wrestle her hand from his grip, but he held firm. "Rather than try to fight our mutual attraction, why don't you give in to it? Have a drink with me."

"But…"

Sir put his finger to her red lips. "There's no reason to put up pretenses when there's no one else around."

When Brie stopped resisting, he released his hold. She watched in silent adoration as Sir set to work making martinis, his signature drink.

He looked so incredibly hot dressed as Rhett Butler. The man was every bit as handsome as Clark Gable—even more so, in her eyes. The butterflies started up as she continued to stare at him.

She was reminded of that first day at the Training Center, when he had spoken to her near the end of class. Sir had been an enigma then and, even now, after all they had been through, he still held a mysterious air.

She liked that about him.

Brie licked her lips, watching him intently as those masculine hands shook the tumbler. Her body remembered well just how talented those hands were.

He poured out the second martini and, with that devilish grin, offered her the glass. "See if that doesn't help break down your resistance, my dear."

Brie took a tentative sip. She smiled, momentarily forgetting her role. "Oh, Sir! I'd forgotten how good your martinis taste."

Sir winked, pretending not to hear her slip-up. "There's nothing wrong with a strong drink to begin a memorable evening together." He took a long sip himself and stared at her lustfully as he put his glass down on the counter.

He looked her over with open admiration. "I must say, the gown suits you. The color and style of it gives you an air of innocence, but the bare shoulders and the way the neckline accentuates your…feminine assets are enough to inspire any man."

"You are a cad, Mr. Butler. One minute you give me the sweetest compliment, then you go and ruin it by insulting me."

Sir picked up his glass, raising an eyebrow. "I must correct you. I only give the highest compliments. I never insult."

She said indignantly, "Didn't your father teach you any manners? There's a proper way for a gentleman to address a lady."

"My father taught me plenty of things, dear Scarlett."

Brie's heart fluttered. Although Scarlett would have certainly given Rhett a snappy retort, she couldn't help flirting with him. "Such as…?"

He set her glass on the counter, saying, "He taught me to give a lady exactly what she deserves." Sir suddenly grabbed her by the back of the neck and kissed her hard on the lips.

The intensity of the kiss took Brie by surprise, and she stumbled when he let go of her. She was legitimately dazed.

Oh, Rhett…

"As you can tell, my daddy taught me well," he stated with a smirk, picking up her glass and handing it back to her. "Now, drink, my dear."

Brie took it from him and sipped absently at her martini, her whole body tingling from that forceful embrace.

Sir continued to stare at her hungrily. His heated gaze only added fuel to the fire.

"You look like you could use something, Miss O'Hara," he growled in a husky voice.

"What?" she asked, her lips curling into a playful smile.

"Come over here and find out," he stated, taking her drink and setting it on the counter before guiding her to the loveseat.

Brie followed him, her heart racing with anticipation. She was so deep into her character, she actually felt that delicious, nervous fear of physically connecting with someone new.

Sir sat down and patted the area beside him.

As she moved to sit down, Brie thought he would kiss her again, but he surprised Brie by grabbing her bodily and throwing her over his knees.

"What is the meaning of this?" she cried in protest.

"I'm going to give you a spanking, my dear."

His hands began traveling up the inside of her skirt.

Brie began struggling, knowing Scarlett would never allow such a thing. "Don't you dare spank me."

"Fair warning. If you struggle, you're only going to make it harder on yourself." He started tugging on her bloomers.

"Not my bare bottom!"

"Yes. I am going to spank your naked ass, and you are going to take it like a good girl."

Brie screamed, fighting to keep her modesty.

He suddenly let her go, and she got back on her feet, backing away from him when he stood up.

"Have you no shame?" she cried.

His lustful smile let her know that the games were just beginning. "I'm going to spank you, but not in that damn dress. Take it off."

She looked at him indignantly. "I will *not* take off my dress."

"Yes, you will," he answered. "If you do not, I will rip it off you, and you wouldn't want to ruin that pretty garment now, would you?"

Brie glanced at the door. "I'll run," she threatened him.

Sir chuckled. "We both know that's an idle threat. You want to feel my hand against your skin. I see it in the way you look at me, and I felt it in the way you kissed me."

She shook her head.

He nodded, his charming smirk daring her to disagree. "Enough of these silly pretenses. Take off your dress like a good girl and come over here."

Sir sat back down on the loveseat and waited for

her.

Brie was actually trembling, imagining how Scarlett would feel undressing for Rhett under these circumstances. She slowly untied her sash and wrestled with the dress as she lifted it over her head. Once free, she let it fall to the ground and put her hands to her hips in challenge.

"The hoop skirt and petticoat, too."

Brie hesitated, but then stepped out of her skirt and shimmied out of the petticoat, kicking it to the side.

"That's *much* better," he stated, patting his lap.

She shook her head, still reluctant to give in.

"Come."

The tone in his voice compelled her to obey. She made her way over to him and sighed nervously as she lay across his manly thighs.

Sir rubbed his palm over her lacy buttocks. "Frilly ass."

Brie smiled to herself, remembering that she had asked him to spank her frilly ass in her phone message to him.

However, Sir was not satisfied with spanking her through the ruffled material and slowly pulled down her bloomers to expose her bare bottom. Her pussy tingled with anticipation.

"Are you ready for your spanking?"

She nodded, biting her bottom lip as a small squeak escaped.

The sound of the first smack echoed in the room.

Brie squealed, squirming on his lap, having forgotten the sting of a good spanking.

Sir was sensual about the way he spanked her, rubbing his hand over her skin, teasing it with a gentle caress before raising his hand slowly and making her wait a few seconds before he delivered another smack. Her whole body shivered with delight with each impact.

He was slow and thoughtful, drawing out this sexual exchange between them, reminding her that he controlled the moment—and her body. Each swat caused her pussy to contract with pleasure.

The idea that a man could bring her to the verge of climax by simply swatting her bottom with his bare hand remained a wonder to Brie.

"Do you want me to stop?" he asked, rubbing her pinkening ass.

She turned her head to look back at him. "Not yet…"

Sir smiled knowingly, raising his hand to spank her again.

Brie closed her eyes, acutely aware of his every movement. She reveled in the sound of his hand smacking her skin, the way her skin burned pleasantly with each contact of his hand. He was strategic in the delivery of each spank, varying the intensity so she was continually surprised—sometimes crying out in pain, while other times purring with pleasure.

Oh, how she marveled at his ability to make touch alone the center focus, bringing her body pleasure with the artful and varied ways he delivered it.

Brie whimpered when he lifted the material back over her ass. He chuckled. "You are a greedy thing, aren't you?"

Brie smiled back at him, answering truthfully. "Yes."

Sir pulled her up to him, whispering in her ear, "I love everything about you, woman. Your passion, your mind, your body, your need…all of it."

He'd told her those very words once before when they were in Russia, visiting the cabin for the first time. After being accused by Tono's father of being too ravenous to be satisfied, Sir had restored her confidence by proving daily that he meant those ardent words he'd spoken then.

They still held power over her today.

"I love you," she told him.

He set her back on the loveseat, looking amused. "One simple spanking and you're already declaring your love for me?"

Brie's answering giggle was cut short when he kissed her, thrusting his tongue deep into her mouth. She instantly melted into his embrace, her body craving the release he could give.

Sir pulled back and smirked. "You are an eager young thing, aren't you?"

"You can't give me a taste, Mr. Butler, and not expect me to want more."

"I thought you might say that," he stated, getting up and walking over to one of the velvet curtains. He yanked on the material and it came cascading down, revealing a wall of kinky tools.

Sir walked over to it and pulled on a lever. A section of the wall lowered, becoming a table with attached restraints. He gestured to her to come to him.

Brie trembled as she approached, reminded of their second night after class, when he had strapped her down to a table.

"Let me finish undressing you," he stated.

Her heart raced as he moved behind her and lightly traced his fingers over her bare shoulders, causing goosebumps on her skin. When he began slowly untying the laces of her corset, Brie closed her eyes, savoring his attention.

There was that almost orgasmic feel when the corset released its hold on her and fell away. "Ohh…" she purred. For Brie, both the restriction and the release of the constriction were equally pleasurable.

Sir ran his hands over the indents left by the tight corset. She purred in delight, loving the sensuous feel of his touch.

"You are truly beautiful," he told her. "You inspire a man to embrace his baser desires, Miss O'Hara." He lifted her up onto the table and began binding her to it. "I want you to feel completely helpless when I take you."

Brie longed for that helpless feeling.

"You flirt with boys, but it's a man you need," he told her. "One who knows how to tame that wild spirit."

While she watched, he started to undress in front of her. He was slow and purposeful about it. Taking off the jacket, and then the vest. Unbuttoning his cuffs, undoing his tie, leisurely unbuttoning his shirt, exposing his manly chest.

Brie was transfixed, watching his every movement, enjoying every new area of flesh that he exposed until Sir stood completely naked in front of her—confident and powerful.

When he walked toward her, she felt her pussy contract in lustful need, readying itself for his penetration.

Sir stood at the end of the table, keeping his gaze on her as he started rubbing his cock against her wet pussy. "You want this as much as I do."

She nodded. The sexual excitement of coupling again after having the baby made it almost feel like this was the first time, with everything unfamiliar and new again.

She needed to know what his cock felt like inside her, longing to feel his possession and his release.

Brie could barely breathe when he positioned his cock and smiled hungrily at her as he grabbed her thighs and gave her that first deep thrust. Brie arched her back as she cried out, her body forced to take his full length. "Oh my God…yes!"

He held her tighter, stroking her pussy with a passion pent up from long weeks of denial. Brie hadn't imagined it could feel this good, but she became lost in his lovemaking, connecting to not only the man he was now, but also the man he had been that first time.

Brie could feel her orgasm mounting and begged, "I want to feel you come when I orgasm."

He gripped her thighs more tightly. "Prepare yourself."

She started panting as he revved up the pace of his thrusts, sensations blurring as her orgasm quickly reached its peak. He held her there on the edge, her body begging for release as he pounded her hard.

The moment he changed the angle slightly, he took her over the edge and she screamed out in passion. Sir's fingers dug into her skin as he released his seed inside her, his own cries of ecstasy matching hers.

Brie reveled in the erotic connection as they came together—one body, one mind.

Meeting Liam

B rie was thrilled when Lea called and said she wanted Brie to meet Liam for the first time. It pleased her even more that Lea had invited Mary to join them. Although the two still had their differences, Lea had also picked up on the change in Mary. "It's weird, Brie. I'm actually beginning to *like* her, not just barely tolerating her anymore. Isn't that strange?"

"Mary's really changing. I hope that means she'll be dumping that creep Mr. Holloway real soon. She deserves better."

"It must be strange knowing he was your boss."

"Yeah, it's made me question things concerning my film. Like, was the whole documentary just a ruse to get Mary into his life? If so, why go to such extremes?" Brie shuddered thinking about it. "All I can do now is be grateful that the film positively impacted people. But I have no intention of working with him again. Not after the way he treated Faelan, and his odd obsession with Mary."

"Yeah, you saw how she reacted when I asked her

about the guy at your party."

Brie nodded. "I did, and I tried to talk to her later, but she's still being close-mouthed about it."

"Maybe we can pry something out of her, but not in front of Liam. I don't want things getting all serious, you know?"

"Sure. Since we haven't even met the guy yet there's no need to scare him right out of the gate."

Lea laughed. "He did mention a few times that he wanted to meet you." Her voice got all sweet and mushy on the phone when she added, "He told me that he's hoping you guys get along because I love you so dang much. I can't help it. I love my Stinky Cheese!"

"You know I love you, too, girl. This is going to be fun! The Three Musketeers together again, plus one."

Sir was rocking Hope in his arms when she headed out the door. "Don't stay out too late, babygirl."

"No chance of that, Sir," she assured him. "I miss you two already."

Brie hesitated for a moment before shutting the door. As excited as she was about the night, she considered time alone with Sir and Hope the best way to spend an evening. Although it wasn't as exciting as sexy nights at the Haven, it was every bit as magical and satisfying to her soul.

When Brie arrived at the place, she spotted Lea standing at the bar and headed straight over to her. The girl was obviously telling one of her jokes, based on the expression on the bartender's face. Brie snuck up behind her and covered her eyes.

"Hey, I know those big boobies. It must be the new mama," Lea said, giggling as she turned around. She reached out and squeezed Brie's breast, commenting, "Wow, have those things gotten even bigger?"

Brie swatted her hand away. "Girl, don't go groping me in public. Just look what you've done."

Sure enough, Lea's little antic had attracted the attention of several men around them. Brie raised her hand. "Sorry, gentlemen, no girl-on-girl action here. Go back to your drinks. Sorry for the false alarm."

"Look at you, breaking the hearts of men wherever you go," Lea teased, giving her a hip bump.

Brie looked around. "So, where's your fella?"

"He'll be here soon. Don't worry." She grinned at Brie. "But, while we wait, I've got a new joke for you…"

"Let's save it for Mary," Brie suggested.

"I second that," the bartender said with a wink. "What'll you have, gorgeous?"

Brie smiled. "Just water tonight, thank you."

As he set off to get it, she turned to find Lea pouting.

"What's wrong?"

"I'm an unappreciated talent among my own people."

Brie giggled, giving her a hug.

A handsome man with sun-kissed hair and sea green eyes sidled up behind Lea and smiled at Brie as he put a finger to his lips. The guy was definitely a looker and seemed to be several years younger than Lea.

He leaned closer to Lea and said, "Boo!"

Lea jumped and then broke out in laughter, slapping him playfully. "Oh, Liam, don't go scaring me like that."

He gave her a peck on the lips, then held out his hand to Brie. "You must be the infamous Brie that Lea is always going on about."

She blushed, caught off-guard by the intensity of Liam's gaze, and instinctually lowered her eyes as they shook hands.

"Yep, Liam, this is my BFF, Brianna Davis," Lea stated, smiling at him with a twinkle in her eye.

Liam let go of Brie's hand and wrapped his arms around Lea. "It's nice to meet someone whom Lea holds in such high esteem." He kissed Lea on the tip of the nose, causing her to break out in giggles.

Brie could see how infatuated the two were with each other, and it made her glad, seeing her friend happy. Lea deserved someone completely devoted to her after her disastrous love affair with Ms. Clark.

"So, Brie, what do you think of my hunky man?" she asked.

"He's hunkalicious," Brie answered, amused by how giddy Lea was about the guy.

Liam cupped his hand around his mouth and whispering loudly, "She loves me for my brains."

Lea grabbed on to his arm and pressed her head against his shoulder. "Of course, silly. I love everything about you, like those lips, those sexy abs, and…" Her gazed traveled down to his crotch.

Liam chuckled. "Yeah…she totally loves me for my brains."

Brie laughed with him, liking the comfortable banter between the two. It was unexpected, considering they hadn't known each other for long.

"So, Liam, what was it that attracted you to Lea?" she asked him.

"I heard her laughing across the bar and said to myself, 'I gotta meet that girl.' In a world of cynics, it's refreshing to meet someone who isn't afraid to laugh."

Lea elbowed Brie. "You'll find that Liam actually appreciates my humor, unlike the rest of you."

"I'll try not to hold that against him," Brie teased.

"You know what they say," Liam said, looking at Lea proudly. "Laughter is the best medicine."

Lea looked at him with an adorable smile on her face. "See, Brie…he gets me. He really gets me."

"There's not much to get, so that's not really an accomplishment," a familiar voice stated behind them.

Brie turned around to see Mary standing beside her with a rum and Coke in her hand. "How long have you been here, Mary?"

"Oh, about fifteen minutes. I was sitting back there," she said, pointing to a corner table. "I was watching you guys and making up my own dialog as you talked."

"I bet that was entertaining," Liam replied with a grin.

"Oh, it was," Mary agreed sarcastically. "So, Liam,

your daddy rich or something?"

Liam chuckled uncomfortably. "Okay, I'll bite. What makes you think my father's rich?"

She looked him over. "You're too damn slick."

He frowned slightly. "And you were able to make that assessment sitting over there in the corner?"

"It's all about the body language."

Lea wrapped her hands around Liam protectively. "Don't go insulting him, Mary. Liam's perfect in every way."

Mary gave Brie a sideways glance and threw back her drink.

Brie was surprised to see Mary acting like the old "Nemesis" of her past, but Brie did her best to play it off, saying, "Liam, you should be honored that Mary's trying so hard to win you over."

Mary shrugged, glancing at the bartender and giving him a flirtatious wink. "Hey, big boy, could you get me another one—but make it a double?"

"Sure thing, gorgeous, and consider this one on the house."

Lea shook her head, telling Brie, "I don't know how she always does that. One little wink and, boom, the guys fall all over her."

"It's a talent I was born with," Mary said nonchalantly as she took her free drink and held the glass up to Lea.

"Wink at me, pussy cat, and I'll get you a drink," Liam told Lea.

"Oh, God, he's already given her a pet name," Mary muttered.

Lea stuck her tongue out at Mary. "Jealous."

It was Mary's turn to laugh. "Now *that* was actually funny, Lea."

"Why did I invite her?" Lea asked Brie.

Brie wrapped her arm around Mary, imitating Lea and Liam. She looked at Mary with adoring eyes. "Because this woman is my hero." Of course, Brie totally meant it, but Lea didn't know that—no one did.

Liam stared at Mary with the same intensity he had Brie. "I was just trying to figure out how I knew you, and I think I've got it. You're that girl in the documentary who's dating the famous producer."

"I *am* that girl," Mary answered smugly. "You got a problem with that?"

It was obvious to Brie that having Mr. Holloway's name come up was making Lea nervous. Wanting to keep things light, Lea blurted, "What do you call an incestuous nephew? An aunt-eater!"

Mary and the bartender groaned, but Liam laughed, giving Lea a peck on the cheek. "Damn, you're funny."

"You are as hopeless as she is," Mary stated.

"I'll take that as a compliment," Liam answered, smiling at Lea proudly.

Lea beamed at Brie. "See why I love him?" she said, her voice all bubbly and cute.

Wanting to know more about Liam, Brie asked them, "How did the two of you meet?"

Lea grinned. "Well, I was sitting at this very bar, chatting it up with some of my Training Center buddies. I told the girls I had the feeling I was being watched, and then this hunky stranger comes up behind me. In a sultry voice, he says, 'Hey, you're pretty and I'm cute. Together we'd be Pretty Cute.' When I turned around and saw those gorgeous eyes, well…I was a goner."

"Seriously, that pickup line worked?" Mary scoffed.

Liam shrugged, chuckling. "What can I say? She's the first."

Brie laughed, holding up her water glass. "Here's to bad pickup lines and the girls who fall for them."

"Cheers!" Lea cried, clinking everyone's glass, including Mary's.

"So, Brie, you asked how Lea and I met. Tell me, how did you meet the infamous Thane Davis?" Liam asked her.

Brie felt heat rise to her cheeks, remembering that first encounter with Sir. "We met over a pack of Winstons, actually. I just happened to be bending over a box full of them and caught his eye—and the rest is history."

"An interesting start to a relationship," he remarked.

"Yeah, Brie and Sir were fated in the stars," Lea said dreamily.

Brie rolled her eyes, although she secretly agreed.

Throwing the question to Mary, Liam asked, "What about you and that producer guy?"

Mary narrowed her eyes and glowered at him.

Liam must have realized he'd stepped into a hornet's nest because he threw his hands up in surrender. "Hey, just trying to make conversation here. Sorry."

Desperate to redirect the conversation, Lea blurted.

"Hey, Mary, If Master Anderson wears cowboy clothes, is he ranch dressing?"

"Seriously, Lea?" Mary muttered.

Liam's laughter filled the room while Mary glanced at Brie, giving her a pained expression.

When the live band started playing, Lea grabbed Liam's hand and pulled him out onto the dance floor. Brie was grateful because it looked like things were just about to head downhill and she needed to know what was up with Mary.

"How are you doing?"

"I need a drink," Mary growled. Once the bartender had handed her another drink, she glided over to a table with several men. Brie had no idea what she said, but the men got up and smiled as they willingly gave up their seats.

Brie shook her head as she walked up to her. "How did you get them to give you their table?"

"You have to know the way they think. They're not complicated—not like women. That's why I prefer the company of men."

"Okay...so, tell me, what's the real story between you and Mr. Holloway?"

"Everything is peachy. Just peachy, Brie. My film debut is slotted to begin early in the fall and everything's a go."

"Since it's just you and me here, you can cut the crap."

Mary leaned back in her chair. "Feeling feisty tonight, are we?"

"Not feisty. I just want to be upfront and uncomplicated—like a guy."

Mary chuckled. "I like that answer, Stinky Cheese."

"So?"

Mary sighed. "Greg and me...it's complicated." She tried to laugh it off, but Brie could see the pain in her eyes.

"Have you thought of leaving him?"

"Nah, not with the film coming out in the fall. That would be stupid."

"What about your pharmacy career? I remember what you said about wanting to save people's lives. It was the whole reason you chose that career path. Is acting really the direction you want to head in?"

Mary frowned. "To be honest, I'm feeling lost, Brie. I don't know what I want..." Her voice trailed off. "I don't feel in control of my life anymore."

"Then forget about the film and go back to what you are passionate about."

"It's not that easy. Besides, if I stick it out with Greg, I can help you get that second documentary released."

"After the crappy way he treated Faelan and the weirdness with you, I've lost all respect for the man."

Mary's eyes flashed with anger. "Don't forget that man saved my life. I wouldn't be here if it weren't for him."

Brie realized she would need to be very careful about the way she talked about Mr. Holloway in front of Mary. Even though everyone else could see what a creep he was, for some reason, Mary still held him in high regard because of the gifts he'd left on her doorstep during those years of unspeakable abuse as a child. "I can only speak to what I've seen and heard. I don't know the man like you do," Brie conceded.

"That's right." Mary sat back in her chair, seeming less defensive. "As you are well aware, Stinks, in this business, it's *all* about who you know. People like Greg have the power to make or break a person. I happen to be sleeping with a man of influence. Let me help you get that second film out."

Brie shook her head.

Mary grabbed Brie's hand, seemingly desperate for her to agree. "I can't begin to tell you how ruthless this business can be…but I've got an opportunity to do some good here. Please let me do this for your film."

Brie was touched by Mary's desire to help, but she was more concerned about Mary's well-being. "Do you know what I want?"

"Of course. Me winning an Academy Award and your second documentary becoming a worldwide blockbuster."

"Not even close."

Mary took another drink, winking at an admirer sitting at the next table. Out of the blue, she said, "You know, even though that Kylie chick may not be a real looker, she's got something I don't."

Brie was surprised by her friend's comment. She realized that Mary might still be hooked on Faelan even though she was the one who walked out. Brie liked Faelan's new girlfriend, so she asked cautiously, "What's that?"

She was unprepared for Mary's answer.

"The ability to love."

Mary turned away from Brie when her eyes started tearing up. "I don't like myself, Brie."

Her painful confession broke Brie's heart, and she scooted her chair over, giving Mary a hug. "We all have layers to protect ourselves, woman. You have more than most because you needed them as a kid. But I've seen you pulling the layers back, Mary. We all have. Don't you dare give up on yourself. I love you."

"You've always been an idiot."

Brie laughed, grateful to see a glimpse of the Mary she knew.

Liam came up with Lea in tow and Mary immediately sat up straighter, nonchalantly wiping the partial tear from her eye.

"You two looked like you were having a pretty intense conversation there," Liam commented.

"Nah," Mary answered, slugging down her drink. "Brie was just going on and on about dirty diapers. Like I give a crap about that." Mary winked at Lea. "See what I did there? That's called subtle humor, Lames."

"Oh, yeah…subtle as in it's so subtle it's not even funny," Lea shot back.

Liam turned to Brie, looking her up and down. "To be honest, I never would have guessed you recently had a child, Brianna."

"I attribute it to all the soup I ate during my pregnancy," she answered, laughing at her private inside joke.

"You really aren't funny when you don't drink,

Stinks," Mary said. "Just being brutally honest."

Brie smirked at her.

Liam excused himself to get Lea another drink, and Brie took the opportunity to tell Lea, "I have to say, Liam seems nice."

"He is!" Lea gushed. "The nicest guy I've ever met."

"Well, I don't trust him," Mary grumbled.

"Oh, posh, you say that about every guy you meet," Lea said dismissively. "Here's the best part…" She leaned forward and informed them, "He's vanilla, but totally interested in BDSM. I've got a newbie to play with!"

"I was going to ask you about that," Brie admitted, chuckling as Liam returned to the table. When Liam handed Lea her drink, Brie noticed Mary staring at him and wondered if Lea was right that Mary really was jealous.

Rytsar came to mind. Maybe Mary could do with a session with Rytsar's cat o' nines. It might break her out of this current funk she was in. At the very least, he could provide her with a challenge.

"Just a sec, guys," Brie said, digging out her phone to text.

Would you be interested in a possible scene with Mary Wilson?

Why?

She could use some focus in her life.

Rytsar took a few seconds to reply.

Is she still surly?

Yes

Okay

Brie giggled at his response, knowing he would have some fun with her.

"Hey, Mary, Rytsar's all healed up from the surgery. Would you be interested in a session with him?"

"Maybe."

Brie suspected she was chomping at the bit but was trying to play it cool.

"I hope you know what you are doing, Brie," Lea stated, looking at Mary worriedly. "He's all about pushing buttons. Relentless about it, really."

Mary crossed her arms, saying nothing as her gaze returned to Liam. Brie noticed the poor guy shifting uncomfortably under her intense stare.

Brie understood that the prickly persona Mary projected out in the world hid how wounded she was inside. She hoped there would come a day when Mary wouldn't need to hide anymore.

Written in the Sky

A few weeks later, Brie was struck by a sudden hankering for one of Master Anderson's delicious grilled cheese sandwiches, so she walked down to the small grocery store near their apartment to get the ingredients.

While she was perusing the bread aisle, she looked up and swore she saw Liam standing at the checkout counter. "Hey, Liam!" she called as she walked toward him.

When he didn't respond, she called out again, feeling a little embarrassed as she drew nearer, wondering if she'd been mistaken. "Liam?"

He turned around with a pack of Winston cigarettes in his hand, looking startled to see her. "Hey…"

"What are you doing in my neck of the woods?"

He smiled awkwardly. "I…had an errand to run. What about you?"

She held up her basket. "Just getting supplies for dinner."

"Ah…"

Feeling awkward, she didn't really know what to say without Lea there, and the two of them stood in uncomfortable silence.

Glancing at the cigarettes in his hand, she smiled. "Funny that you have Winstons there."

"Why's that?"

She giggled "You know, the story about how Sir and I met?"

"Oh, yeah, right. I remember now."

She looked to the clerk, grinning. "You wouldn't happen to have Treasurer cigarettes, would you?"

The clerk, who knew her well, just laughed.

Brie looked down at her basket. "Hey, would you like to have dinner with us and meet my husband while you're at it? We live only a few blocks from here."

"Nah, thanks for the offer, though. Lea was hoping to make formal introductions, I think."

"Gotcha…"

More uncomfortable silence followed.

"I guess I'll go finish my shopping, then. Nice seeing you, Liam."

"Same here."

As she was turning to walk away, he called out, "Hey, do you mind not saying anything to Lea? In fact, don't tell anyone."

"Why?" she asked, suddenly suspicious.

He pointed to a jewelry shop across the street. "That was my errand."

She looked over at the place, knowing the high-end pieces they carried. "Well, I have to admit you have good taste."

Liam gave her a crooked grin. "Yeah…it's a big deal, and I wanted to make sure I got the right ring for the job."

Brie's jaw dropped. "You're…?"

He nodded. "Don't say anything. I want it to be a surprise."

She pretended to zip her lips. "Consider them sealed."

"Great. See you around then." He exited the store, leaving her standing there with that huge secret.

After getting the needed supplies, Brie headed up to the apartment. The instant Sir saw her face, he knew something was up and questioned her on it.

She was bursting, wanting to tell him. "I just learned something that's going to totally flip Lea out, but I have to keep it a secret." She bounced on her toes in excitement. "But this is huge!"

Sir chuckled. "I can tell you want to tell me more."

"I *do*…but I promised." She walked into the kitchen, crying out in misery, "Argh, this secret is going to be impossible for me to keep."

He laughed. "And this all happened while you were getting groceries?"

She popped her head out. "I know! Craziest thing."

Brie went to start on the sandwiches, shaking her head. She was surprised that Lea's relationship was moving so quickly. But if Lea was happy, that's all that mattered to Brie. Besides, she wasn't one to judge.

She knew firsthand about love at first sight…

"I have news as well but, unlike you, I can share it," Sir told her with amusement.

Brie stopped what she was doing and headed out of the kitchen to hear what he had to say. She paused for a moment when she saw him, struck by the sight of Hope lying against Sir's shoulder as he looked over documents on his laptop. It was so endearing, the way he had incorporated the baby into his everyday activities with seamless ease.

"What's your big news, Sir?"

"Unc and Judy finally got custody of the baby. They received the news today."

"That's wonderful news, Sir! They must be over the moon right now. They've waited so long for this."

"It's a relief knowing the child will be raised in a stable home by people I deeply admire and love."

"I didn't think today could get any better," Brie exclaimed.

Needing to release this happy energy, she made a suggestion. "We should have a party for them, don't you think? Just because Judy didn't give birth to the little boy doesn't make this any less special. In fact, considering the circumstances, there's even more reason to celebrate."

"I think that is a fine idea. I greatly respect my aunt and uncle. They have no idea how much of Lilly and my mother this boy carries within his character, yet they are embracing him with open arms."

"I just have to look at you, Sir, to know he will turn out well."

Sir stood, careful not to disturb Hope, who was fast asleep on his shoulder. He walked over to Brie, wrapping an arm around her. "I have you to thank for that, babygirl. As I have expressed numerous times, you gave me hope for the future—and now I literally hold Hope next to my heart."

When Rytsar heard from Sir about the party Brie was planning, he called her up and insisted she use his beach house.

"We're planning on inviting a lot of people, Rytsar. And I hate to tell you this, but the Reynolds and their friends don't drink. So I was thinking something a little mellower than one of your vodka parties."

Rytsar chuckled. "Make it a beach party, then. That way people can get drunk on the waves."

"Oh, that sounds perfect! I'm being a little sneaky and want the Reynolds to think we're inviting everyone to meet Hope. But, really, this is going to be a party to celebrate their adoption."

"Of the child?" he asked with some distaste.

"Of the innocent boy who should not bear the sins of his mother."

Rytsar cleared his throat. "*Da*, you're right. I would be condemning myself if others judged me by my father."

"Exactly. I believe Mr. and Mrs. Reynolds wanting to give Lilly's child a strong foundation should be honored. Their sacrifice of love is a beautiful gift."

"It is," he agreed.

"And now that I have the location set because of

you, I can start inviting people!"

"Have fun with it, *radost moya*," Rytsar said, chuckling into the phone. "Although, your babe is my sunshine, and you will always be my joy."

Brie immediately sent out the invitations asking people to gift the Reynolds with specific baby items they needed for his arrival. Sir had set up a college fund for the boy. His aunt and uncle were taking on a significant financial burden by adopting Lilly's child, and Sir wanted to lessen the impact of it without insulting his uncle's sensibilities.

When Boa received his invitation, he gave her a call. She was extremely grateful that they were talking on the phone because just hearing his voice had triggered memories of her fantasy, and it had Brie seriously blushing.

"I wanted to offer my services for the party."

Brie had to stifle her laughter, her thoughts immediately going down a kinky path. "Services, Boa?"

"Yes, I'd like to cater the party for the Reynolds. I don't normally tell people this, but I was adopted as a kid. What they are doing for that boy will change his life."

"I wholeheartedly agree with you."

The tone of his voice changed when he explained, "My dad died of a heart attack when I was in culinary school. I never really got the chance to thank him for everything he did for me. This is my way of passing that on."

"I'm so sorry to hear of your loss, Boa. But that's such a beautiful thing to do for Sir's family. Thank you."

"My sincerest pleasure."

With the food and location taken care of, the plans for the party were falling into place. It seemed sweet irony when Mr. Reynolds reached out to her, letting Brie know that he was making a run for baby supplies and wanted to know if she needed anything.

Brie took the opportunity to give him a list of consumable items she knew they would need. "This is such a big help. Thank you, Unc. I'll shoot you the money online, and we'll swing by your place after the party to pick it up."

"Sure you don't want me just to drive it over?"

"No need. You've got enough on your plate, preparing for your son's arrival."

"My son…" he said with satisfaction. "I will never tire of hearing that."

"I'm so happy for you and Aunt Judy, and I can't wait to meet your little boy."

"It's a dream come true for Judy to become a mother after all these years."

Brie felt a little teary when she said, "He needed you as much as you needed him."

"Very true, Brie."

"So, have you decided on a name yet?"

"We are partial to the name Jonathan."

"Oh, that is a good name. I can't wait until Saturday when I can hug you two and meet your son, Jonathan."

"We're looking forward to seeing how much Hope has grown since our last visit. Amazing, how life plays out. You came to the tobacco shop looking for a temporary job, and now we are family and raising children together."

Brie laughed. "Such a crazy, beautiful life."

Brie was anxious to escape to the ocean with Sir and Hope. It had been a while since they'd been to Rytsar's beach house, so they left a couple of hours early to spend time alone with him before the party began.

They knocked on the door, but no one came to answer it. Little Sparrow came loping around from the back and gave them a playful yip as she approached.

"Where's your Master?" Brie asked as Sir gave the dog a pat on the head.

Little Sparrow walked over to Brie, sniffing the air as she looked up at the baby.

Brie knelt down slowly and let the pup smell Hope so she would become familiar with their baby's scent and know she was a part of the family.

The dog wagged her tail vigorously, her hindquarters dancing with excitement. She licked Brie's hand, smiling at her with a big doggy grin. She then walked back to the corner of the house and gave another playful yip.

"I guess that means we follow," Sir stated.

As they rounded the corner, heading toward the beach, Brie let out a happy squeal. Rytsar had set up the beach in grand Durov style.

"Welcome!" he stated, his arms outstretched to them.

"Oh my goodness! You have outdone yourself, Rytsar," Brie cried happily.

Rytsar grinned at Brie as he caressed the baby's head and gave Hope a light peck on the cheek. "Welcome to you as well, *moye solntse*."

Gesturing to the setup, he told Sir proudly, "All in honor of your aunt and uncle."

Brie marveled at the rows and rows of beach chairs with umbrellas and the netted canopies with linen-covered tables waiting for Boa's catered food. There was even an area strewn with beach toys for children of all ages.

"You've thought of everything," Brie gushed.

"I want your guests to enjoy themselves, despite the lack of drink." He held out his arms for Hope, and Brie dutifully handed her over.

Rytsar lifted the baby up, twirled her slowly in the air as he smiled at her. "Hope is here…"

Brie took Sir's arm and leaned her head against his shoulder, bursting with happiness as she watched Rytsar with their child.

"It's good to see you fully healed, old friend," Sir stated, noting the effortless way he moved now.

Rytsar answered proudly, the babe cradled against him, "I am, brother!" He winked at Brie. "And, as you know, I can swing my nines again."

She blushed, inadvertently shuddering.

He grinned, enjoying her reaction. "Did you know we will be spending time together soon?" He gave Sir a wink.

When Brie saw it, her heart skipped a beat. She enjoyed the power play of knowing the two Doms had spoken in private and had something planned, but not knowing what it was.

Rytsar shielded Hope's face with his hand when he noticed her squinting from the sun. "Let's retire to the shade for the babe's sake." He led them to a special area he'd had prepared for them.

Under the spacious shade tent, the ground had been covered with a large blanket. He pointed to several comfortable lounge chairs and pillows strewn about. "Make yourself comfortable."

Brie's eyes were riveted on a small table laden with fruits and nuts. Her stomach growled so she asked, "May I?"

"Of course."

"I always seem to be hungry these days."

"Naturally, now that you are feeding the babe. Eat up."

She immediately grabbed a piece of fresh pineapple and began munching on it, moaning in pleasure as the sweet juice dripped from her lips. "Oh, Rytsar, all of this is wonderful."

Brie snagged a plate and grabbed a few more pieces of fruit before settling into one of the chairs. Sir chose one beside her while Rytsar lay on the ground, propping himself up with a pillow while he watched Hope on the blanket. Little Sparrow lay beside Rytsar, waggling her tail, content to be beside her Master.

After Brie finished the fruit and was done licking

her fingers, she closed her eyes to listen to the peaceful lull of the waves as a light ocean breeze played across her skin.

This was pure heaven...

Sir broke the silent reverie, announcing, "I have something I'd like to discuss with you both."

Brie opened her eyes and turned her head toward him, curious what had him suddenly sounding so serious. "Yes, Sir?"

"I know this may come somewhat as a surprise, but I would like to have our baby christened."

Brie tilted her head, surprised by Sir's request since he had never been a religious man.

"I've given it much thought and know it would give my grandparents peace of mind. Nonna has written me several letters since Hope's birth, expressing her concern for our child." Sir looked at Brie. "I would like to give my grandparents that gift, but only if you agree."

She smiled at him. "Your grandparents have been through such terrible loss, and I can't think of a more joyful event than a christening. I'm happy to have Hope christened, if that would bring them joy."

He took her hand and kissed it. "Thank you, baby-girl."

Sir addressed Rytsar next. "As our daughter's god-father, we would need you there."

"But of course, brother."

"In Italy."

Brie squeaked, excited to have the chance to visit his grandparents again.

Rytsar chuckled. "A trip to your father's homeland, eh, brother?"

Sir nodded. "I feel a call to return there."

"I respect that, comrade, and am honored to join you."

Their conversation was interrupted by the drone of a small plane flying above them. Rather than buzzing past, it sounded as if it was hovering above them. Curious to see why, Brie left the comfort of the chair and peeked out from under the shade tent.

Looking into the expanse of bright blue sky, she saw that the small aircraft was leaving a trail of smoke. Brie pointed excitedly at it. "The plane is writing a message in the sky!"

Sir joined her, looking up at the plane. "It sure is," he agreed. He took out his phone and started recording it.

Rytsar picked up Hope and walked over to stand beside them as they watched the plane slowly making its way across the sky, creating a giant heart.

"That's so adorable!" she cried, pointing up at it to show Hope. "Do you see it? It's a heart."

The aircraft did not appear to be done as it began another pass under the heart. It started with a vertical line as it slowly created a letter. As it buzzed back and forth, Brie said, "Wouldn't it be amazing if it was writing the word 'HOPE'?"

"I believe it is," Sir stated as the plane curved to finish the letter 'P'.

Brie looked at Rytsar, smiling. "Did you do this?"

He shrugged. "Why wouldn't I want the world to

know Hope is here?"

Before it was done, the plane had made another heart underneath her name. Brie took several pictures of Rytsar holding the baby with the skywriting in the background. "This makes me so very happy," she told him, hugging Rytsar while he held the baby.

"A memory for us to look back on," Rytsar told her. He looked down at Hope. "And one we will share with you when you are older, *moye solntse*."

Sir held up his phone, telling Rytsar, "And I have it recorded for posterity, including what you just said to her."

They returned to their place under the tent and Brie sat back down on the lounger, with Rytsar laying Hope on her chest. As she listened to the gentle waves with her eyes closed, she was overwhelmed with a feeling of completeness. "I don't think it gets any better than this."

"*Nyet.*"

"I can imagine doing this every weekend," she murmured.

"Yes, it would be nice," Sir agreed.

Rytsar sat up. "Make it so, comrade. You are welcome any time."

Sir chuckled. "It would not be practical."

Rytsar lay back down. "Still, you should consider it…"

A few hours later, the beach was crowded with people waiting for the guests of honor to arrive. Brie had purposely told the Reynolds to come a half hour later to make sure everyone was present to surprise them.

Rytsar took Hope from her so she could meet them up front with Sir. As Brie approached his aunt and uncle, she experienced a momentary feeling of queasiness—coming face-to-face with Lilly's baby. Sir must have had a similar feeling, because he squeezed her hand tightly.

Sir's aunt and uncle were positively beaming as they walked up to present their baby boy to them. "This is our son, Jonathan," Mr. Reynolds said proudly.

Brie looked down at the little boy and instantly relaxed. Although he had some facial characteristics of his mother and grandmother, the boy had gentle eyes. He seemed fascinated by Sir and reached up, staring intently at him.

Sir took the boy from Judy. Since Jonathan was several months older than Hope, he was able to hold himself up and play with Sir's chin, apparently liking the feel of his five o'clock shadow. When Sir glanced at Brie, she read the relief in his eyes.

"Congratulations. He's a handsome boy," Sir told them proudly.

"Jonathan is absolutely adorable," Brie agreed. "You must be so happy to finally have him safe in your arms."

"I was worried there for a bit when it seemed to drag on forever," Judy admitted.

"I never doubted we would get custody," Mr.

Reynolds told Brie. "We're family, and we have the means and the desire to be good parents to this boy."

Sir handed the boy back to Judy and put his hand on his uncle's shoulder. "He's where he belongs."

Judy asked her husband, "Do you mind grabbing the diaper bag and Hope's gift?"

Brie laughed. "There was no need to get her another gift, Aunt Judy. You were so generous at the baby shower."

"Nonsense, we never got to celebrate with you, and a little girl can never have enough dresses."

Brie wrapped an arm around her aunt as they made their way toward the beach.

"Wow, that's quite the turnout, Thane," Mr. Reynolds said, clearly impressed.

"Yes, a lot of people came to celebrate," Brie agreed.

"Hey, isn't that Tom and Sherry over there?" Judy asked.

"That was mighty thoughtful of you to invite our good friends, Brie," Mr. Reynolds said.

Brie grinned. "I just wanted it to be perfect."

"Well, I'm not surprised you have such a good turnout," Judy commented. "You two are quite the popular couple. Thank you for including us today."

Brie glanced over at Sir and nodded.

"Actually, Unc and Auntie, these people came to celebrate with you."

There was a collective shout of "Congratulations!" from the group.

The Reynolds looked at each other in confusion,

understanding finally dawning when the banner bearing the words *Welcome to the family, Jonathan!* was unfurled.

Judy started to cry.

"Now, now, dear. There's no reason for tears..." Mr. Reynolds told her.

"You two..." she said, wiping her wet cheeks. "I can't believe you did this for us."

Brie squeezed her, while Sir handed her a tissue. "It was Brie's idea, and I wholeheartedly agreed." He turned to his uncle. "Unc, I have never been prouder to be a part of your family."

"Considering all that has happened with regards to my sister and niece, I am extremely touched to hear you say that."

"You are creating a new path for the Reynolds legacy," Sir told him.

Jack nodded. "Thank you, Thane." His voice was strained with emotion.

"Come, come," Brie insisted, pulling Judy toward the party. "Everyone is anxious to fawn over your son."

As people surged forward to get a peek at the new baby, Brie and Sir stayed back. Rytsar walked over to join them, Hope asleep in his arms.

"*Moy droog*, who would ever have guessed this would be your reality after so much suffering?

Sir nodded, looking down at Brie. "A miracle, to be sure."

The Switch

Brie had to try to contain herself when Lea invited her to hang at her place for a special BFF night. Lea had been hinting all week about having some big news to tell her, and had promised Brie a night of takeout and cheesy romance movies to go along with her big reveal.

Knowing that Brie would be gone for the evening, Rytsar decided to come over to spend time with Sir. It made Brie glad to know that Sir would have some quality time alone with his best friend.

Brie was feeding Hope when Rytsar showed up. Rather than cover up as she would with most visitors, she just smiled up at him when he entered the apartment.

"What a beautiful sight. Wouldn't you agree, comrade?"

"Certainly. I have taken quite a few photos of Brie breastfeeding. I find it exceedingly charming."

Rytsar looked at her with a critical eye. "*Radost moya*, I think you should get a portrait done. A classic painting to pass down to future generations of the Davis Family."

Brie giggled. "Do you really think my kids and grandkids want to see a painting of me breastfeeding hanging over the mantel?"

"I would," Rytsar insisted.

"Actually, if you turn your head, it only gives a hint of your face. I think it would be an excellent addition to the art on our wall," Sir stated.

"Did you hear that, Hope?" Brie asked her daughter. "They want a painting of you and me. Do you want to be immortalized for all time as the breastfeeding baby of the Davis Family lineage?"

Hope looked up into her eyes, a drop of milk escaping from her lips.

"I think that is a yes," Rytsar stated, taking the baby to burp her after Brie was finished feeding. "And you should be immortalized, *moye solntse*. You're too beautiful not to be."

Brie fastened her bra, pulled her shirt down, and quickly stood up, giving Rytsar a peck on his cheek. "Be good while we're gone."

"You could leave her," he suggested.

Brie glanced at Sir. "No...I want you two to have some man time—just the two of you."

She walked over to Sir. "I hope you two have fun tonight."

He grabbed her waist and pulled her to him to kiss her on the lips. "Do the same, babygirl. I know you will be laughing the entire night."

"And I'll finally be able to share in the big news!"

"I look forward to hearing about it."

"Give Ms. Taylor a slap on the ass for me," Rytsar told her.

"What am I supposed to tell her when I do it?" Brie giggled.

"Tell her Durov says hi."

"I'm not so sure her new boyfriend will appreciate such a greeting."

"Oh, is she serious with him?"

"Yes, it's pretty darn serious. Are you jealous?" Brie had asked it teasingly, although she was curious to know.

"*Nyet.* Ms. Taylor is free to partner with whomever she desires. However, it is an odd choice since I've heard he is not a Dominant."

"True, but Lea says he wants to explore BDSM," Brie explained.

Rytsar shrugged, looking at Sir. "A perfectly good submissive wasted."

Sir smirked. "We have to let our graduates walk their own paths, old friend."

Brie picked up the diaper bag and took Hope from Rytsar. "Well, I expect to be back around twelve. You can party all you want, but have the place cleaned up by then," she joked.

"Drive safe, babygirl."

"Always, Sir."

Brie smiled down at Hope as she was buckling her up in the car seat. "You're going to love spending the night with your Auntie Lea. She's all kinds of silly fun."

Brie picked up two orders of fries on the way to Lea's, having a sudden craving. She knocked on the door holding the baby carrier and the bag of hot fries, eager for the night's activities to begin.

She was surprised when Liam answered the door.

"Oh, I didn't realize you would be here."

Liam grinned. "Heya, Brie."

He moved aside so she could enter the apartment. Brie walked in slowly, trying to hide her disappointment when the alluring aroma of cooking garlic and onion hit her nose. "Hey, girl, you promised me Chinese takeout tonight."

"Liam and I agreed our news is too special for takeout."

Brie shrugged. "Well, I hope you don't mind, but I brought fries as an appetizer."

She unbuckled Hope and picked her up, feeling disconcerted by the unexpected change of plans but trying to adjust. "Well...alrighty then. I guess we'll munch on my fries while Auntie Lea cooks."

Lea put down her spoon and walked over to them. "Oh, wow! She is getting so dang big, Brie." She rubbed noses with Hope. "Look how gorgeous this baby is, Liam."

Liam looked at her, nodding. "A stunning child."

Lea bumped Brie's hip. "Didn't I tell you on your wedding day that you and Sir Davis would make beautiful children? Have you thought of entering her in one of those baby pageants?"

"Are you kidding me? I want Hope to have a normal childhood."

"Well, I bet she'd win," Lea declared, heading back into the kitchen.

When Hope suddenly got fussy, Brie looked around for her diaper bag and realized she'd left it in the car. "Dang it, I gotta get Hope's bag out of the car."

"I can hold her for you," Liam offered.

"You sure? Most young guys don't want to get anywhere near a baby."

"Not an issue, I assure you. I come from a large family. I know my way around kids."

"See? Just another reason to love the guy," Lea gushed as she stirred her sauce.

Brie handed Hope over and ran out of the apartment. She came back a few minutes later and found Liam standing in place, rocking her.

"You look like a natural, Liam," Brie admitted.

He looked at her with those intense sea green eyes and smiled. "I must say she looks like her mother."

"Thanks for the compliment, but I love that she has her daddy's eyes and beautiful Italian skin."

"Where is Sir Davis tonight?"

"He stayed home to hang."

Brie suddenly remembered Rytsar's request and walked into the kitchen, smacking Lea hard on the ass.

Lea squealed in pain. "Hey, what was that for?"

"It's a hello from our mutual Russian friend."

Lea giggled as she went back to stirring her sauce.

"Hey, I have a joke for Rytsar. Will you pass it on?"

"Depends."

"On what?"

"If it's funny. I don't want to get punished."

"You know it'll be great."

Although Lea's jokes were generally groan worthy, Lea had surprised her on occasion, so she waited, hoping for the best—ever the optimist.

"What do you call a bossy potato?"

Brie chuckled. Rytsar had complained about being a potato when he was forced to rest after the surgery. She had a feeling this was going to be good and asked, "I don't know, Lea. What *do* you call a bossy potato?"

Lea snickered. "A dic-tater."

Brie giggled. "Yeah, I think he will like that."

She grinned. "See, Stinky Cheese? I've still got it."

"You sure do," Brie said, slapping her ass again.

Brie looked over and noticed that Liam hadn't even noticed the exchange, because he was so focused on entertaining the baby. Brie walked over, taking her back so he could join them.

Giving Liam a wink, she asked Lea, "So tell me your big news already, Lea. You've been so tight-lipped about it."

"Well…you probably guessed it has to do with Liam and me," Lea said, stepping out of the kitchen.

"Yeah, I kind of figured that," Brie teased.

"Well…" Lea wiggled her fingers, showing off the ring on her left hand. "We're getting married!"

Brie grabbed her hand and stared at the stone. It was a much simpler ring than she had expected, but she pretended to be surprised. "No way! I can't believe you're getting married, girl!"

Lea looked at Liam. "He just asked me out of the blue. I didn't even see it coming."

Brie gave her a one-armed hug. "I'm really happy for you, girlfriend."

Lea squeezed her back and then walked over into Liam's open arms. "When it's right, it's right. You just know it."

Brie nodded, smiling at them both.

"I have another surprise for you," Lea announced, beaming with excitement. "I want—" The sound of a pot boiling over caught Lea's attention and she ran back to the kitchen. Brie glanced at Liam. "I love seeing Lea so happy."

Liam stared at Lea, smiling with satisfaction. "She's a special girl."

"Oh, dang!" Lea cried from the kitchen. "I forgot the sherry."

"Are you sure?" Liam asked, going into the kitchen to help her look.

"I really thought I bought it…"

"I'm sure the dish will taste fine without it," Brie assured her. "Remember, I was coming for takeout. No need to impress me."

"No," Lea insisted. "It won't be worth eating without it." She turned off the burner and took the pan off the heat. "It won't take me long to get it."

"Don't worry about it, pussy cat," Liam told her. "It'll be fine."

But Lea already had her purse in her hand and was

heading out the door. "Nope, everything needs to be perfect. Just give me fifteen minutes, or so. I'll be right back."

The apartment was uncomfortably quiet the instant Lea's bubbly energy left the room. Brie looked at Liam and smiled, laughing nervously.

Liam sat down in the couch and indicated she should take a seat beside him. "So, have you heard any good jokes lately?"

She laughed, shaking her head as she bounced Hope on her lap. "Lea sure is full of them, isn't she?"

Brie was surprised to hear a noise coming from the back of the apartment and glanced up to see another man who looked exactly like Liam. He was dressed the same, down to the clothes and shoes. The only difference were the pair of black leather gloves he wore.

Shaking her head as if she were seeing things, she stammered, "Wait…you…have a twin?"

"I do."

Brie was stunned and just sat there, struggling to process what she was seeing. "Is Lea dating both of you? Was that what she was about to tell me?" She shook her head, laughing. "That's such a Lea thing to do."

"Actually, Lea has no idea I have a twin," Liam told her with a charming smile.

Icy chills ran down her spine as the other man produced a bottle of Sherry from behind his back and smiled at her. Brie instinctively pressed Hope against her, glancing at the door.

Force

"What's going on, Liam?"

He just smiled.

Brie immediately stood up, clutching Hope as she started toward the door, muttering, "I think I left the formula in the car..."

Liam moved to block her way. "There's no reason to be frightened. Everything's been arranged for your travel."

Brie backed away from him. "What are you talking about?"

"We've come to unite you with your rightful Master."

Brie felt her mouth suddenly go dry as fear gripped her heart. "I'm collared to Thane Davis. I have no other master."

"I beg to differ," Liam stated. "My employer paid a hefty price for you and has been patient. It's time for that debt to be paid now."

Brie shook her head. "Lilly had no right to make that deal. I will *not* go with you."

Liam's twin laughed. "Do you really think you have a say in this?"

Brie glanced down at Hope, who was staring up at her innocently. "You can't have my child. She was never a part of Lilly's deal."

"Your child is the only reason our employer agreed to wait."

"You cannot have her!" Brie screamed, edging slowly toward the door even though she knew she would never make it in time.

Hope began to cry in her arms.

Trying to reason with them, she warned, "Lea will be back any second."

Liam glanced at his watch. "Actually, she won't be coming back. Not anytime soon, at least."

"Why? What did you do to her?" Brie cried.

Liam chuckled. "I'm simply going to meet her at the store and let her know that your husband had to call you back home. I'll put the bottle of Sherry back on the grocery shelf and take her out for a fancy dinner instead. I know she will be disappointed that her best friend left so abruptly, so it's the least I can do."

Brie looked around the room, trying to formulate her plan of escape. But there were two of them, and the apartment was small. She watched helplessly as the twin picked up her purse from the coffee table and took out her phone. Turning it off, he stuffed it in his pocket and smiled at her while Liam explained, "I'll take my fiancé out for the evening, while my brother transports the merchandise to our employer."

"I'm not going anywhere with either of you!" Brie

spat savagely.

"It's not as if you have a choice," his twin informed her. "By the time they discover you're missing, you will be safely on your way."

Brie glanced around the room wildly, looking for a weapon—anything to protect her while clutching Hope against her chest. "I would rather die than go with you."

"There's no reason for the dramatics," Liam said. "You are being offered a life of luxury, being pampered and coddled. I've heard he spoils his property."

Brie clutched the collar around her neck.

He looked at her possessive hold on Sir's collar and laughed. "You have a new Master now. Nothing's really changed except the location."

It frightened Brie how calm they both seemed, as if they were discussing a simple trip instead of a kidnapping.

Brie tried to defuse the situation by engaging Liam. "You know how much I love my little girl. I'll do anything to protect her. Hope wasn't part of this, so leave her here. I'll go quietly if I know she's safe."

He sucked air in through his teeth, making an irritating sound that grated on her nerves. "Actually, our employer does have plans for the child. There's a substantial bonus if she's delivered." He looked over at his brother. "Naturally, we plan to collect on both."

"But," his twin warned, "I will not hesitate to dispose of the child, should you prove difficult."

Liam looked at his watch nonchalantly and then nodded to his brother. The two came at her from both sides, cutting off her escape. Brie picked up a candy dish on a side table and hit Liam with a solid blow to the head before his twin grabbed her arm. Brie screamed bloody murder, hoping someone would hear and call the police.

His twin covered her mouth, hissing in her ear. "Shut the fuck up."

Before she could react, Liam snatched Hope from her. Brie's muffled cries of anguish filled the room.

"You'll have to go in my stead," Liam said, wiping the blood from his forehead.

"Fuck, fuck, fuck!" his twin howled. He angrily turned Brie around, binding her arms behind her back. Stuffing cloth into her mouth, he wrapped duct tape around her head to keep it in place. Pushing Brie to the floor, he tied her feet next before binding her so she was curled into a ball.

Liam set Hope, who was crying hysterically now, in the carrier. He pulled out a large suitcase and unzipped it. Both men lifted Brie up, as she squirmed desperately against her bindings. However, she could do nothing as they set her in the suitcase and zipped it back up.

Brie was in the dark, hearing Hope's frantic cries as the two men talked, reformulating their plans. She heard one leave, slamming the door on his way out.

She lay there helpless, terrified for Hope, praying rescue would come but fearing it would not.

Liam had planned the kidnapping out perfectly. Sir would not be expecting her home until twelve, and Lea would be out for several hours. By the time her friend returned to the apartment, Brie and her baby would already be on a plane to the Middle East—never to be seen again.

Brie thought of Tatianna and understood what the future held for her…and for Hope. Tears of anger, frustration, and fear rolled down her cheeks as the air in the suitcase became hot and stale.

Liam lifted the suitcase upright and rolled it toward the door. Hope continued to cry, which worked to Liam's advantage when he was stopped in the elevator.

"She sure doesn't sound happy," a woman commented beside them.

Brie screamed into the cloth, but it only sounded like muffled whimpering, and it could not compete with Hope's screams.

Brie bounced along in the rolling suitcase as Liam walked to the car and, with much grunting and effort, he lifted it into the car. Brie heard him buckle Hope into the car seat beside her.

Liam told Hope, "Thanks for saving my bacon with that crying jag."

He slammed the door, getting into the driver's seat and revving the engine. Brie silently screamed to Sir, to Lea, to Rytsar, to Tono, praying that one of them would hear her cries of desperation.

It was frightening how easily these men had been able to snatch her away from everyone she loved. How long had Liam been planning this? His quick romance with Lea made complete sense now.

Liam had attached himself to Lea in order to assess the situation with Brie and the baby before extraction. No one knew his twin existed, giving the two of them time to execute the plan while cementing Liam's alibi.

Her chance meeting with Liam's twin at the grocery store could have been her salvation, but she hadn't picked up on his confusion about the significance of the Winston cigarettes, and he'd been quick on his feet, giving her a reason to keep their encounter a secret.

Sir would never know what had happened to them.

She was Hope's only chance.

Brie began concentrating on the ropes, but she began to panic when she couldn't release herself from the bindings. Her rising panic only caused her to breathe faster, taking up the little oxygen left in the suitcase.

When she began to feel faint, Brie forced herself to slow down her breathing. She imagined Tono was with her, and began taking shallower breaths.

The only thing that mattered now was Hope. What happened to her was secondary, as long as Hope was spared this horror.

Brie felt the car slow down and heard Liam cuss. "What the fuck?"

After several tense moments, she heard the window being rolled down and Liam asked, "What seems to be the problem?"

"You need to step out of the car, now!"

"You have to be kidding me. You're not even a fucking cop."

"No, I am not."

"Fuck this shit!" The car lurched forward before a shot rang out and it came to a halt. Liam screamed in pain and she heard the door open.

Someone must have pulled him forcefully out of

the car, based on the cries and curses that followed.

"They're right here."

Brie heard both back doors open at once.

"Shh...*moye solntse.*"

Tears of relief filled Brie's eyes at the sound of Rytsar's voice.

Someone lifted the suitcase, and it was set down gently outside the car. Brie whimpered as the suitcase was unzipped and a flood of fresh air rushed in.

She looked up into Sir's eyes and time stopped.

Safe...

The horror on Sir's face was replaced with concern as he made quick work of the duct tape around her mouth. Brie gasped for breath, her body numb with relief.

"Are you all right?" Sir asked, his voice strangled with emotion.

Brie nodded, unable to speak.

Sir began cutting through the knots while Rytsar moved into view, holding Hope, who had stopped crying. Even though he held the babe gently in his arms, the look in Rytsar's eyes was one of a rabid dog ready to rip someone's throat out.

"How...did you know?" Brie finally gasped as Sir helped her to her feet and held her against him.

"Miss Wilson alerted Rytsar to her suspicions weeks ago."

"Mary?" Brie asked, turning her head toward Rytsar.

"She did not trust Lea's new man and voiced her concerns to me. Said she didn't trust him because he was too gregarious, and she didn't like how he had attached himself so quickly. Thane and I could find nothing on the man, but we decided to play it safe and put a tracer on his vehicle."

"But how could you know what happened tonight?"

"I added a hidden tracer app on all your friends' phones," Rytsar told her. "I wasn't willing to take any chances."

Brie stared at him in shock.

"It was deemed necessary by both of us, Brie," Sir explained. "Your safety was our *only* concern."

"But…" Brie was still struggling to wrap her head around it. "How did you know what was happening in Lea's apartment tonight??"

"We'd been keeping tabs on you both tonight with your phones and saw that Liam was at the apartment. We grew suspicious, so Rytsar called one of his men to check on you."

The man kneeing Liam in the back to keep him immobilized, nodded his head at Brie. "Ma'am."

"He confirmed when Lea left, but we knew your phone was still in the apartment and assumed you were too. Then he reported seeing Liam leave the apartment without you. When he saw Liam leave a *second* time with a suitcase and the baby a short time later, we were only minutes behind."

Brie shivered.

"I realized there was a twin involved and immediately called the police to inform them."

"What about *Lea*?" Brie whimpered, realizing she

was still with the other twin.

"The police have already located her and arrested the man. She's fine, Brie," Sir assured her.

Brie began shaking, the reality of what had just happened filtering through her brain and causing a delayed sense of panic.

Sir held her tight. "You are safe, Brie."

She held out a shaking hand to touch Hope. "She's safe."

"No one will ever hurt her," Rytsar stated emphatically.

Brie looked at him, her bottom lip trembling. "Thank you."

Rytsar's jaw was clenched as he stared at her with tears in his eyes. "I was not too late."

"No, you saved both of us."

He nodded his head, sighing deeply.

Brie knew Rytsar was thinking of Tatianna. He had that haunted look in his eyes as he relived her kidnapping, the near rescue, and her eventual death.

Reaching out, Brie touched him. "We are safe because of you."

Rytsar swallowed hard, nodding again, but said nothing.

Brie leaned her head back against Sir's chest. "I was terrified I would disappear and never see you again."

His voice was gruff with the anguish he felt. "I could not have borne it."

"I know," she whispered, tears running down her cheeks.

Sir pressed her so tightly against himself that she

could barely breathe. Even so, she welcomed the feeling as she listened to the sound of his heartbeat and the far-off sirens echoing in the distance.

Liam started cursing viciously on the ground.

Sir let go of Brie and walked over to him. "Stand him up," he commanded.

Rytsar's man lifted his knee from Liam's back and pulled him up to face Sir.

Sir cocked his fist back and let it fly, connecting with his jaw. In the blink of an eye, Liam was back on the ground, writhing in pain.

Sir shook his hand out and looked over at Rytsar. "That felt good."

Rytsar walked over to Sir and carefully handed the baby over to him. "Let me try."

Liam cried out when the men forced him back onto his feet. "Don't. For God's sake, have mercy...!" he begged.

Rytsar smirked, nodding his head. "*Da*, I will show the mercy you showed *radost moya.*"

"I was just doing a job. It wasn't personal...oh God, no!" Liam screamed as Rytsar narrowed his eyes and cocked his fist back.

"Don't kill him," Brie cried out, remembering what had happened in Russia.

Rytsar hesitated for a moment before letting his fist fly through the air.

Liam shrieked even before Rytsar made impact. Again, he fell to the ground but, this time, he didn't move or make a sound.

Brie looked at Rytsar in horror. "Please say you

didn't…" She turned her head toward the sound of the approaching sirens. "They'll put you away, Rytsar. We'll never see you again."

Rytsar walked over to Brie and lifted her chin so her worried gaze met his. "I am a responsible *dyadya* now."

Liam started moaning on the ground and Brie let out a sigh of relief.

"There was no reason to worry," Rytsar assured her.

He wrapped his arm around Brie and held out the other to Sir. "Come, brother."

Sir joined them with Hope cradled against him. Rytsar hugged them both, the baby in the center. "We are an unbreakable force."

"Yes…" Brie whispered.

The police and emergencies vehicles rolled in with sirens blaring, their lights flashing everywhere around them, but Brie's focus was solely on her baby and the two men before her.

Rescue had come.

Hope was safe.

Aftershock

B rie woke up tucked in bed, the lights out, but a
lone candle burning on the bedside table. She
struggled out from under the covers when she heard
Hope cry and padded out of the bedroom, the cold
marble chilling her bare feet.

She walked toward the low tones of Sir hushing the
baby while trying to distract her with a stuffed animal.

Sir looked up and smiled. "Feeling better?"

Brie nodded slowly until memories of the night's
events flooded in and her smile disappeared. She shook
her head and began to cry.

Sir motioned her to him.

Brie walked over and knelt at his feet. He reached
out to her while still comforting the baby by gently
stroking her hair.

Safe.

It was the overwhelming feeling his touch evoked,
and the fears that tormented her began to evaporate.

"I almost lost everything," he stated quietly.

"But you saved me," she answered, kissing his hand

gratefully.

"I have been so closely monitoring Lilly, thinking that keeping her at the convent would ensure your safety, that I let this happen right under my nose. I basically delivered you to your kidnappers tonight." He shook his head, a look of devastation on his face.

"I was blind because I just wanted Lea to be happy... When Mary told me she didn't trust Liam, I assumed it was out of jealousy, Sir. Even when I bumped into him at the grocery store, I never questioned why Liam was acting so strange, but I wasn't even talking to the same man! Why didn't I pick up on that?"

Sir cradled her cheek. "We could go round and round second-guessing ourselves, but it changes nothing. The only thing that matters is that you are safe."

Brie shuddered, envisioning the horror she and the baby would be facing right now if they hadn't come to the rescue.

Sir pulled her to him, vowing fiercely, "I will do anything to protect you and Hope. *Anything!*"

"I apologize for coming unannounced, but I had to see you for myself." Faelan stood in the doorway, staring at Brie. He glanced over at Sir, who nodded, before he embraced her.

Brie closed her eyes, soaking in Faelan's love and

concern for her.

When Faelan let go, he muttered, "Fucking Lilly. Even though I did everything to neutralize her impact, I failed you. I'm sorry."

"I'm fine. Hope is fine. You did not fail us."

Faelan shook his head, clearly drowning in guilt.

Brie reached out and took his hand, squeezing it as she pulled him inside. "You protected me from Lilly. I am grateful to you."

He frowned. "I still can't help feeling partially responsible for what happened yesterday."

Glancing at Sir, he said, "I'm sorry, Sir Davis." His voice was full of regret.

"Don't think you are alone in feeling guilt. Durov, Anderson, Nosaka, Captain, Samantha, and even Marquis have communicated to me about how they feel accountable. In the end, I hold the greatest responsibility in this."

"Do you think Lilly orchestrated this remotely somehow?"

Sir shook his head. "No. Reverend Mother has written me faithfully twice a month. Lilly lost privileges as punishment and has been in isolation ever since she arrived. She has had zero opportunity to contact anyone."

"If that is the case, then it must have been the slaver returning for his debt."

Sir nodded sadly. "Yes. Durov and I believe this kidnapping attempt is directly linked to the slaver Lilly made the deal with. Unfortunately, he did not give up his claim on Brie after his informant reported back to him. He's simply been biding his time until our baby was born to collect them both."

Brie felt the blood drain from her face and had to sit down. "If that's true, you believe he will try again?"

"We hope the public arrest of his two men will deter any further attempts. The slaver will not want to risk exposure now, and there will be an inquiry as to who their employer was. As soon as we get a face and a name, I will ensure that man never touches you."

"But I don't want you to get involved," Brie cried. "Haven't I suffered enough?"

"I won't let Sir Davis go alone," Faelan assured her. "The man must be dealt with as soon as we know his identity. Rytsar and I discussed it at length before this even happened. We will not let another woman suffer because of this man."

"No, Faelan. I don't want any of you to go," Brie begged. "There has to be another way. Maybe the overseas authorities can help."

"That is wishful thinking, babygirl."

Brie whimpered at Sir's answer.

"This man has been able to keep his identity hidden this entire time. Even Durov's normal channels have found nothing up to this point."

"Are you saying that I either live in fear for the rest of my life or I risk losing one of you? Neither seems like a viable option, Sir."

"No, babygirl. I trust that the publicity will help us in the hunt, and that we will resolve this situation once and for all."

Brie knelt on the floor, baring her heart to him. "I

cannot lose you again. Promise me you won't go, Sir."

He shook his head. "I can't make that promise."

Brie slowly stood up and took Hope from his arms. Standing before him, she beseeched him again, "I need my husband, and Hope needs her father."

Sir closed his eyes, saying nothing.

Faelan spoke up. "I know this is shocking coming from me, but I feel that the only solution in this case is annihilation, plain and simple. Until that day, you won't be safe, Brie. What happened yesterday proves how vulnerable you are, even with all of us here to protect you."

"First Lilly, now this…" Brie cried.

"Lilly is the reason for this," Sir hissed.

"And she is paying the price for that, Sir. You said yourself that she remains in isolation with time to think about what she's done."

"You aren't asking for me to spare the slaver as well?" Sir demanded.

"No. He not only poses a threat to us, but to other women. I want him gone."

"At least we agree on that," he stated.

"Sir Davis, I can keep you abreast of any news I hear, and I hope you will do the same," Faelan told him.

"Certainly. I appreciate the help, Wallace."

Faelan turned to leave, the guilt still etched into his face. It broke Brie's heart and she called out to him. "Faelan…"

He turned to face her. "Yes, Brie."

"How are you and Kylie?"

She saw his brief smile at the mention of her name.

"Please," she said, wanting to ease his burden. Getting up to sit on the couch, she patted the area beside her.

He sat down, a charming smile gracing his lips when he spoke about Kylie. "Our relationship is progressing well."

"You haven't scared her off yet?" Brie teased.

"No, the girl seems to be able to handle me, obsessions and all."

Brie looked at him with tenderness. "That's wonderful. I would tell you that Kylie is lucky to have found you, but it's obviously true for you as well. You finally found the lock to your key."

He chuckled. "I did. There's a real freedom when you meet someone who not only accepts you for who you are, but actually loves you for it."

Brie smiled, glancing at Sir. "I know exactly what you mean."

"As far as my professional life, I have some news you might find interesting."

"Please share," Brie pleaded, welcoming the distraction.

"You know that strange vision you had about me a few months ago?"

"Of course," she answered, looking back at Sir excitedly.

"Well, from out of the blue, I got this call from a TV exec asking if I would be interested in doing a talk show—a talk show, of all things."

"I told you, didn't I?"

He laughed. "It's all just discussions at this point, and who knows if it will lead anywhere. Still...you did predict it. It kind of creeped me out, actually. How could you have known that would happen?"

Brie shrugged. "I get a feeling sometimes—it's like a tingling sensation on my scalp that travels straight to my heart. Whenever it happens, I know something important is going to happen. I felt that when I had my vision about you."

"Well, wherever your powers come from, they were freakishly right about this one."

"Did they give you any idea when?" Sir asked.

Faelan shook his head. "Nah. Like I said, we're still at the planning stages. I'm not mentioning it to anyone else because I know LA. People make plans all the time here, but it is rare to have one actually pan out."

"I'm sure you're wise to keep it under wraps. It's not a business I am familiar with," Sir said.

"Me either," Faelan admitted. "But ever since Brie mentioned her odd vision, I've been doing some research, just out of curiosity."

"So you've been googling it?" Brie asked, giggling.

Although Faelan hadn't been there when Brie first uttered those words to Sir during a practicum, the phrase "I googled it, Sir" had become a sub favorite at the Center. "I have been googling it. In fact, I've googled the shit out of it," Faelan replied with a smirk.

Brie laughed with delight.

"I love the sound of your laughter, babygirl."

She looked at Sir. They'd been so close to losing each other yesterday...

Brie wasn't sure she could handle any more close calls, but she took solace in knowing they were safe and people like Faelan were looking out for her.

Turning back to Faelan, she stared at his eyepatch. It reminded her of what he'd done for them. "You are not allowed to say that you failed me. Not only did you keep Lilly far away from me, but you also saved Rytsar. You will never know the depth of my gratitude." He tried to shrug it off, but she wouldn't let him. "You are a hero, Faelan, and your sacrifice changed the course of all our lives. Don't you ever forget that."

Faelan looked at her sadly, his beautiful lone blue eye filled with remorse.

"May I take this off, Faelan?" she asked, lightly touching his eyepatch.

He furrowed his brow. "I…" he faltered. "It's not pretty, Brie."

"Please."

He looked at her for several moments before slowly untying the leather straps of his eyepatch. It slowly fell from his eye, exposing a partially closed eyelid and the tender red flesh of the back of the eye socket.

"Does it hurt?"

"No," he answered casually. "I've grown used to it. I considered getting a replacement at one point, but…the eyepatch does the job, so I haven't seen a need."

She noticed that he held his breath while she lightly traced her finger around the lid of his missing eye. "This is a testament of your bravery, Todd Wallace." Brie met his gaze and smiled. "And I agree that you don't need a replacement."

Sitting back, she looked at him critically.

"What are you doing?" he asked with a crooked grin.

"Just taking in all of who you are now. I'm truly humbled."

He laughed uncomfortably. "There's no need to feel that way."

"But there is, and you need to hear me when I say it. I am grateful and honored to call you my friend."

"As am I," Sir said, clapping Faelan on the back. "Never feel the eyepatch is necessary around us."

Faelan actually blushed. "To be honest, I prefer wearing it. I like knowing the eye socket is protected, but thanks. It means more than you know."

He then looked at Brie. "You have my undying gratitude as well. Even though you didn't know it at the time, you saved my life when you tripped just outside the school that night."

"But that was not an act of bravery. It was just sheer clumsiness."

"Doesn't matter. That encounter changed the course of my life. I was running on autopilot before I met you—my life consisted of just misery and guilt."

Brie's heart swelled with admiration for him. "I'm glad we came into each other's lives."

"I am too, blossom," he said, smiling at her tenderly. "I am, too."

Lea swung by the same day, desperate to see her.

The two did not even speak for the first ten minutes after she arrived, hugging each other tightly, grateful to be together again.

"Oh, Brie…" she whispered, her voice trembling.

"Lea…" That was the only word she could get out before her throat closed up again.

Sir nodded to Lea. "Ms. Taylor, are you okay?"

She shrugged, looking crushed.

Sir walked over and took her into his arms. Lea let out a strangled gasp as she accepted his embrace.

Brie felt so sorry for Lea. Not only had her life been in danger, but the man she had fallen in love with and had just agreed to marry did not even exist. What a terribly cruel thing for her to bear.

After Sir released Lea, he retrieved a tissue for her and then excused himself. "I'll take care of Hope while you two talk. If you need anything, just say the word."

Lea gravitated to the kitchen table, so Brie started hot water for tea, not really knowing what to say or do.

It broke her heart when the first words out of Lea's mouth were, "I'm sorry."

Brie turned around and shook her head. "Don't. None of it is your fault."

"But I—"

"If anyone should apologize, it should be me. Because of Lilly, I brought Liam into your life."

Lea's face crumbled with sorrow. She covered her face with her hands and started sobbing. Brie walked over and hugged her where she sat, knowing words could not make the pain go away.

When the water started boiling, she left Lea and poured them both a cup of hot tea. She had learned from Tono how comforting the drink could be.

She placed a cup next to Lea, along with a box of tissues, then sat opposite her, remaining silent as she let her friend release the tears that Brie knew she needed to shed.

When Lea came to the end of her sobs, she wiped her tears away and blew her nose several times. Picking up the cup, she held it in both hands, absorbing its warmth. After taking several sips, she met Brie's gaze. "Thank you."

Brie nodded.

Lea took a deep breath. "It's like I can't get my head or heart around this. I almost lost you, Brie." She reached across the table to grab Brie's hand. "When I think how close that was, I want to throw up."

"Hope and I are safe, Lea."

She nodded before taking another sip. "As far as Liam...if that's even his real name...I'm all mixed up. I hate him on a level I can't express. I feel so stupid and humiliated for having been duped by him. And yet..." She looked at Brie sadly. "My feelings were real. I loved him, and I thought we were going to start a life together." The tears welled up, so she took a moment to calm down and breathe before speaking again. "In one fell swoop, I lost the future I saw for myself and the person I loved..." She shook her head, correcting herself. "*Thought* I loved."

"I'm so sorry, Lea..."

"I keep running it over and over in my head, all the

small things I missed and should have questioned—but I didn't, Brie."

Brie squeezed her hand. "I didn't, either, and I was the one in danger. I really liked the guy. It's just so weird to think the person we knew isn't real. That we don't even know the man."

"I'm really struggling with that..." she said, her voice cracking with emotion. She took another sip of tea. "We didn't just have sex, Brie. We made love. How can a person fake that?"

"I don't know, Lea."

She grabbed another tissue and dabbed her eyes. "I really suck at relationships. I seem to always fall in love with people who don't love me. I'm fucking hope-less..."

"No, you can't take responsibility for what happened with Liam. It was calculated and cruel. As far as Ms. Clark, that's all on her. Don't let that beautiful soul of yours get crushed by this."

She shook her head. "I don't know how to move on from here. I don't want to love anyone..." Her face crumbled again. "But I desperately *need* it."

Brie got up and hugged her again. "Sometimes the love of family and friends is all we have to get us through. I love you, Lea. I love you so damn much."

Lea could only manage a half-smile. "You know what the kicker is?"

Brie shook her head.

"Mary knew. The first night they met, she knew not to trust him, and all I could think was that she was being a jealous cow."

"Honestly, I thought the same thing myself. If I had just listened to Mary…" Brie started to cry. If she had just listened, maybe none of this would have happened. "I'm forever indebted to Mary because she spoke to Rytsar about it. Otherwise…" Brie had to shake the horrible thoughts out of her head.

"Damn it, Brie. Who would have ever thought that Mary would turn out to be smarter than either of us?"

Brie snorted her agreement through her tears. "I owe her, again…"

Lea looked at her strangely. "Again?"

Brie quickly covered up her accidental slip by explaining, "Yeah, remember when I screwed up and disobeyed Sir by reading his mother's note? When he kicked me out, Mary took me in. But instead of telling me it was going to be okay, she suggested Sir might be better off without me."

"Oh Lord, that girl…"

Brie chuckled. "Mary can be brutal with her words, but she says it like it is. I'm starting to appreciate that more and more now."

Lea sighed. "Yeah. I guess I am, too."

"What are you going to do now, girlfriend?"

She groaned. "I don't know…maybe I should ask if I can have a session with Rytsar's nines. I could sure use a little pain therapy right now."

"That sounds like a good idea, actually. There are times when pain can bring relief."

"You're not kidding, and I could use some to combat this heartbreak. It's going to take a fucking inferno."

Brie got up to pour Lea another cup of tea. "We're going to get through this and, someday, we will be able to look back and marvel at how strong we were."

"I don't feel strong at all, but I'll drink to that." She hit her cup against Brie's. "And let me add another. Here's to Mary Quite Contrary. Bless her heart, that bitch knows her shit."

"To Mary!"

It weighed heavily on Brie—what Sir had shared about Lilly still being in isolation after all this time. In an attempt to deal with the warring emotions she felt, Brie wrote a letter that night.

Lilly,

I write this letter because I am feeling compassion toward you.

I understand that you carry demons borne of your mother, just as my husband does. However, I believe there is good in all of us, and it is my sincerest hope that you find that part of yourself and embrace it fully as Thane has.

I can never forget what you've done, but I hope you will be able to forgive yourself and move on.

I trust there will come a day when I will be able to forgive you and be free from this painful connection between us.

May you find peace in this life so we can finally be free of each other.

Sincerely,
Brianna

After writing the letter, she set it on fire and watched the flame consume the paper. Brie imagined the smoke taking the thoughts contained in her letter and releasing them out into the world.

Although Lilly would never read her words, it brought Brie much needed peace.

Her Christening

S ir came to Brie, wanting to discuss Italy. "Would you be up to traveling, babygirl? I know it's sooner than we planned. However, I feel a strong urge to reconnect with my grandparents."

"I feel it too, Sir." Having their lives threatened had awakened the instinctual need to gather as a family.

"Then I'll make the arrangements for the six of us."

Brie was confused. "Six?"

"The three of us, Durov, and your parents."

"Oh, that's so thoughtful of you, Sir. Even though my parents aren't churchgoers, it would mean so much to them to be there for Hope's christening."

"I would like us to spend extra time with my family, so Durov has offered his private jet. Your parents would take a different flight, if that's agreeable to you."

"My dad actually hates to travel. He never got over being separated from us when I was young and prefers being a homebody, so that would be perfect."

"Since you are agreeable, I'll start the arrangements."

"I'm so glad we're heading to Italy again. I want to be surrounded by your large Italian family, and I know they will fall in love with Hope."

Sir looked down at his daughter and smiled. "When I look at her, I feel my father's presence. It will be the same for *Nonno* and *Nonna*."

"Yes. This trip is needed by all of us." Brie stood on tiptoes and gave him a kiss on the cheek. "Now, I need to buy a christening outfit for her."

"Let me go with you," Sir insisted.

"No need. I'll do it online. Gives me time to start packing. Having to travel overseas with a baby will require a lot more planning and equipment. But I'm not complaining. I can't wait to see *Nonna* hold Hope for the first time."

Tears welled up in her eyes just thinking about it. "This is exactly what my heart needs."

Brie double-checked to make sure Hope was secure before the plane started down the runway. As she glanced out the window, she was overcome with a feeling of dread. Grabbing Sir's hand for comfort, she found his was ice cold.

Looking up at his calm face, Brie would never have guessed he was terrified to take this flight, but she could clearly feel his terror rolling off him now. Brie squeezed his hand tightly to give him reassurance.

He glanced at her and nodded before looking ahead

again.

The fact he was on this plane spoke to Sir's level of courage and love of family. In all aspects of his life, he had never let unwarranted fears stand in his way. This, however, was different. He had every reason to fear flying, having almost died in a plane crash at this very airport.

And yet…

Here he was, quietly facing that fear so he could present their daughter to his father's family.

As the engines revved and the plane started bouncing just before takeoff, Rytsar made an offhand comment. "Comrade, I don't want to alarm you, but I heard that a small two-seater plane crashed into the Forest Lawn cemetery in the Hollywood Hills yesterday."

Sir narrowed his eyes.

"Rytsar!" Brie cried out in protest.

Rytsar smiled at her and continued undaunted. "Search and rescue workers have recovered two hundred bodies so far and expect that number to climb as digging continues."

Sir shook his head slowly, glaring at Rytsar as the plane lifted off.

Brie felt her stomach drop as they broke contact with the ground. Her nerves increased, along with Sir's, as they rose higher and higher over the ocean, and then the plane banked sharply to the right, finally settling into its set flying pattern.

Sir suddenly let go of her hand and relaxed.

Raising an eyebrow at Rytsar, he said, "That joke

was worthy of Ms. Taylor, but she would have the sense to wait until *after* the plane had taken off."

"Ah, but that was purposeful on my part, comrade. If you are concentrating on being upset with me, you naturally would think less about the plane crashing."

"Surely, there must have been a better way to handle it," Brie insisted.

"Not for a sadist." Rytsar smirked, adding, "I rather enjoyed myself."

"I could tell," Sir replied. He turned to unbuckle the baby, holding her against his chest as he closed his eyes.

Brie said nothing as she watched, knowing he needed that connection and peace that only holding their little girl could provide.

Rytsar gazed at Sir for several moments, a tender look in his eye. As cruel as he could be sometimes with his humor, Rytsar was a true and loyal friend.

"Must you hog the babe?" he finally complained after several minutes had passed.

Sir opened his eyes. "For that little stunt? I think a timeout for *dyadya* is in order."

"You wouldn't," Rytsar protested, turning to Brie for support.

Brie did *not* want to step in between the two Doms, choosing to say nothing about it as she stared out the window at the land racing by down below them. "So amazing. Everyone is going about their lives, busy with their daily routine, but us...?" She turned to face them. "We're headed to Italy!"

"And a christening," Sir added, handing Hope over

to Rytsar. "Not that you deserve to be her godfather after that joke."

Rytsar gratefully took the babe into his arms. "You know you love me, comrade. Who else would be brave enough to jest with you in such a way?"

"No one, thankfully."

"But it helped get your mind off the takeoff, did it not?"

"Barely. Like an irritating gnat."

"Then it was worth your ire toward me," Rytsar stated with satisfaction. Looking at Hope, he said, "Your papa doesn't want to admit it, but he is extremely lucky to have me as his brother."

Sir slapped him on the shoulder. "Actually, I'm well aware of that fact." He placed his finger next to Hope's hand and she squeezed it, wiggling happily in Rytsar's arms while making cooing noises at her father. Sir then glanced over at Brie. "I wouldn't be here today if you hadn't come to the Collaring Ceremony, old friend."

Brie's interest was piqued as she looked at both men. "Tell me, please. I want to hear what happened that night."

Sir gazed at Rytsar thoughtfully. "You know, looking back on it, I realize you specialize in provoking people to get what you want."

"It is the duty of a sadist."

"Well, you were in rare form at the Collaring Ceremony," Sir said, chuckling lightly.

"I've always wondered what you talked about that night," Brie confessed.

Rytsar snorted. "Your Master is a very stubborn

man."

Brie glanced at Sir and blushed. It was true, and she could not dispute that, so she said nothing.

Rytsar smiled at Brie. "When I walked up to you that night, you were absolutely radiant, *radost moya*. The picture of perfection. And what was my comrade doing? Hiding in the corner, ignoring you."

"That's not exactly how it went," Sir replied.

"But it *was*," Rytsar insisted.

"It was my duty as Headmaster to remain impartial so my student could make her choice without any outside influence."

"Well, I certainly saw the Wolf Pup *influencing* her, so where were you?"

Sir answered through gritted teeth. "I was letting her decide for herself."

"Right...but the entire time, her choice was you, and you chose not to accept it."

"You knew the circumstances, old friend."

"I did. It was clear as day. She wanted you to fuck her, and you were hungry to fuck her but, instead, you hid in the corner like a man-baby until I came to save the day."

Sir muttered, "I'm sorry I even brought this up..."

But Brie was loving it—this rare peek into the past. "I remember every detail of that evening," Brie informed them. "I was a mess after Tono's dad rejected me and Mary stole Faelan for her interview. I could hardly think straight, much less make a decision." She grinned at Rytsar. "And then you showed up."

He gave her a slight nod. "I do whatever it takes

for my friends."

"Your intentions were questionable, *brother*," Sir snorted.

Rytsar winked at Brie. "Did I not tell you to choose wisely, *radost moya*? I only had my comrade's best interests at heart."

"I definitely remember you saying that," she agreed.

"What he is failing to mention is that he threatened to claim you himself if I didn't that night."

Brie's eyes grew wide as she looked at Rytsar. "Really?" She could just imagine the shock if that had happened and then she discovered she'd been collared by a sadist.

"You should have seen your man when I said that. Talk about the green-eyed beast rearing its ugly head." Rytsar's robust laughter filled the plane.

"Yes, it was your irritating 'gnat tactic' striking again," Sir said, shaking his head.

"But it was effective," Rytsar said proudly. He turned his attention on the tiny infant cradled in his arms. "I told your papa that he was in control of the situation and to take what was his. And do you know what he said to that?"

Brie couldn't wait to hear.

"Your papa insulted me." He smiled sweetly at Hope. "His exact words were, 'You are the fool. Just because something is offered does not mean one should claim it.'" Rytsar nodded, staring at Hope as if she were talking to him. "I agree completely. Your papa is crazy."

Brie looked lovingly at Sir, understanding why he

had felt that way at the time. He was afraid of destroying her because of the demons he had carried inside.

"There was only one answer to his ridiculous statement," Rytsar continued, glancing over at Brie with a smirk. "I was honest with your papa and told him I would not respect him if your mama wasn't wearing his collar the next time we met. And, guess what, *moye solntse*?" His smile grew wider. "He listened to your *dyadya* and took matters into his own hands." Rytsar held the baby up in the air, smiling at her. "And *that* is how you came to be."

"Not exactly," Sir stated drolly.

"Nope, that's not how it played out, Rytsar," Brie told him, remembering how devastated she'd been when Sir had said no.

Rytsar lowered Hope, cradling her in his arms as he stared at Brie in confusion. "How did it go, then?" he demanded.

Is this news to Rytsar? she wondered. "Well…" She glanced at Sir, remembering the pain of that night. "I was about to choose Tono, but I was plagued with second thoughts."

"Go on," Rytsar encouraged.

"I threw caution to the wind and turned around to offer Sir my collar, instead."

"And…?"

"He turned me down."

Rytsar looked at Sir in disbelief. "Why have I never heard this before?"

"Let her finish, old friend."

"I was completely crushed and had to get out of

there before I totally lost it in front of everyone."

Rytsar wore a look of shock. Turning to Sir he said, "Obviously, something happened because she wears your collar."

Sir's lips curled into a smile. "I resigned as Headmaster so I could claim what was mine."

Rytsar nodded approvingly. "You do like to be dramatic."

"Sir is anything but dramatic," Brie laughed. "However, he did break my heart that night."

Sir gazed at Brie, his eyes expressing his regret.

"All that being said…" he stated to Rytsar. "Had you not been there, I might have made the biggest mistake of my life. Thank you, brother."

Rytsar grinned mischievously. "So you owe me."

Sir chuckled. "I do, and your payment comes in the form of remaining this little girl's godfather despite your poorly timed joke today."

Rytsar let loose a bout of low laughter. "Fine, comrade. So be it." Hope suddenly got fussy in his arms.

"Little one, there's no reason to fret," Rytsar told her. "I know exactly what you need." He walked over to Brie and handed the baby to her. As soon as Hope had settled in Brie's arms, the baby turned her head, opening and closing her mouth hungrily.

Rytsar sat down next to Brie.

Since breastfeeding in front of him was natural to her, she eased the material of her blouse down and unlatched her nursing bra to expose her full breast.

Hope instantly latched on and began sucking noisily. Brie closed her eyes, groaning at the ache caused by her milk rushing in.

"That is very sexy, *radost moya*," Rytsar growled.

Brie opened her eyes to find him staring at her lust-fully. She felt the heat rise to her cheeks under his scrutiny and glanced over at Sir. He also had the same ravenous look.

Pleasant tingles coursed down her spine as she wondered if she was about to find out their secret plans for her. "What are you thinking, Rytsar?"

His wicked smile grew wider. "I'm having sexy thoughts."

"About what?" she ventured.

"About what we will be doing to you."

Brie squeaked.

"But not yet..." Sir replied with a smirk. Her Master was always challenging her in the area of patience, and it was one thing she had yet to learn.

Her heart started racing. Here she'd thought they'd only come for a traditional family gathering, but these two obviously had something more in mind.

Brie looked back at Rytsar, his intense gaze giving her goosebumps. "Do I have a say in this?"

"Of course," Sir answered.

But Rytsar shook his head.

Brie giggled nervously. She trusted Sir without question, and she knew Rytsar would never force her to do something she wasn't willing to do—although he would do everything in his power to convince her.

"Should I be worried?"

Rytsar nodded.

She felt butterflies in her stomach. Looking down

at Hope, she giggled to herself. Being married, and now a mother, did not seem to deter either man.

It filled her heart with joy knowing they still longed to dominate her.

Rytsar refused to come with them once the ferry docked at Portoferraio.

"Please join us," Brie begged.

"*Nyet*, this is a time for you to introduce *moye solntse* to your family. It should be private."

"But you *are* part of our family," Brie insisted.

Rytsar smiled but looked to Sir, wanting his agreement.

"You are my brother," Sir stated simply. "Dearer to me than blood."

Rytsar lowered his head for a moment. "You know I feel the same, brother. However..." He put his hand on his chest. "I would feel more comfortable if I came later, after you have had some time to reconnect with your blood relations."

"It's not necessary," Brie insisted.

Sir surprised her by suddenly taking Rytsar's side. "If he says he is uncomfortable, we shouldn't force him."

"But he would, if the tables were turned," Brie countered.

Rytsar grinned. "*Da*, I would but, thankfully, your man is not me."

Brie looked at him sadly. "But I want you there."

"And I will be. But before I do, I would like to wander the town for a while." He nodded at Sir. "I want to get to know you better by exploring this part of your youth, brother."

Sir nodded slowly as if absorbing his words. "I visited here often with my father. I hope you will be equally as charmed by the place."

Rytsar scanned the town built against the side of the hills surrounding the port and smiled. "I was in too much of a rush to pay attention the last time I was here for your wedding. I do not want to leave here without absorbing this part of your past."

He put his hand on Rytsar's shoulder. "Enjoy, old friend."

Sir held his arm out to Brie. "Let's leave him to discover the magic of my island."

Brie eyed Rytsar with suspicion. What if he was using this as an excuse to get things set up for their mysterious scene? If so, why would she ever want to interfere? She smiled shyly. "I hope you find what you are looking for."

Rytsar chuckled, shaking his head. "Sex on the mind, eh, *radost moya?*"

"Me?" she protested, blushing at being called out.

"*Da,*" Rytsar laughed, grinning at Sir. He gave them a curt bow before walking away, whistling a pleasant Russian tune.

A smile played on Sir's lips as they started up the narrow street that led to his grandparents' place. Along the way, people pointed at the baby, talking excitedly in hushed tones just like the first time they visited here.

Sir acknowledged them with a nod but did not engage them.

Brie had forgotten how popular Alonzo Davis had been on Isola d'Elba, and how Sir garnered the same adoration, being the son of the great violinist. Now that he had a child, it made him even more venerated here.

She kept glancing at Sir as they walked up the steep hill, the significance of this meeting hitting her fully. Brie felt that he should be the one holding the baby for this momentous occasion and stopped, holding Hope out to him.

"No, you are the mother," Sir said.

Brie looked at him tenderly. "This is an important moment for your father's family. Your grandparents lost their only son twenty years ago, and they almost lost you... I can't imagine what they've been through emotionally."

Sir nodded. "Yes, they have suffered greatly."

"Now, not only are you returning, but you are bringing your father's grandchild. His legacy—their legacy." Brie handed her over to Sir and stroked Hope's soft cheek. "You're bringing a miracle they can hold."

Sir closed his eyes. Brie knew he was missing his father. Truly, it seemed cruel that the man who had loved and shaped Sir into the caring father he was today could not be a part of this.

When Sir opened his eyes, he looked up at the sky, cradling Hope in his arms. He then turned to Brie and said, "*You* are the miracle."

Brie shook her head, wrapping her arm around him, as they continued up the hill in silence. When they reached the vivid red door, Brie knocked on it loudly. There was excited chatter from inside, but no one came to answer the door.

Brie looked at Sir questioningly.

"My grandparents must be making their way down the stairs," he told her.

Normally, Aunt Fortuna was the first person to greet them at the door, but it was only right that his grandparents were the first to lay eyes on the baby.

Brie and Sir stood patiently waiting as a small crowd gathered behind them.

It seemed no one wanted to miss this moment.

The door finally opened and his tiny grandmother appeared, breaking out into a huge smile. "The *bambina!*"

Sir's grandfather stood proudly beside her. "Welcome, *Nipotino.*"

"*Nonno,*" Sir replied, his voice full of love for the man.

Sir carefully placed their child into the tiny woman's withered but strong arms. "I present to you your great-grandchild, Hope Antonia Davis."

Nonna had a look of pure wonder on her face. "*Bellissima…*"

"Yes, she is beautiful," Sir agreed, smiling down at them both.

Behind them, the women in the crowd collectively let out an "Aww…"

Nonna turned and placed Hope in her husband's

arms, tears running down her wrinkled cheeks. "Alonzo's *nipotina...*"

"*Sì*," he replied gruffly. He held the baby, gazing into her eyes as if he were communicating with her in a secret language.

Hope stared up at him, completely mesmerized.

Nonna took the opportunity to hug Brie. "*Grazie*, Brianna."

The old woman's embrace was filled with overflowing love for her. Brie remembered that feeling from her last visit—the feeling of belonging to a bigger whole, and of being totally accepted.

After Nonna let go of Brie, she hugged Sir. She cried tears of happiness in his arms and did not let go until Nonno cleared his throat. The tiny woman looked up at Sir, her cheeks wet with tears. "*Ti amo, Nipotino.*"

Sir looked down at her, cradling her thin face in his strong hand. "I love you, *mia nonna.*"

His grandfather held up their daughter for the crowd to see. The group clapped and cheered, shouting blessings for the child.

Aunt Fortuna joined them, having been patient long enough. She immediately took Hope from Nonno and cuddled her, telling Sir, "Congratulations, Thane. She is as beautiful as your mother."

Sir's smile faltered.

Aunt Fortuna didn't notice as she turned to Brie and added, "She has Alonzo's eyes."

Brie glanced at Sir, realizing how much he must take after his father. What would it have been like to meet Alonzo in person? It made her sad that she would never know—that Hope would never know.

"I agree, Aunt Fortuna. Our little girl is a beautiful blend of families," she replied, grateful that the famous violinist lived on in their daughter.

"She is," Sir agreed, his smile returning.

"We need to get you inside," Aunt Fortuna stated. "There is much celebrating to do!"

Brie stayed back, observing the group as they headed up the stairs: Aunt Fortuna in front with the baby, Sir helping Nonna up the steps, and Nonno at the rear, a look of pride in his eyes.

He turned back and held out his hand to Brie. "*Bellissima mia nipotina.*"

She grinned, taking the hand he offered, honored he'd called her his beautiful granddaughter. In this family, once you were accepted, it was as if you had always been a part of it.

He gripped her hand firmly and placed his other hand on the small of her back as they made their way up the stairs. There was no doubt Sir took after this man. She glanced at him, admiring his full head of hair and classic good looks despite the toll that time and sorrow had etched in his face.

Sir would make an exceedingly handsome older gentleman too, she realized. How lucky was she?

Once they reached the top of the stairs, Brie was greeted with a pleasant surprise. The room was decorated for a baby shower, complete with streamers, baby items, presents, and cake. All the females in Sir's large family had managed to squeeze themselves into that room—the men taking over the kitchen.

Aunt Fortuna was surrounded by women wanting to see and touch the baby. Brie glanced at Sir. He stood back from the crowd, an arm around his grandmother, who was looking up at him in loving adoration.

Nonno guided Brie through the cluster of women so she could stand next to Sir. Some of them reached out and stroked her as she passed, chattering at her excitedly. Although Brie had practiced the language, these women were speaking too quickly for her to translate more than a couple of words. However, their smiles were easy enough to read.

Brie basked in the joy that surrounded her. It was reflected on Nonna's face, in the pride shining in Nonno's eyes as he gazed on his great-granddaughter, and in the tenderness in Sir's eyes when he caught Brie staring at him.

Their little girl would grow up with this depth of love and be forever supported by it.

Famiglia…

Later that afternoon, Brie moaned as she sat back in her chair, completely stuffed, having just finished off her meal with a delicate cannoli. She sat there in a pleasant food coma with a smile on her face as she digested all the fabulous food Sir's family had prepared.

Sighing in contentment, Brie looked up at the wispy clouds floating in the blue sky. She was grateful that Sir's grandparents had their family meals on the rooftop.

Everyone around her was in the midst of animated conversations. Her ears were filled with their beautiful Italian when she heard a faint, but familiar, voice. Brie got up and walked over to the edge, placing her hands on the half-wall as she looked down at the street below.

Rytsar was holding something large in one hand and pounding on the door with the other. But, because everyone was upstairs, no one had heard him knocking.

"Rytsar!" Brie shouted down from above.

He looked up, sounding alarmed. "What are you doing on the roof?"

"We're having a party. Just a sec, I'll let you in." Brie skipped down the flights of stairs and opened the door for him.

"It is good to see your face, *radost moya*. I was beginning to think I had the wrong place."

"Sorry we didn't hear you. Everyone's upstairs. Come. Follow me!"

As they climbed the stairs, it was easy to hear the noise from above. "How is *moye solntse* handling all this chaos?"

She stopped and turned, grinning at him. "She's eating up the attention."

"Takes after her mama, I see."

Brie went to give him a poke, but he grabbed her wrist and squeezed tightly, pulling her close to kiss her. Her stomach did a flip-flop when he claimed her mouth with his tongue.

Rytsar let her wrist go and turned her back around, slapping her on the ass. "Hurry, I have something to give my comrade's grandparents."

Brie bit her lip as she ran up the rest of the stairs, her heart racing.

Rytsar called out to Sir loudly, "Your brother is here!"

Sir held up his hand and waved before making his way over. "What took you so long?" he chided.

"I have been knocking on the door for over an hour, comrade."

"You have?"

"*Nyet,*" he admitted, chuckling as he gave Sir a slap on the back. "Thankfully, *radost moya* heard me shouting and let me in before I gave up."

"I'm sorry, old friend."

"If I can hold *moye solntse,* all will be forgiven. However, I must first give this to your grandparents."

"Please don't mention having to wait," Sir asked him. "My grandmother wouldn't forgive herself, if she knew."

"I am a gentleman, comrade. I would never say a word to embarrass your *babushka,*" Rytsar promised him.

Brie and Sir joined Rytsar as he walked over to Sir's grandparents.

"*Nonno* and *Nonna,* this is Anton Durov, my friend and brother by choice."

Nonna smiled, her words simple as she spoke to him in English. "Welcome, Anton."

Rytsar gave them both a curt bow. "It is an honor."

Nonno held out his hand. "Hope's godfather."

He nodded with obvious pride.

"Family now," Nonno stated, embracing the burly Russian.

Rytsar's look of surprise quickly turned to one of tenderness. "*Grazie*, Mr. Davis."

The old man shook his head. "*Nonno*, to you."

Rytsar's boyish half-grin melted Brie's heart.

Sir's grandmother wrapped her tiny arms around his waist, saying nothing. Rytsar glanced at Sir, clearly touched by their kind gestures, and it looked like he might cry. "I have a gift for you both," he suddenly announced, handing his wrapped present to the tiny woman.

"For us?" she asked.

Nonno shook his head. "Not necessary."

"*Da*, it is," Rytsar insisted.

Nonna pulled at the paper, and her smiled widened when she saw what was revealed. She touched it lightly with her fingers, a look of wonder on her face.

Brie leaned forward to see a wall clock. However, instead of the numbers, it had pictures of Hope for every hour, each one with a different expression on her face. The gift was so remarkably sweet.

Rytsar explained. "I know the distance is hard. This way, you will see your granddaughter every hour of every day."

Sir translated his words for them.

Nonna nodded, handing the clock over to her husband so she could give Rytsar another hug.

Sir's grandfather was also clearly affected by the gift since it took him a few moments before he was able to speak. Grabbing Rytsar, he slapped his back hard several times as he embraced him. "*Grazie*, Anton."

Brie's heart swelled with the knowledge that Rytsar had secured his rightful place in this family. All the pain from the past, the wrongs done to him by his own kin, could be forgotten in the loving embrace of Sir's family.

The day of the christening arrived, and everyone gathered at the old church by the sea. Instead of the outfit Brie had purchased online, Hope was dressed in a traditional christening gown covered in white Italian lace, lovingly crafted by Aunt Fortuna. The baby looked like a fairy princess to Brie.

In the very same church that Sir's father and Sir himself were christened, Rytsar presented Hope Antonia Davis to the priest. The ceremony took place in front of Nonno and Nonna, all of Sir's family, and Brie's own parents.

Brie stood next to Sir and watched proudly as the priest anointed Hope's head with holy water.

Before the assembly and God, Rytsar made a personal vow to his goddaughter. "As Hope's godfather, I will help her parents, Thane and Brie Davis, to bring this child up knowing God, and I vow to support her in times of crisis and sickness until my dying breath."

When he placed Hope back in Brie's arms, he said, "We are now officially family in the eyes of God, *radost moya.*"

He looked to Sir and nodded.

Sir's tone was solemn. "Thank you, brother."

The Isle 2.0

As she was packing to head back home, Rytsar walked into the room and nodded to Sir. The sexual tension in the room suddenly increased.

Brie took one look at Sir and felt weak in the knees, knowing she was finally going to find out what all their planning had been about.

"Téa, we are not headed back to the States."

"Where are we going, Master?"

"Someplace Hope will not be joining us. However, your parents have kindly agreed to take her with them. We will be returning to get her in a couple of days."

"Why the separation, Sir?"

Rytsar smirked. "I am finally going to visit the Isle with you, *radost moya*."

Warm jolts of electricity coursed through her body thinking about being on their private island alone with Sir and Rytsar for days…

Luckily, her parents were so thrilled to have Hope all to themselves for a couple of days, that it made it easier for Brie when the time came to say goodbye.

As they were preparing to leave, her mother told Brie excitedly, "Thane has taken care of everything, sweetheart. Supplies have even been sent to the house," she leaned in and whispered, "including your reserves of milk."

Brie gave Sir a sideways glance. "So *that's* why I've been storing extra in the freezer. And all this time, I thought it was a precaution in case I got the flu."

Sir chuckled. "It never hurts to be prepared."

"Don't worry about a thing, little girl," her father reassured her as he grabbed Hope's bags from Sir. "We'll take good care of our granddaughter."

"So you're not worried about the long plane ride back with her?" Brie asked him.

Her dad looked down at his granddaughter and grinned. "Nope, because I'll do whatever it takes to make her happy."

Brie wrapped an arm around him. "Thank you, Daddy."

He gave her a kiss on the cheek. "You've opened up a new world to us making us grandparents. Know that this father is extremely grateful."

Brie gave Hope one more cuddle and kiss before handing her over to her mother. But Rytsar intervened before she could make the transfer.

"Could I hold her once more?"

Brie smiled. "Of course, Rytsar." She handed Hope to him and watched as he cradled the baby against his chest.

Rytsar said nothing as he held her with his eyes closed for several minutes.

Her parents looked at Brie strangely, wondering what was up.

Brie explained, "He takes his *dyadya* responsibilities very seriously."

They both nodded, but her father gave Rytsar an amused look as he set Hope's bags in the back of the trunk.

Finally, Rytsar released his hold and lifted Hope in the air, smiling up at her as she giggled. "Your *dyadya* loves you, *moye solntse,* forever and a day."

He gave her a kiss on the cheek and gently handed her over to Brie's mother.

"I sure wish I had an uncle like you," her mother joked as she went to buckle Hope into the car seat.

Brie put her arm around Rytsar. "Missing her already?"

"*Da.*"

Sir came up behind them and they watched as her parents left with Hope. Brie waved goodbye with a light heart. Between Sir's family and her own, Hope was surrounded by an abundance of love.

Brie's scene started before they even left the airfield for the Isle.

Once they were on board Rytsar's jet, Sir commanded her to strip. Brie smiled to herself as she undressed in front of him. He buckled her into the seat and kissed her on the lips before placing a blindfold over her eyes.

Her body was already tingling with excitement as the plane took off. Once in the air, Sir told her to unbuckle and walk toward his voice. She made her way over to him, her arms outstretched.

Strong arms encased her. Rytsar asked in a gruff voice, "What do we have here?"

He lifted her off her feet amid happy squeals and carried her to the front of the cabin. He set her down and bound her wrists behind her back in cuffs. He then secured her to the wall with a hook mounted there, moving down to bind her ankles next.

He stepped back when he was done, and asked Sir, "What do you think?"

"Nice, but I think we could use some more ornamentation." Sir moved over to her, his touch causing goosebumps on her skin as he played with her nipples. "Something delicate and decorative." She felt the pressure of a tweezer clamp on her nipple, but he kept the tension light as he tightened it, not wanting to evoke her milk rushing in. He then secured the other clamp, and she felt the delicate chain, weighted down by a jewel, swinging between her breasts.

Sir had a flare for making her feel beautiful during play.

Brie heard them go back to their seats and felt their heated gaze on her.

"Yes, she looks good there," Sir commented.

"Agreed," Rytsar stated huskily.

Brie heard the stewardess walk up and ask the men what they wanted to drink.

It reminded her of the time she'd acted as a platter at an important party during her training, and that feeling grew as she listened to Sir and Rytsar talking about business.

It actually turned her on, this feeling of objectification—knowing they were aware of her, but choosing not to interact.

Soon, however, Rytsar returned to her, placing a gag in her mouth and securing it behind her head. When he sat back down, he told Sir casually, "I like to see her bound and gagged."

"I agree. It is an arousing sight."

Brie basked in their pseudo attention, knowing she was the center of it even though they were treating her as if she were a mere decorative piece.

They upped the ante when Sir came to her and placed silencing headphones over her ears. Now, she was devoid of her main senses and completely dependent on their contact.

They did not disappoint her need. Throughout the trip, each man came to her, playing with her chain, fingering her pussy, or biting her on the neck. It made her dripping wet and desirous for more of their attention.

Near the end of the flight, Brie found herself handled roughly as Rytsar took off the headphones and threw them aside. He then quickly unbound her wrists and ankles, growling, "I have watched your breasts swell this entire time. Now I must partake." Lifting her up, he carried her to the back of the jet and dropped her onto his bed.

Sir and Rytsar tied her wrists to the bed, then lay on either side of her. Sir removed her blindfold while Rytsar relieved her of the gag.

Brie was struck by how ravenous both men looked. It was obvious they had taken pleasure in torturing themselves by teasing her during the flight.

Sir removed the delicate clamps and began rolling her nipples between his fingers. Not having nursed in so long, her body primed itself to feed.

Brie held her breath as both men descended on her breasts at the same time and began sucking her nipples. She cried out as the ache of her milk rushing in was coupled by the sensuous feel of their lips.

It was unlike anything she had experienced before.

Sir's hand sought her pussy, creating a glorious heat as he began rubbing against her clit. It seemed so wrong but felt so right as her pussy began pulsating with need.

Brie closed her eyes and prayed there would be no punishment when her body rocked with an intense orgasm that wouldn't stop as they continued to suckle her breasts.

When the last pulse finally ended and her milk was spent, she opened her eyes. Rytsar pulled back, wiping a drop of her milk from his lips.

"Delicious," he growled lustfully.

Brie blushed, embarrassed that she had enjoyed them sucking her full breasts so much.

She turned to Sir, who looked at her hungrily. "I want you…"

Brie spread her legs wider in invitation, longing for him to fill her up with his cock. Sir quickly undressed and climbed on top of her, his shaft easily finding its way into her wet pussy. Her body craved his animal-like lust as he began thrusting like a beast.

There was no holding back a second orgasm when she felt the burst of heat, his seed coating her inner walls. Brie came with Sir as he pushed in deep with each thrust of his release, making her moan in pure pleasure.

Afterward, as she lay there sweaty and spent, Sir asked, "Coming twice without permission?"

She turned her head to look at him. "I'm sorry, but it felt so good…"

Wiping the sweat from his brow, he told her, "I agree, but now I must think on an appropriate punishment." He chuckled, adding, "I'll let you ponder on that."

"Mercy," she begged, although she had to admit she was already anticipating his punishment.

Rytsar took over then.

He undid her bindings before he thoroughly cleaned her, making her fresh before he undressed himself. The burly Russian still carried the scars from his torture, as well as his surgery, but they were fading. His muscular physique had returned, but he was thinner than before, as if his body was permanently altered by the experience.

Rytsar stood before Brie, his cock hard and his eyes

sparkling with mischievous mirth. What was he planning?

She held her breath as he pressed the length of his body against hers, his cock between her legs. Whispering in her ear, he murmured, "You are beautiful, *radost moya*."

His intense blue eyes were mesmerizing as Rytsar slowly rubbed his hard cock on her pussy, coating it with her juices. She held her breath as he pushed the head of his shaft into her. Rytsar began kissing her deeply, claiming her lips as he claimed her body with his manhood.

Sir lay back against the headboard, watching them—a satisfied look on his face.

Brie had expected Rytsar to play hard and rough with her, but he was gentle. Taking her deep, demanding her body conform to him, but stroking her slowly as he nibbled and kissed her skin.

This unexpected lovemaking left her curious. She smiled, running her fingers over his bald head. "You are sweet for a sadist."

He chuckled, biting down on her shoulder as he gave her a couple of spirited thrusts. Brie loved his response and purred with delight.

Rytsar went back to his leisurely pace, stroking her G-spot, but not quite taking her to the edge. Instead, he made her climax build upon itself over and over again. His knowledge of her body, and his natural desire to make her suffer, meant that he soon had her body tormented with need.

"Please…" she begged.

"*Nyet,*" he murmured, biting her again.

He knew what his teeth did to her, and she cried out in painfully delicious frustration.

"This feeling? That is what you do to me, *radost moya.* You simply being near me makes my cock ache like this for you."

She shook her head, moaning with passion, both loving and hating having to ride this intense edge.

"Still yourself," he commanded her.

Brie immediately stopped moving and looked up into his eyes.

"Feel my need for you," he murmured huskily.

Brie readied herself, longing to feel the strength of his orgasm.

"But do not come yourself," he added with an evil twinkle in his eye.

He covered her lips with his, plunging his cock into her, rubbing against her G-spot with calculated expertise.

Brie stared into his blue eyes as he pumped his seed into her, her body trembling in excitement and in need for her own release. When he was done, he collapsed on top of her, breathing heavily.

All her nerve endings were twitching, needing to climax.

He propped himself up and stared at her, smiling. "*Radost moya...*"

"Yes?" she gasped.

"This Russian loves you."

She whimpered, her pussy still pulsing with need, having nearly come.

He leaned over and whispered the word she'd been desperate to hear. *"Da..."*

Her orgasm crescendoed, finally reaching the top of the precipice. His lips smashed against hers as every muscle in her body seemed to join in her climax. She was like a woman possessed, shaking uncontrollably as she came.

Brie lay with her head on Sir's lap, listening to the pleasant drone of puddle jumper as they headed to the island. She was still pleasantly weak from the hours of play on the jet.

"Babygirl."

She turned to look up at him and said with adoration, "My Master..."

"Did you enjoy your erotic trip?"

"Very much."

Sir played with her hair as he explained, "Durov and I decided to take full advantage of the flight with so little time at the Isle."

"Couldn't we stay longer?"

"I'm afraid not."

She heard the pitch of the engine change, and Rytsar announced lustfully, "We're here."

After the plane landed in the water, the three undressed, leaving their clothes on board. Rytsar strapped a waterproof bag onto his back while Sir helped Brie into the water. Both men assisted her in getting to the shore, knowing she was still weak from their hours of play.

Once they were safely on the white beach, Sir picked Brie up and slung her over his shoulder as he started walking down the path through the vegetation.

Brie giggled. "I'm sure I can walk, I'll just be a little slower than normal."

"No time to waste," Rytsar answered her, grinning at Brie hungrily.

The miniature house with the front made entirely of glass was a welcomed sight as they walked into the clearing. There were so many good memories contained in that place during the honeymoon, and Brie sighed contentedly as Sir carried her over the threshold, laying her down on the large bed.

Rytsar looked around the tiny home, opening the cupboards and drawers, exploring every inch of the place.

"I had the place stocked in advance of our stay," Sir informed him.

"This place is everything I envisioned, brother," Rytsar stated in satisfaction.

Rytsar pointed to the stunning tub of frosted blue glass, nestled in the unique metal frame resembling bare tree branches with a skyline of pine trees in the background. "What do you think of the tub?"

"It is beautiful, Rytsar."

He stared proudly at the oversized tub. "A good heirloom for your family."

Brie giggled. "What, the Isle or the tub?"

He smirked at her. "Both."

When he was done filling it with water, he held out his hand to her. "Come, my naked *radost moya*." She stepped into the delightfully warm water and waited as both men joined her, one on either end. It was a tight squeeze, which made it that much more enjoyable for Brie as she lathered up Rytsar first.

Running her hands over his muscular chest, with the dragon tattoo peeking over his shoulder, was sensual and intimate. "You look good all covered in soap."

"I'd look even better covered in you."

She giggled as she rinsed him off, giving him a bunch of wet kisses when she was done.

Brie then turned herself around to lavish attention on Sir, but the movement created a ripple of water that cascaded over the edge of the tub and onto the floor.

"I might have to spank you for that," Sir teased.

"Please do, Master."

Brie lathered Sir's body slowly, enjoying the rough texture of his body hair. As she ran her hands over the defined muscles of his pecs, she smiled to herself. She took great pleasure rinsing off the lather to expose his body to her again.

"I think it's time to turn the tables," Sir told Rytsar.

"Agreed, comrade."

Brie purred in pure pleasure as she felt the hands of both men rubbing her entire body. They tickled her toes with their thorough cleaning and made her pussy wet with their extra attention on her breasts.

Brie was surprised when Rytsar left the tub. She watched as he wrapped a towel around his waist and went to the cupboards to get the pitcher. He walked back and handed it to Sir.

Sir told her to relax against him. He slowly poured the warm water over her body, rinsing the soap from her skin. She shivered in pure pleasure and asked him to do it several more times.

When the water began to get cold, Rytsar held out a towel to Brie, wrapping her in its fluffy goodness. As for Sir, Rytsar did not hand him the towel, but whipped it instead, smacking his thigh hard with the end of it.

Sir let out a surprised yowl, snagging the towel from Rytsar, then chuckled ominously as he looked down and watched a red welt appear on his skin. "You are going to pay for that, old friend."

Rytsar smirked. "There is nothing you could do that would faze me."

"We'll see about that."

As Sir rubbed the welt, Brie noticed the smile playing on his lips as he toweled off and wondered what he was planning.

Once he was thoroughly dried off, Rytsar brought out a custom-made sex swing. With Sir's help, he attached it to the anchor in the ceiling. Brie stared at it with interest, remembering her first time in one with Baron.

"Before we begin our next round, I say we have a drink and make a toast," Sir suggested.

Rytsar turned to him, grinning. "Vodka is always an excellent idea, comrade."

"I thought you'd agree."

Sir made the drinks while Rytsar beckoned Brie to

his lap. She sat and curled up against him, feeling completely relaxed and pliable—exactly how they wanted her.

As Rytsar held her close he began humming his mother's lullaby. Its haunting melody was now familiar to her since he often serenaded Hope with his mother's song.

"Hum with me," he commanded. Brie did her best to keep the same rhythm and tone as they hummed it together. "Good," he complimented. "Keep humming."

Rytsar surprised her when he sang the words in his native language, his voice low and melodic. Their harmonious exchange was enchanting and magical, especially since Brie lacked the actual talent to sing herself. When they were done, he chuckled warmly, kissing her on the head.

"Very nice," Sir praised, handing a glass to Rytsar.

Sir pulled Brie from Rytsar's lap and wrapped his arm around her, handing her a drink as well.

The shot glasses were made of the same blue glass as the tub. "They're such a pretty color," Brie commented, staring at it with appreciation.

Sir told her, "Another heirloom from our friend."

"What shall we toast to, brother?"

"Why not brotherly love?" Sir answered Rytsar with a slight smile.

Brie raised her glass. "To brotherly love, then."

"Amen," Rytsar replied with a chuckle as he tossed back his drink. He immediately spewed liquid all over himself and started gagging as he grabbed his throat.

"What's wrong?" Brie cried.

Sir started laughing when Rytsar threw him a nasty glare.

Brie ran to get a towel and handed it to Rytsar. "What happened?"

He looked at her with an expression of utter disgust. "Coconut water."

Sir held up his glass. "Here's to getting even, old friend."

There was silence for a moment before Rytsar pointed his finger at Sir accusingly and started laughing. Brie joined in, looking at both men in amusement.

"I should never have doubted your craftiness, brother," Rytsar confessed when he could finally speak again. "But if you ever replace my vodka with coconut water again, I will kill you."

Sir started laughing again. "The look on your face…"

Rytsar shook his head as he made his way to the sink. After rinsing out his mouth and spitting several times, he asked Brie, "How can you drink this awful stuff, *radost moya?*"

"It's yummy," she told him, taking another sip of hers.

"Coconut water is a travesty of nature and should be banned," he growled, spitting into the sink again.

Sir downed his drink and said with a smirk, "I do prefer a fine vodka to coconut water, myself."

"Is that what you are drinking?" Rytsar demanded.

"Of course."

"Then give me the bottle, you *mudak*."

Sir opened the freezer and took out a bottle of Zyr.

Rytsar snatched it from him, glugging it down as if it were milk. He wiped his mouth after several swigs and sighed in satisfaction.

He then looked at Brie lustfully. "Are you ready to get frisky, *radost moya?*"

Her answer was to kneel down on the floor in an open position.

As if the humorous exchange had never happened, both men instantly fell into their Dominant roles.

Brie's body responded to their dual dominance, her pussy contracting in pleasure when Sir placed his hand on her head. "Stand and serve your Master."

She stood up and squeaked when he lifted her off her feet. Rytsar helped hold the swing still as Sir placed her into it, positioning her feet in the hanging stirrups. The feeling of helplessness turned her on as she swung slowly in midair, her pussy splayed out for them.

Rytsar removed his towel, standing before her with his rigid cock ready to begin. "Are you prepared to please me, *radost moya?*"

"It would be my pleasure," she answered, envisioning him pounding her deeply.

Her heart started beating faster when Sir adjusted the sex swing, pulling her into an upright position, her legs spread out, while she hovered a few inches above the floor. He moved her hair forward to bare her back.

Rytsar's low laughter filled the room as he took his cat o' nines from out of his bag. "Yes, you have a date with my nines."

Brie's eyes grew wider as he swung his instrument,

cutting the air with its cruel, knotted tails.

"As you can see, the surgery was a success. I feel no pain," he told her with a wicked grin. "But you will…"

Sir read her growing fear and grabbed her chin, kissing her deeply. "Enjoy this session with him. Accept the love with which it is delivered." His sensual kiss and the truth behind his words helped her embrace this challenge with the right frame of mind. Not being a masochist, it was easy for Brie to fear the pain instead of welcoming the experience Rytsar was presenting to her.

She nodded, taking his advice. Closing her eyes, Brie heard the nines cut savagely through the air, but concentrated on the sound of Rytsar's heavy breathing.

Sir whispered huskily, "Watching you submit excites me, babygirl."

Her pussy ached, the power exchange between the three of them as exciting for her as it was for them. She fed off the sexual energy in the room as she waited for the first stroke of the nines.

"Feel my passion for you," Rytsar growled as he took the first swing. Her back exploded with the fiery sensation those wicked knots could create, and she cried out in pain, surprised once again by how excruciating his whip was.

"Color, *radost moya?*" Rytsar asked lustfully.

It took her a moment to speak. Her body was already tingling as the endorphins rushed through her bloodstream. Swallowing down her fear, she answered him.

"Green."

The next stroke blurred out all thought, and she screamed. He had to time his strokes with the movement of the swing as he gave her another. He spoke to her in Russian, the passion in his voice, along with the seductive sound of his native language, reminding her of their first meeting.

My warrior.

She took the pain Rytsar delivered, harnessing each stroke to carry her further into subspace. She went beyond her endurance, embracing his pleasure over hers—connecting with his sadistic need and giving fully in to it.

When the lashes stopped, she was trembling and whimpering softly. Sir slowly repositioned the swing so she hung in a horizontal position again.

Both men descended on her then, hungry to connect physically with her. Rytsar took position near her mouth while Sir stilled the swing and pressed his cock against her pussy. She was flying high on the euphoria of having transformed his pain into pleasure, and was desperate for the connection they sought.

Brie reached a new level...the transcendence of their dominance—her back burning with Rytsar's love as she took his cock deep in her throat and Sir pounded her to a glorious release.

Pure submissive bliss.

It was with great sadness that Brie said goodbye to their

Isle the next day.

"Please promise me that when we return, it'll be for longer," she begged Sir, not wanting to leave this submissive paradise yet.

Rytsar seemed reluctant to leave, as well, and smiled at her. "It's a shame it must come to an end, *radost moya.*"

"Agreed. Next time we go for a week, brother," Sir said.

"*Da.*" Rytsar grabbed him in a hug, slapping Sir hard on the back.

Brie felt as if the two men had somehow been changed by their encounter on the Isle. They seemed closer and more in tune with each other.

After an exhilarating swim back to the plane, Rytsar removed the waterproof bag from his back and insisted on helping Brie dry off. She dressed back into her clothes that were waiting and sat down between the two men.

Brie was a contented sub with her head resting on Rytsar's shoulder and her hand on Sir's thigh as they flew back to the main island. She felt completely loved and incredibly spoiled.

Although Brie was anxious to get back to Hope, she was excited that they had a long plane ride ahead because it gave the three of them a little more time together. She wasn't quite ready for it to end.

Once the plane had landed and they were safely on the tarmac, Rytsar surprised Brie by handing his bag with his tools over to Sir. "Hold on to this for me, brother."

"Will do."

Brie looked at Rytsar in surprise, then laughed out loud knowing he would never give his nines to another—not even Sir. "Okay, what are you up to now?"

He looked at her tenderly. "It's time."

"Time for what?"

He kissed her on the forehead and turned to Sir. "Keep her safe."

"Wait…you're not heading back with us?" Brie asked, suddenly alarmed.

"No, *radost moya*. I must go."

Brie looked at Sir, noting the serious expression on his face. She felt a cold, prickling sensation course through her body. "What is this?"

"He's going after the slaver, Brie. We got the information we needed before leaving for Italy."

She looked at Rytsar again, shaking her head. "You can't!"

"I must."

The thought of losing him was too much for her heart to bear and she begged, "Don't go, please…"

"Titov is temporarily coming out of retirement to assist me. It is what must be done to end this."

"But I don't want you to go…" Brie cried.

Rytsar cradled her face in his strong hands. "But I must." His gaze was resolute, unmoving.

Tears rolled down her cheeks, realizing that his actions during their trip to Italy and the Isle had been his quiet way of saying goodbye. She shook her head, looking at him in disbelief.

Rytsar understood he was causing her pain and

pounded his chest fiercely, explaining, "I need this, *radost moya*. It is not just for you and the babe. I do this also in memory of my Tatianna. I could not protect her, but I can protect you. I have to be the one—to avenge you and the babe, and finish what I could not years ago. The slaver must die, and I cannot go on knowing he still breathes."

Rytsar turned to Sir, putting his hand firmly on his shoulder. "I see it so clearly. This is how it ends. Everything that has happened to me has led to this moment."

"I can still join you, brother."

"*Nyet*. Your job is to protect your woman. I made a promise to God that I would protect *moye solntse*, and that is what I will do."

He smiled at Brie, vowing, "You will not see me again until the man is dead."

Brie started to cry.

Rytsar was leaving her—and there was nothing she could do about it.

He put a finger to her lips. "I know you will not send me off with tears."

Stilling the panic and fear bubbling up to the surface, Brie quieted her thoughts and dried her tears for him.

"Good, *radost moya*." Rytsar gripped her head in both hands, pressing his forehead against hers as he stared into her eyes. "Do you trust me?"

She wanted to say "No"—and she would have—if it would have stopped him from going. "Yes, Rytsar, I trust you."

"Then there is no need for tears. I will return."

"Yes."

"Now give me a kiss to send me off properly."

Rytsar grabbed her, kissing Brie passionately, his lips expressing his deep love for her. His final goodbye.

Brie wanted to weep when he broke the embrace, but she held the tears back and told him, "My heart beats with you, Rytsar."

He put his hand on his chest and smiled at her. "I feel it always."

Rytsar then turned to Sir. "Brother, do not second-guess this path you and I are on."

Sir's eyes were shrouded in pain and uncertainty.

"Do not!" Rytsar insisted. "Victory is certain."

Brie could tell Sir was still struggling with the decision, but he clasped his friend's shoulder and said confidently, "We will drink to your success on your return."

"*Da*, comrade," he answered with a grin. "And I will drink you under the table."

Rytsar turned and walked away then, shouting, "*Poka my ne vstretimsya snova!*"

Brie didn't let the tears fall until he was out of sight. But, once they began, she was inconsolable.

Blood Moon

They had no communication from him because the risk was too great, just as it had been during the rescue mission in Russia.

Brie was forced to put all her trust in Rytsar's abilities. Her only consolation was knowing that Titov was with him. The two men had extensive experience with the underground world they were entering, and they were on a mission to right a wrong that had haunted them for years. They were both seeking redemption by granting Brie and the baby the safety they could not provide Tatianna.

As the weeks dragged on, the silence became deafening and doubts began to creep in. As much as Sir tried to reassure her, she could tell he was struggling as well.

Brie lived with the guilt that her situation had put Rytsar's life at risk, but Sir carried the burden of knowing his own flesh and blood had created this. By not wanting to break his promise to her, Sir had to bear the weight of not being with his brother now, and she could tell it was eating at his soul.

They simply went through the motions each day, clinging to the hope that the next day would bring word from Rytsar.

Brie began humming Rytsar's lullaby to Hope, wanting to ensure she remembered her *dyadya*.

Master Anderson knew about Rytsar's mission and understood the pain they were suffering. Being a kindhearted man, he called Brie out of the blue to let her know that Shadow was welcomed to visit.

"Do you really mean that?"

"I do, young Brie."

"When?"

"Anytime."

"Would now work?"

He chuckled. "Now would work just fine."

Brie squealed, overjoyed that Shadow would finally be reunited with his family. The large black cat had taken on the role of comforter in their home after they'd come back from Italy. He drifted back and forth between Brie and Sir, providing a soothing presence that was complemented by the calming sound of his purr.

However, Brie knew it was a burden for the cat because they were so deeply entrenched in their sorrow that his need to comfort them could not overcome it.

Sir joined Brie on her trip to Master Anderson's

house. Shadow sat up front on Brie's lap, content to look out the car window. Brie had to wonder what he was thinking. He could not know their destination. And yet, the cat was so calm as he was taken from the apartment that Brie let him out of his carrier once they were in the car. She marveled at the fact he was so trusting. How could Shadow be certain she wasn't taking him to the vet?

She shook her head in amazement as she petted him.

"What are you thinking?" Sir asked.

"I can't believe Shadow is so trusting."

He chuckled. "He's only that way with certain people. Therefore, his level of trust now speaks volumes about you."

Brie stroked his soft fur, grateful for Shadow. "He was there for me as support at the commune. And, later, when he came to live with me after Master Gannon died. I owe him a lot."

"Well, he obviously loves you, and has even come to accept me because of you."

She let out a long sigh. "It feels good to finally be able to do something for him. You know?"

Sir smiled. "While I have never felt that way about an animal, I can understand your sentiment. He has been an asset to our family."

Rytsar…

Brie had to push away the feelings that threatened to ruin this moment. This was about Shadow, and all the focus needed to be on him.

When they finally reached Master Anderson's

house, Brie didn't even bother with the carrier, choosing to carry the giant black cat up to the house while Sir brought Hope.

Shadow glanced around his surroundings with interest until Master Anderson opened the door. As soon as their eyes met, Shadow narrowed his.

"Looks like someone is happy to see me," Master Anderson joked.

Sir patted his friend. "He didn't care much for me either, at first. However, the animal has an uncanny soul and I've grown to respect him over time."

Master Anderson frowned slightly. "He may be an extraordinary animal, but he defiled my Cayenne."

Brie giggled. "No, he didn't, Master Anderson. He made sweet, passionate love to her, and there are six beautiful offspring to prove it."

Master Anderson crinkled his nose, but Shey came up behind him, wrapping her hands around his muscular arm. "They're beautiful *and* adorable. We've had so much fun with those little rascals, and we've posted their antics all over Instagram." She looked up at the muscular Dom, adding, "Life wouldn't be the same without their crazy cuteness, admit it."

He gave her a charming grin. "True, they do make me laugh."

Brie lifted up the heavy cat. "And Shadow is the one responsible. He totally deserves your love, Master Anderson."

He laughed. "As long as Blacky doesn't get too close to Cayenne, I can tolerate him. But that's *all* he's getting out of me."

Brie carried Shadow over to the guest bedroom—now Cayenne's nursery.

As soon as she opened the door, Cayenne sniffed the air twice, her tail twitching back and forth as Brie put Shadow down. The two cats met halfway.

Cayenne sat down in front him. Shadow sniffed her while purring loudly.

"Oh my goodness, it's like two long-lost lovers being reuniting," Brie cooed, holding her hands to her chest.

The kittens seemed a little intimidated by the giant tomcat and kept their distance. It broke Brie's heart, but she understood why. They had never met their father, and he was a daunting figure.

Master Anderson chuckled. "So, seems like the kittens are scared of him. Not a surprise. Sorry, young Brie, but I don't think this is going to be the family reunion you were hoping for."

The little calico that had licked Sir during their visit at the hospital was the first to cautiously approach Shadow.

"Naturally, she'd be the first to brave contact with the black bastard," Master Anderson said, shaking his head in disbelief.

The large cat sniffed the calico for several moments before rubbing his cheek against her.

"And there he goes...marking his damn territory," Master Anderson joked, trying to laugh it off, but Brie could tell it was actually making him uncomfortable.

Cayenne lay down beside Shadow, rolling onto her back and wiggling playfully as if she was a kitten herself. Instantly, the entire brood ran to her, a mass of furballs climbing and tumbling over each other.

To Brie's amazement, Shadow stepped around Cayenne and sat down. She rolled next to him and meowed. With his two massive paws, he began kneading her shoulder area as if giving Cayenne a massage. It was the most loving thing Brie had ever seen, and both she and Shey murmured at the same time, "Aww…"

Master Anderson stared at the cats. "Well, I never."

Sir wrapped his arm around Brie as he watched. "A father who looks after his woman is a man to be trusted."

"I told you he missed her, Master Anderson," Brie exclaimed happily.

He stood watching Shadow intently, as if he were in shock. "I can't believe I'm saying this, but I agree, young Brie. Shadow deserved this visit." He laughed when he told Sir, "Of course, I'm having Cayenne fixed after this."

"That's wise, Master Anderson. I've read that cats can go into heat just weeks after giving birth," Brie informed him.

"Oh, hell!" Master Anderson cried. He looked at Shadow with distrust. "No unsupervised visits for you, old man." He gave Brie a wary look. "Maybe he should go now."

Brie giggled, smiling down at the feline couple. "Just look at them, Master Anderson. You can't deny they have a special bond. I couldn't bear breaking them up quite yet."

Master Anderson looked to Sir for help. "Surely,

you agree."

"On the contrary, I find this quite unusual and...touching."

Master Anderson brushed his hair back, chuckling to himself. "This is not how I saw this visit going."

Shaking off his surprise, he asked Sir. "So, I've heard rumors that Baron and Captain have asked you to teach demonstration classes with Brie. Is that true?"

Sir inclined his head. "It is."

"I'm extremely interested in hearing what they have planned. Why don't we give these felines time to bond while you tell me more about Baron and Captain's idea? The girls can watch over this Shadow character to ensure there are no more 'surprises' while we discuss it further over some soup." Master Anderson winked at Brie as he walked out of the room with Sir.

Master Anderson knew how to effortlessly take care of his friends. It was a natural talent of his.

Brie took advantage of the time he'd given her to spend it with Shey while they watched Shadow interact with his little family.

Marquis had shared with Sir that a Blood Moon was eminent and advised him to make the effort to see it. "It is a remarkable sight. Truly inspiring."

Sir talked to Brie afterward, wanting to know her level of interest. "Gray insists it will be worth the early hour to observe the event."

Brie shrugged. "To be honest, Sir, I've never seen one. If you want to, I'm willing to get Hope ready and join you."

"Excellent."

Sir woke Brie up several hours before dawn and drove them up to the California hills overlooking the city. This place held history for her. Sir had taken her twice after dealings with his mother, and she'd taken her own mother here after shopping for the wedding dress.

It had a breathtaking vista that could not be matched.

Sir helped Brie out of the car and then got Hope from her car seat. The baby was wide awake, looking around with a curious expression. Brie wondered if she was questioning why her parents had insisted on taking her out into the chilly air so early in the morning.

"Look, Brie…" Sir pointed up at the dark sky.

She followed his line of sight and a cold chill took over when she saw the full moon. It was the color of blood. While Brie appreciated that it was a spectacular sight, it reminded her of Rytsar. Without warning, she burst into tears.

"What's wrong?" Sir asked, surprised by her sudden outburst.

Brie couldn't even answer him, the lump in her throat preventing any speech. She just shook her head.

"Babygirl…" he murmured, wrapping his free arm around her. Brie smashed her face into his coat, embracing Hope with her other arm in a group hug, needing their connection to survive the overwhelming pain she felt.

Brie had no idea how long she sobbed, pressing her cheek against his cold jacket. However, the tears eventually stopped and numb relief followed. She pulled away from Sir, wiping her face before giving Hope a gentle kiss on the head. Without speaking, she got back into the car and shut the door.

Sir did not question her silence, buckling Hope into the car seat. He drove them back to the apartment, giving her time to work through her emotions, but he kept glancing at Brie, his concern easy to see.

Knowing he was worried about her, Brie fought through the painful lump in her throat and whispered, "Rytsar." The tears threatened to start up again, so she said nothing more.

Sir nodded, staring ahead at the road, having no words of comfort to give.

Although the outing had been an emotional landmine for Brie, she found her heart growing lighter with the passage of time.

It left her to ponder if Marquis had somehow known it would provide her with a much needed release. Time became a friend to her again as she and Sir began reengaging with the world, their friends, and each other.

It left her receptive when Sir came to her one evening sounding excited when he told her, "I have something I want to show you, babygirl."

Brie responded to his enthusiasm, fighting against the dark cloud that had been hovering over her. "If it pleases you, Sir," she answered, assuming that the gleam in his eye had something to do with a new scene he wanted to play out together.

For the first time in a long time, she felt a surge of sexual excitement.

Expecting Sir to head toward the bedroom, she was surprised when he picked up the car keys. "Where are we going?"

"My secret," he answered. "Get Hope ready."

His unusual request stirred her curiosity, and Brie bundled Hope up for the night ride, excited about this unexpected jaunt.

As Sir drove, he kept glancing at her, a secretive smile playing on his lips.

Brie's heart started racing when she realized they were headed toward Rytsar's beach house.

"Sir…"

"Don't say anything. Just wait."

Brie could hardly breathe as they drove up to Rytsar's place, but it shocked her when he didn't slow down and passed by the beach house. The place was dark, and only helped to remind her that he wasn't there anymore.

The joy she'd felt evaporated.

Sir pulled into a driveway two houses down. The house was lit up brightly with every light in the house turned on—a drastic contrast to Rytsar's home.

The complete opposite.

Brie tried to contain her disappointment, seeing how animated Sir was as he opened the car door and popped out of his seat, walking over to the passenger side to open hers. Brie got out slowly, forcing herself to smile up at him.

He got Hope out of the car next and turned to face the house, stating proudly, "This is our new home."

Brie's heart skipped a beat. She stared at the house, wanting to be happy for his sake, appreciating what Sir had done. "This is ours?"

"Yes," he answered. "We are next to the ocean so we can take advantage of the calming waves whenever we have the need."

"That's wonderful, Sir," she said, but her heart wasn't in it.

"Come, Brie. You can't appreciate how perfect this place is until you see inside."

Brie took the baby from Sir, kissing her on the head. She took a moment to readjust her mindset. Sir had done this wonderful thing for their family. This place would connect them to Rytsar through the years. Hope would grow up here, soaking up his presence on the beach—his passion and zeal for life still lingering here.

She started walking toward the entrance, smiling at Sir, sincerely grateful for this gift he'd given them. Bouncing Hope in her arms, she asked, "Are you ready to see our new place, little girl?"

As Brie stepped up to the door, it swung open.

Rytsar stood before her with Titov right behind him. Rytsar wore a mischievous grin with his arms wide open.

"*Radost moya,* welcome me home."

COMING NEXT

Tied to Hope: Brie's Submission
18th Book in the Series
Available Now

Reviews mean the world to me!

I truly appreciate you taking the time to review
Bound by Love.

If you could leave a review on both Goodreads and the site where you purchased this eBook from, I would be so grateful. Sincerely, ~Red

ABOUT THE AUTHOR

Over Two Million readers have enjoyed Red's stories

Red Phoenix – USA Today Bestselling Author
Winner of 8 Readers' Choice Awards

Hey Everyone!

I'm Red Phoenix, an author who also happens to be a submissive in real life. I wrote the Brie's Submission series because I wanted people everywhere to know just how much fun BDSM can be.

There is a huge cast of characters who are part of Brie's journey. The further you read into the story the more you learn about each one. I hope you grow to love Brie and the gang as much as I do.

They've become like family.

When I'm not writing, you can find me online with readers.

I heart my fans! ~Red

To find out more visit my Website
redphoenixauthor.com
Follow Me on BookBub
bookbub.com/authors/red-phoenix
Newsletter: Sign up
redphoenixauthor.com/newsletter-signup
Facebook: AuthorRedPhoenix
Twitter: @redphoenix69
Instagram: RedPhoenixAuthor
I invite you to join my reader Group!
facebook.com/groups/539875076052037

SIGN UP FOR MY NEWSLETTER
HERE FOR THE LATEST RED
PHOENIX UPDATES

FOLLOW ME ON INSTAGRAM
INSTAGRAM.COM/REDPHOENIXAUTHOR

SALES, GIVEAWAYS, NEW
RELEASES, PREORDER LINKS, AND
MORE!
SIGN UP HERE
REDPHOENIXAUTHOR.COM/NEWSLETTER-
SIGNUP

Red Phoenix is the author of:

Brie's Submission Series:
Teach Me #1
Love Me #2
Catch Me #3
Try Me #4
Protect Me #5
Hold Me #6
Surprise Me #7
Trust Me #8
Claim Me #9
Enchant Me #10
A Cowboy's Heart #11
Breathe with Me #12
Her Russian Knight #13
Under His Protection #14
Her Russian Returns #15
In Sir's Arms #16
Bound by Love #17
Tied to Hope #18
Hope's First Christmas #19
Secrets of the Heart #20

*You can also purchase the AUDIO BOOK **Versions**

Also part of the Submissive Training Center world:

Rise of the Dominates Trilogy
Sir's Rise #1
Master's Fate #2
The Russian Reborn #3

Captain's Duet
Safe Haven #1
Destined to Dominate #2

The Russian Unleashed #1

Other Books by Red Phoenix

Blissfully Undone
* Available in eBook and paperback

(Snowy Fun—Two people find themselves snowbound in a cabin where hidden love can flourish, taking one couple on a sensual journey into ménage à trois)

His Scottish Pet: Dom of the Ages
* Available in eBook and paperback

Audio Book: *His Scottish Pet: Dom of the Ages*

(Scottish Dom—A sexy Dom escapes to Scotland in the late 1400s. He encounters a waif who has the potential to free him from his tragic curse)

The Erotic Love Story of Amy and Troy
* Available in eBook and paperback

(Sexual Adventures—True love reigns, but fate continually throws Troy and Amy into the arms of others)

eBooks

Varick: The Reckoning

(Savory Vampire—A dark, sexy vampire story. The hero navigates the dangerous world he has been thrust into with lusty passion and a pure heart)

Keeper of the Wolf Clan (Keeper of Wolves, #1)

(Sexual Secrets—A virginal werewolf must act as the clan's mysterious Keeper)

The Keeper Finds Her Mate (Keeper of Wolves, #2)

(Second Chances—A young she-wolf must choose between old ties or new beginnings)

The Keeper Unites the Alphas (Keeper of Wolves, #3)

(Serious Consequences—The young she-wolf is captured by the rival clan)

Boxed Set: Keeper of Wolves Series (Books 1-3)

(Surprising Secrets—A secret so shocking it will rock Layla's world. The young she-wolf is put in a position of being able to save her werewolf clan or becoming the reason for its destruction)

Socrates Inspires Cherry to Blossom

(Satisfying Surrender—A mature and curvaceous woman becomes fascinated by an online Dom who has much to teach her)

By the Light of the Scottish Moon

(Saving Love—Two lost souls, the Moon, a werewolf, and a death wish…)

In 9 Days

(Sweet Romance—A young girl falls in love with the new student, nicknamed "the Freak")

9 Days and Counting

(Sacrificial Love—The sequel to *In 9 Days* delves into the emotional reunion of two longtime lovers)

And Then He Saved Me

(Saving Tenderness—When a young girl tries to kill herself, a man of great character intervenes with a love that heals)

Connect with Red on Substance B

Substance B is a platform for independent authors to directly connect with their readers. Please visit Red's Substance B page where you can:

- Sign up for Red's newsletter
- Send a message to Red
- See all platforms where Red's books are sold

Visit Substance B today to learn more about your favorite independent authors.

Made in the USA
Monee, IL
23 September 2020